BLACK ICE KINGDOM

by

ANGELIKA DEVLYN

Black Ice ~ The Dark Kingdom Chronicles
first published in 2010 by
Chimera Books Ltd
PO Box 152
Waterlooville
Hants
PO8 9FS
United Kingdom

Printed and bound in the UK by
Cox & Wyman, Reading.

ISBN 978-0-955451-06-5

This novel is fiction – in real life practice safe sex

This book is sold subject to the condition that it shall not, by way of trade or otherwise, be lent, resold, hired out or otherwise circulated without the publisher's prior written consent in any form of binding or cover other than that in which it is published, and without a similar condition being imposed on the subsequent purchaser.

The characters and situations in this book are entirely imaginary and bear no relation to any real person or actual happening.

Copyright © Angelika Devlyn

The right of Angelika Devlyn to be identified as author of this book has been asserted in accordance with section 77 and 78 of the Copyrights Designs and Patents Act 1988.

BLACK ICE ~ THE DARK KINGDOM CHRONICLES

Angelika Devlyn

Chimera *(kī-mîr'ə, kĭ-)* a creation of the imagination, a wild fantasy

Her heart raced, but knowing he was angry she didn't complain. Nor did she struggle or cry out for him to stop. The book of *Protocol and Etiquette* said punishments were easier to bear if they were not fought against. Time to test out that theory.

Her belly pressed against his leather-clad thighs and her firm breasts hung, pointing to the floor where her fingertips splayed out in an effort to support herself.

Fingers grasped her panties, yanked them down to her knees and left them there. Cool air wafted around her exposed bottom, now thrust high and vulnerable. Her face reddened at the thought of him inspecting her. So closely. With one hand between her shoulder-blades he held her down. A broad palm rested across both cheeks. His touch made her jump.

'Hold still,' he admonished, taking his warm hand away and raising it high above his head. She gritted her teeth and waited for the first spank.

Part One – Not Long After the Beginning of Time, Pandreas Cave

Chapter One

'You are not welcome here!' The witch flew through the air, clawed talons aimed for the renegade soldier's face. With fast reflexes Prometheus unsheathed his razor-sharp sword and speared her dirt-covered cloak. A hiss escaped her twisted mouth as he punctured her flesh. Terrified, her disbelieving eyes bulged and her mouth fell open, distorted with pain. An unearthly screech, a call for help, echoed round the dark. Desperate to save herself flailing limbs attempted to push him away. In a violent surge of energy she scratched at his face and clawed at his hands. Anything to make him lose the firm grip he held on his sword. A futile effort. The damage done, her nostrils flared and with a last hope of victory her eyes changed colour. Prometheus recoiled at the sight, but held his sword firm. Pinpricks of glowing red light radiated from within her black eyes like turbulent flames upon coal. As he stared into her eyes he felt their blaze warm his face. With each second the heat's intensity grew and threatened to burn him alive, consume him until he was nothing but black char. Burned alive. His worst fear.

Hēphaistos Fire! A mighty power harnessed from the Olympian god, Hēphaistos himself. A gift from the Magic Box of Destiny from which the Pandora coven was born. But how was she controlling it? His eyes flicked down to the bronze amulet around her neck. A magical talisman? To test his theory Prometheus stretched his free hand out towards her. The sweltering heat through his glove escalated and scorched. Quickly he yanked it free from her breasts and threw it on the floor, out of her reach. It sizzled in the cool sand when it landed.

At the realisation her reprisal was short-lived, the witch screamed again.

Without pause the soldier thrust his weapon deeper and gritted his teeth as it pierced her rotten black heart with a sickening slurp.

With her life draining away her twitching body slumped heavy on his sword, the bright red pool of blood a sharp contrast against her white cloak.

Prometheus gaped as her body shrivelled before him. The raging fire within her haunting eyes dwindled, then extinguished. Dark eyes returned and milked over. Dead? The soldier breathed a sigh of relief and pulled the sword out of her collapsed body with caution, watching her fall facedown onto the sandy floor. Her body hissed in protest. With a large booted foot he rolled her body over to check she was dead. Cracked and wrinkled her face stared up at him with dead white eyes. As beautiful as the White Witches were, he felt no remorse. He knew them to be young and inexperienced, yet given the chance to survive she could have easily matured into one of the higher ranking witches which grow even more attractive with age. And far more dangerous.

He heard a noise and turned back to the entrance of the cave as his brother Epimetheus burst in, his sword also dripping with red witch blood. 'I found another one,' he panted. 'Hiding behind a boulder round the front.'

'Are you hurt?' Prometheus asked with a look of concern.

Epimetheus shook his head. A long curl of silky blond hair fell down over his forehead. He brushed it out of his eyes with the back of a bloody, gloved hand. Blood mixed with sand smeared his face. 'No, brother, but great care must be taken. They are surprisingly fast.'

'And the eyes. I would not have believed it if I'd not witnessed it myself,' Prometheus said with a hollow laugh, as he remembered the Hēphaistos Fire. 'I do not want to go through that again.' Did the Pandoras know his fears? Sense it in him? They were capable of many things and he was so new to it all. How could one fight what one did not fully understand?

Epimetheus froze and pointed further into the cave, and Prometheus squinted through the darkness for any hint of white clothing. With caution Prometheus silently unsheathed his sword. His brother did the same. Scanning their surroundings for any sign of movement the men straightened, alert and ready.

How wrong he was to assume the weaker white witches, trained to protect the entrance of the Pandora coven, could be ruled out as a threat. Had she had time to call on the darker powers of the more experienced grey or red witches he would surely be dead. Still they had made it to Pandreas Cave; there was no going back now. Not without Hamira.

Out of the corner of his peripheral vision something scuttled across the shadows. Prometheus turned. Up against the far end of the cave they saw a pair of dark eyes glinting. Another witch. She saw them, screeched, and fled towards a tunnel at incredible speed. Within seconds Epimetheus charged ahead and blocked her escape. She shrieked and attempted to go back the way she'd come. Prometheus surprised her from behind. He grabbed her long dark hair, twisted it tight around his hand and held her steady. Epimetheus snatched the cold bronze amulet from her elegant neck, before it could ignite.

'Kill her?' Epimetheus growled.

'No. She shall take us deeper into the caves to the nest. We could use her as an exchange.'

A long shot, but it had to be worth a try. Hamira, the love of his life, and the host to his Goddess of Hope's spirit, were being held captive somewhere within. Going back was not an option.

The soldiers pulled the witch kicking and screaming into the tunnel and demanded to be taken to her high priestess. Four dead witches later she calmed down, admitted defeat and led them through a series of underground tunnels. They rounded a bend and came to a large opening. The foyer to the centre chamber.

'Brother, look at this!'

Prometheus turned, and his mouth fell open. The walls were covered in ancient drawings depicting hosts of a much darker evil. A sign of things to come. Prometheus held onto the witch and stepped forward, not quite understanding what he was reading.

The witch straightened her shoulders. 'Pandora's Prophecies,' she purred, confidently snaking a long nail down his bare chest, where his shirt had been ripped open during their scuffle.

'For what purpose are those drawings?' Prometheus demanded, grabbing her hair and roughly directing her head towards the wall.

'Oh, you have not heard? This section here,' she pointed, 'explains how times are changing. A new age where humans living in the Otherworld will share their lives with a force to be reckoned with will soon be upon them—'

'Impossible!' Epimetheus interrupted. 'No one believes such nonsense!' But while the validity of her claims remained uncertain, the High Priestess Pandora was known for her foresight and the accuracy with which it came true. To dismiss them outright, without a second thought, could be detrimental to their mission.

'But that is Zeus!' Prometheus gasped, pointing at a detailed figure that could only be the god he once knew so well. 'Pray do tell,' he said, letting go of her hair. 'What does he have to do with all this? He cannot be working with the Pandoras.'

The beautiful girl fixed her eyes on his and smiled. A dainty hand delicately stroked the pictures with admiration. 'You are right. These creatures, mere parasites, were born from a weakening Zeus, and his need to recreate himself and his power before he is overthrown and banished to Tartarus like so many distant and powerful gods already...' An icy chill filled the once warm cave. Prometheus shuddered. Tartarus, a place in the Fire Kingdom of Pyredom, deep beneath even the Land of the Dead. How could he forget that prison of brass? He still had the scars to prove it. He never did discover the identity of the one who pulled him out of there and set him free.

'These orphaned abominations of the gods,' the White Witch continued eagerly, 'will employ numerous strategies for getting from one host to another.' She then pointed to a new section, a much darker and bloodier wall showing images of seemingly normal humans doing despicable things to others; spreading pain, torture and death wherever they went. 'But take heed,' she said, sidling up to him, and with a growing excitement used the palm of her hand to rub his crotch, 'in times to come they will interbreed…' instantly his cock swelled, '…and grow stronger day by day until their survival will no longer depend on finding a host, and they will become a race of their own. Under Pandora's rule they will rise in numbers and rage an everlasting war against you and the pitiful humans upon the Otherworld.'

'And what of these pictures?' asked Prometheus, as she slowly unbuttoned his trousers, reached in and took hold of his hard cock. He strove to ignore his body's traitorous reactions, but when her hand slipped up and down his shaft he slipped under the mesmerising spell of her fingers. He groaned, wanting to bend her over and fuck her right there. To give her what she was after. To teach her what it meant to be…

'Brother!' Epimetheus shouted and pulled them apart, breaking her spell. 'I can't believe you fell for that! Watch out for their Mindlust tricks. These Pandoras work their own dark magic to lure you into their traps for their own devices!'

Prometheus snapped out of the trance and angrily shoved his cock back into place. 'Heaven's above, girl, stop playing games and tell me,' he said, frustrated with a hard cock and no release.

'Ah! This is the best bit. The Paraphanites, which Her Highness named the Black Army, will begin their march of annihilation *very* soon. Their weapons of choice – silence, stealth, and their ability to blend in with other humans, take over their bodies and cause all the evil in the world. No one can spot them. No one is safe. No one knows when or where they will strike.' She turned back to the brothers and licked her ruby-red lips seductively. 'You Destaurians were never the types to move with the times, were you? You could have come over my tits and still continued with your fruitless plight!'

'And pray, what do you mean by that young lady?'

She rolled her eyes. 'If you thought the struggle for power and ownership over that stupid box of hers was important, think again.' She laughed, and flicked back her long black hair. 'Of course, you will not want her opening the Magic Box of Destiny and releasing more evils unto the world, but take heed of the Pandora Prophecies. When the Paraphanites arrive that box is the least of your troubles. Now,' she said with her hands on her hips, 'are we going to stand out here all day or shall I take you in and announce you to the High Priestess Pandora herself? I take it she's not expecting you?'

Taking back his control Prometheus took hold of the witch again, careful to avert his eyes from hers. 'With her ability to see much of what is hidden she will know we are here,' he said.

Not amused, Epimetheus grunted. 'Our names are—'

'Oh, don't think I don't know who you are. Your names are *infamous* around these parts. I may only be a White Witch,' she added, waggling her finger at them rudely, 'but we're highly trained in demonology.'

'We, I hasten to add, are *not* demons,' Epimetheus corrected her.

'*Whatever*. Destaurians, Fallen Angels, Denounced Gods; you're all the same to us if you live in the Dark Kingdom.' She tried to shake Prometheus off her arm, but he held onto her tight.

'Enough of this nonsense; show us the way,' he demanded.

'Rightio. Oh, and by the way, technically your brother is still married to the High Priestess, but I guess you already know that.' She grinned.

'Go!' Epimetheus said, his tone harsh, and Prometheus felt the push from behind even as the witch stumbled forward.

'In case you're wondering I'm Darkita,' she said, leading the way with a wiggle of her bottom. 'Something tells me we're going to see a lot more of each other, boys. At least, that's what I hope.'

The Private Quarters of the High Priestess Pandora, Central Chamber

Chapter Two

The smoky air smelled of burning incense. The sand beneath their feet changed to a wide expanse of exotic floor tiles. Tall cave walls were covered with large instruments of torture. Prometheus knew exactly what they were all called and used for. The walls of his special basement room back home looked almost identical.

On a raised platform at the back they found Pandora, enjoying some playtime with a bullwhip upon a naked girl. The sound of the whip rushing through the air and then thrashing her tender red skin grew louder as they drew nearer.

Swish! Whack!

From the spaced-out look upon the pained, pretty face, and the gold talisman around her neck, Prometheus knew the girl was of Red Witch status; being taught the pleasure of pain – something all witches revelled in. Once they learned to love it.

Swish! Whack!

A slight twitch escaped Prometheus' lips. The gods above didn't nickname her Pandora the Punisher for nothing. He couldn't wait for her to turn round. It had been such a long time since they'd seen each other, and even though his brother's marriage to her was hardly made in heaven, they once had their good times. Whatever had gone on since, none of them could deny they went back a long way. There was a time Prometheus would not have believed they would ever be enemies.

Pandora glanced at them, an amused expression on her beautiful face, and then she continued her 'training'. Prometheus read her message clearly; she was asserting her power over them by making them wait for her to finish. Looking at Darkita, amusement curled his own lips. Despite her recent show of bravado she did not look so brave now.

Swish! Whack!

Having lived with Pandora when she and his

brother were married he quickly learned of her sexual preferences. She loved pain then, and now it would seem she'd moved on to inflicting it. Big time. It didn't surprise him. They were both born from an analogous time period in an age when sexual debauchery and promiscuity were encouraged. Old habits died hard. It stood to reason, he considered, that although he and she were very different, their teaching methods were not. In many ways they were much more similar than he'd care to admit. The only difference was that he did it for the good of mankind, whereas Pandora, the Black Queen, did it for her own evil amusement. Her two best friends were Chaos and Destruction. What pleasure he would have to give her a dose of her own medicine!

Swish! Whack!

He watched the girl's half-opened eyes as she sunk deeper into the bliss of it all, totally unaware the two soldiers were watching.

Would you like to take this witch's place?

Prometheus shook his head, unsure of what he'd just heard. He looked up at Pandora. Her wicked grin said it all. Mind Talk. He'd forgotten about that. Immediately he built a visual image of a brick wall in his own mind to block her out of his thoughts. For good measure he added a locking spell. Who knew what trickery she was capable of these days? He must defend his secrets at all costs.

Swish! Whack!

While she worked Prometheus studied his enemy. As the only Black Witch, the highest rank, Pandora wore a strange, shiny, figure-hugging black dress with a high collar. Her cropped black hair, modern and recently trimmed, framed her attractive pixie face, a face that had brought many men to their knees, evaporating their self-respect in an instant. Some women, too. Prometheus lowered his eyes. The low scalloped neckline barely covered her heaving breasts, which he could not help but notice jolted with each flick of the whip. He wasn't sure about women's fashion, but he knew her dress to be neither a fabric nor a design of their era. A worrying sign of her travels through time. Especially into the future.

'Take a seat,' Pandora said, her tone devoid of politeness.

'We'd rather stand,' Prometheus responded, throwing the young witch to the floor at their feet. Annoyed, Darkita yelped.

'What, may I ask, have I done to deserve a pleasurable visit from such fine men? A Titan and a fallen god, no less.' Pandora purred, her eyes firmly fixed on Epimetheus. 'Hello my dear *husband*. It's been a while.'

'Not long enough,' Epimetheus scowled, avoiding her bewitching eyes.

A weak and feeble human she may have been once, Prometheus thought, but now she wielded a power so strong that when paired with the Magic Box of Destiny with its dormant evils just waiting to escape, she had the command to destroy the world should the remaining Olympian gods wish. As long as the Box existed, that would never change.

'I have returned this young witch unharmed,' he said. 'Now give me back what is rightfully mine. Hamira is not yours to take. She should not be here. This is not a matter for your kind. Release her or pay the consequences.'

The Priestess threw her hands in the air in mock fear and glanced at the witch on the floor. 'This thing in exchange for Hamira?' she snorted. Angry, Darkita crossed her arms and grunted under her breath.

'I'm afraid that is out of the question. There's plenty more where she came from. But the girlfriend of a fallen Titan god, now that's something *special!* And as for her not being a matter for my kind, I may well have to change that.'

Prometheus growled, raking gloved fingers through his dark hair.

'Oh, come on, you can't fool us,' Epimetheus said, ignoring Pandora's last comment. 'We go back far enough to know how you run this sick nest of yours. This thing…' he pushed the White Witch with his foot and she scowled at him, 'this *thing* as you so call her,' he sneered as he continued to address Pandora, 'may be lower in rank, but she wouldn't be guarding the entrance if she wasn't one of the higher ranking Red Witches' daughters. Release Hamira or this one dies. Simple as that.'

Prometheus stared hard at Pandora, waiting for her reaction.

'Do you really want the job of explaining to her mother what happened?' Epimetheus went on more calmly, although his tones were laced with a sneer. 'I'm sure they'd love to know why you'd rather keep an Otherworld girl like Hamira alive over one of your own kind.' He shook his head. 'I can't see that going down too well, can you?'

A gaggle of witches entered the chamber behind them. The two soldiers turned, ready to fight. They were Grey Witches, and their low status disallowed them direct entry into Pandora's private chambers, unless invited. Upon seeing the visitors they reared like wild horses, bleated and screeched. Once they received orders to attack there would be no stopping them. The Priestess held up a hand to prevent them coming any further, so with reluctance and angry protests they backed off.

'Very well, *husband*.' She looked at the Red Witch she'd been whipping. One by one her restraints snapped and fell to the tiled floor, as if cut by an invisible force. 'Damnilar?' The witch blinked, taking a while to come round. 'Damnilar!' Pandora repeated impatiently. 'Fetch the girl, and be quick about it!' Dazed, the girl left her post and hurried away.

Prometheus looked at his brother. How was he holding up? There was something about Pandora's beauty which both excited and unnerved him. If it were not for their past experience with her and that predatory smile she wore, those shapely hips, large breasts and attractive face could easily lead them to their deaths. And even immortality had its weaknesses. Beauty like hers was hard to resist. A deadly tool. From the moment he'd walked in it had taken all Prometheus' strength to stay alert for her spellbinding tricks. How hard it must be for his brother, who once loved her.

When Damnilar returned Prometheus couldn't believe the state his beloved Hamira was in.

With downcast eyes she studied the floor, as Damnilar pushed and prodded her into the room as if she were nothing but cattle to them. She wore a sheer ankle-length skirt of white silk, which hung from a chained belt around her slender waist. Her top half was bare apart from another chain that threaded its way from the belt up between her breasts, and around her neck. No doubt it was locked. *Dressed in white like a trainee witch, and chained like a slave!* Prometheus growled at having to witness her mistreatment.

Hamira lifted her eyes. Seeing familiar faces she broke free and ran towards Prometheus, but he pushed her away into his brother's capable hands.

'Protect her.'

The brothers looked at each other, concern flickered across their faces. They didn't need to share the gift of Mindtalk to know something was wrong. Pandora had given up Hamira far too easily.

The High Priestess smiled as if reading their minds, and pointed to Prometheus. 'You have your soul mate back, soldier, but on one condition.'

Both men shuffled their feet uneasily, their swords weighing heavy on their backs. 'We have nothing else to give to you,' said Prometheus.

'Oh, how wrong you are. Leave the Magic Box of Destiny to the Pandora witches, who know how to control the evils within properly,' she smirked. 'Stop trying to track it down. How many times do I have to tell you, it does *not* belong to you? You've got what you wanted out of the Box, Hope's spirit. Leave the rest to me.'

'Impossible!' retorted Prometheus, his anger rising. 'You know we cannot just stand back and let you and that blasted box destroy everything that comes across your path!'

The Priestess flicked her head back and cackled, but when she looked back at them her black eyes were burning like red-hot coals. Her smile had turned into an angry grimace. Horrified, Hamira gasped and hid her face in Epimetheus' chest.

'How dare you enter Pandreas Cave and desecrate it with your presence, you ungrateful fools!' she hissed, her true colours shining through at last. 'You take that lovesick wretch of a girl and get out of here! She's no use to us anyway.' She sneered. 'Not since my girls have *used* her. She's spoiled meat.'

Prometheus noticed the red welt marks on Hamira's back.

'Why, you bitch! If you've scarred her I'll...' Driven by a burst of anger he stepped forward, the tip of his sword pointing towards Pandora.

'You'll what? Without the Andrastus Dagger you cannot defeat me.' She laughed cruelly. 'Stand down, *little* boy. This is just too sad to watch.'

He hesitated. For the love of Hamira he would have been happy to die knowing he'd killed the Priestess first, but for Hamira's sake he also knew not to rise to the bait. It was his duty to survive in order to protect her. Besides, even if he could cause Pandora's death a Red Witch would surely take her place on the throne as their new Black Queen. True, one less witch was always a bonus, but grudgingly he stepped back.

Pandora flashed a winning smile. After discovering the art of the Dark Magic of the Witches fuelled by the powers once released from the box, one could easily forget Pandora was no longer the human she appeared to be. They had neither the experience nor magic to fight her and win. This was something he knew he should work on, if they could get out of here alive.

'You seem determined to anger the gods,' she snarled. 'That Zeus has cursed your lover, the Goddess of Hope, to live within a host's body in order to survive, does not seem enough for you. Well,' she sang, 'life is definitely going to change for you very soon, young man.'

Blinded by fury, his blood coursed through his veins at an alarming speed. Never before had he hated Pandora like this.

He wanted to cut her down.

Maim her!

Kill!

But gods above! This was Hamira's life! She may be only the host, but with all those years spent watching over her, protecting her, he could not help but love her, too. To him, both Hope's spirit and Hamira were one. The trio needed each other to survive. He could not, would not, fail her. Regardless of the consequences.

'One might even say, a turn for the worse,' Pandora continued. 'I only wish Hamira would be alive to see it.'

'A trap!' Epimetheus shouted, and at the same time Prometheus drew his sword and lunged forward.

With a swift precision Pandora raised a hand. Wisps of strange red smoke formed at her fingertips and a wall of power surged through his trusty sword, freezing it in time, the point of his blade just inches from her palm. His faced contorted with the pressure as he tried to break through her defences. He pushed harder. His own magic energy hummed along his arm and vibrated along his sword. But nothing could penetrate her powerful magic. She leaned closer and looked at him, flames flickering in her taunting eyes. They needed more men. An army like she had. How silly they were to think they could take her on themselves!

'Wouldn't it be fun,' Pandora whispered in his ear as he struggled to move from the powerful force she held him down with, 'if Hamira dies *now*, and Hope's spirit enters one of my witches?' His heart missed a beat. That was her plan? They would never be able to protect the goddess' spirit if her next host was a Pandora witch!

'No!' Prometheus shouted, desperate to remove his sword from her spell, but it stuck firm. He turned back, his arm aching, fearful for what he would see. 'Hamira!' A flash of glowing red Hēphaistos Fire shot out past his eyes, temporarily blinding him. To his horror he felt its heat streak past towards the frightened girl, and shrouded within the glowing light Hamira let out a bloodcurdling scream. A scream which the Dream-crawlers latched onto and dragged him into for the rest of his life.

Every single night.

Relentlessly.

The torture of seeing his Hamira and Hope dying in front of him for the first time since they were cursed was like suffering in Tartarus all over again. Yet, the scars were to serve him well as a reminder of his pledge to do things better from then on.

And so from that day forward Prometheus and his brother gathered together enough Destaurians to join them in their mission to protect his Goddess and her hosts from the Black Queen and her army of minions.

Over time his warriors split into two groups. Those showing more aptitude for leadership became Governing Council members, with

Epimetheus at their side for guidance, in accordance with the wishes of Prometheus.

The second band of Destaurians became a dedicated army of Warrior Guards, forming the first of the Orders sworn to serve the Council and protect all future hosts for the ultimate safety of the Goddess of Hope's returning spirit.

The hosts themselves; female descendants of Hope later named the Children of Destiny, became the second Order. Women bound only by their lineage and their inbuilt need to serve, which for Prometheus became a blessing in disguise. For, miraculously, when Hamira died the Pandora Witches' plans failed. Instead of entering a witch's body Hope's spirit floated up into the skies and waited patiently for her next Child of Destiny to arrive.

During this time, and over the continuing years, Prometheus wrote many a training manual by which all Destaurian Guards and their Children of Destiny would use for training. Amongst a whole series of books, and all the rules and regulations within, there was one rule that over the years never changed, and that was that love did not exist between a single warrior Guard, a *solitaire*, or unbonded Guards and his Child of Destiny.

In his eyes all hosts would be trained to be nothing but empty vessels to be filled; a plaything, a toy, something to be used and discarded as their guardian pleased until their quest was over. Love could only surface after a Guard and his Child received their Bonding rights at the infamous and most longed-for Destaurian Bonding Ceremony. And even then it was up to the individual Guard to decide if love should get in the way of the mission, or not.

As far as Prometheus was concerned, soldiers who think with their hearts would be no use to anyone. His own big mistake. To think with one's cock, however, was positively encouraged. These encouragements included ingenious inventions to brighten a Destaurian Guard's training. A popular example was the Sexual Extra-curricular Xtasy rota, which explicitly forbade two people to have sex together more than once without a break of at least three days apart and someone different in between, and his ingenious newly designed Whip and Cock training. Only when the pain and pleasure were one, and accepted as such, could a Child of Destiny know her true self worth and live and die by the SWORD. Servitude. Worship. Obedience. Respect. Defend.

This pleased Prometheus and he often taught his students, the Destaurian Guard Learnas and Learners that from even the tiniest problems new opportunities can grow. If only you know where to look for them.

But unfortunately, several thousand years later, his next problem wasn't so tiny and came in the form of a large-breasted, blonde-haired female with an insatiable appetite for sex in public places and a penchant for calling everyone dude whether they be Learna or Learner.

Sadly, sex in public places, in front of anyone outside the aptly named Temple of Sexual Extra-curricular Xtasy, was also forbidden. Dude, on the other hand, although not forbidden, annoyed Prometheus immensely. To the point of distraction.

Part Two – 4,000 Years Later, Planet Destauria, Black Ice Training Ground

Chapter Three

'Where are the twins and Eros?' Prometheus asked his team, trying to avoid eye contact with the young attractive Learna Artemis. She sat at the opposite end of the black oval bench attempting every trick in the book to get his attention, when she thought no one else was looking. He studied the way her straight, hip-length blonde hair framed her suntanned face as she leaned forward, the way it flowed behind her like a golden stream as she walked. The way she used her body to taunt him, something Destaurians, although highly sexed creatures, never did in public, simply because it was not their way. That behaviour was left for the Children of Destiny or strictly reserved in the Temple of SEX. Although intrigued, it wasn't so much her outlandish public behaviour which shocked him, more how disrespectful she was being to him on his first day as their Learned, and the founding, most respected teacher of Black Ice Training Ground.

In response to Prometheus' question the male students, the Learners, Samilious and Ares, grinned a knowing look, but said nothing. Even Hestia, a follower of the ways of the original Goddess of the Hearth and Home, did not look up from behind her tatty Encyclopaedia of Magical Herbs and Wortcunning. Prometheus raised his eyebrows at their unwillingness to cooperate. Only Artemis, with her seductive blue eyes, appeared to be interested in nothing but him. But not for the right reasons. It was Hestia who broke the silence.

'I think they've been called away, sir.'

'I think that's code for the threesome they're having together as we speak, dude.' Artemis laughed. 'Dude, you know, or maybe you don't, how horny our sexpert Eros gets? He certainly takes after the God of Love; you should see the size of his—'

'That's quite enough, Artemis. Thank you,' Prometheus added, turning with frustration to a pile of chalk tablets and rummaging through them as his mind whirred. These students were supposed to be the best, handpicked by the Council Destaurian Guards. At their highly trained level they should be fully operational as a team, ready to go out in the field at any given moment's notice. Out of the seven in his session one Learna was blatantly disobeying him from the point he'd first met her, and three had chosen to catch up on their SEX rota during his lesson time and had not even bothered to turn up yet. Inconceivable! They were acting more like layabouts with no ambition than the elite taskforce they were supposed to be. Things had definitely changed since the good old days when he had first established the Training Ground, and he didn't mean just moving with the times and speaking in a more modern fashion. Dude, however, was way too trendy for him to contemplate. But manners never cost a thing.

Prometheus sighed inwardly. Did this happen a lot? Or were they testing him because he was new? Why had none of the other Learned warned him of this? Eros and the twins' rendezvous or Artemis' unbelievable behaviour were not to be found anywhere in their reports. That did not please Prometheus.

Their previous Learned was what Artemis had already called Eros, a slackster. There could be no other reason. Someone was going to pay for doing this to him, make no bones about it! How could he control the situation if he was not given all the information? He pulled out a tablet and pretended to study it hard. As far as he was concerned no one kept secrets from him, or even dared to. And as for this misbehaving malarkey, they may be new to his sessions but they would soon find out he would not be messed about like this. Not on his time. Not on his patch.

He thought about getting one of his team to go and fetch the absent trio. But everywhere was monitored. He would find out for himself sooner than they realised and woe betide the missing trio when he did. With this in mind Prometheus slapped on a smile and continued with his planned and hopefully impressive first-day speech.

'Since it's your first day with me as your Learned, and you've had to sit through a morn full of rules and regulations I had planned something special for this aft, however,' he paused for effect, 'during nourishment break I received some important news sent via Hermes, which must take precedence.'

An excited murmur swept through the remaining team. Now in their twelfth year and with exams out of the way they could call themselves fully-fledged members of the Destaurian Guard Unit, more commonly known as the DGU. Artemis, the group's tease, blew him a silent kiss and winked at him.

'So dude, whatsup?' she asked annoyingly.

'Unfortunately the twins and Eros are going to be sorry they missed this, but on their heads be it. A new Child of Destiny is about to be born and anytime now one of you, a member of *my* team,' he said eagerly, 'will be picked to go on duty as their personal Guardian by Royal Appointment Delegate.' The four students whooped with excitement. Prometheus beamed.

To be a guardian was an honourable job, more so than a High Council member, who had it relatively easy basically doing their admin jobs. But to be here, now, at such a time when one of *his* team would up and leave on the most prestigious mission of their life as a GRAD out in the field was exhilarating. And a goal they all attained to. He hoped. 'On one hand it's a shame, because it means that whoever is chosen will have little time to get acquainted with me.' The team groaned in unison. 'Well, you may laugh,' he said, laughing himself, 'but no one teaches at Black Ice Training Ground like I do. I feel there is so much more inside information from my personal experience that one of you will miss out on. For this reason I promise, as one of the highest ranking of The Learned, I will be in constant touch with the chosen one. Available at any time. Day or night.'

'Ooh, I hope it's me, dude!' Artemis blurted out.

The handsome dark-skinned Learner named Ares, who according to his records was a mighty destructive and savage Destaurian Guard when riled – a perfect warrior – clenched his large fists and growled. Prometheus noted Artemis' interruption and Ares' dislike of her, but if she noticed she didn't seem to care. She crossed her arms on the table and leant forward, sticking her chest out in his direction, flaunting her assets for all she was worth. How very un-guard like!

Prometheus smiled. In all his years he had never come across a female Learna so eager to please him sexually, as if she modelled herself on a Child of Destiny. Everyone knew how easy they were. Quite clearly Artemis had been after a place in the high-ranking protection league of the DGU for quite some time. Pity he had no say in who would be picked for the next mission. Not that he planned to spoil his chances and tell her that.

If she wasn't the one the Council picked she was going to be spending a lot of time after hours, tied up on his rack. Meanwhile, if she didn't behave herself, show him the respect he deserved and stop this brash behaviour, tough times would befall her. It was in her best interests that he nipped this in the bud. Standards must not slip. Outside his sessions he could have her any time he desired. But if she was the one time would be very limited, and he must get his end away before the day was out. Excited with this prospect Prometheus stood up and addressed the rest of the team.

'On the other hand,' he continued, as he made a quick circuit around the smooth black contours of the training room, 'I don't need to tell you this is the most important and influential mission any of you Destaurian warriors could be called up for.'

He stopped at one of the large floor-to-ceiling windows to cast what he hoped looked like a watchful eye over the surrounding Sterile Forest. 'I've studied your scrolls and I know you are more than capable of the job,' he said, with his back to his Learna and Learner, while he adjusted his growing cock into a more comfortable position. When all was in place he turned round and gave them his best serious look. 'If picked, one of you will soon leave your life as you know it. Nothing will be the same again. No more shared barracks. No more unexpected late night drills, and absolutely no more nasty nourishment meals.' If he didn't know better he could have sworn someone added 'and no more SEX rota' under their breath.

There was unanimity of bright-eyed and eager nods around the table. Those that had been slouching through the morn's introductory session were now all sitting straight-backed and eager to hear more.

'So, in order for me to learn more about you I'm going to ask a question. If you are chosen as the next GRAD, what aspect of the mission are you most looking forward to?' Ares raised his hand, and Prometheus gave him a nod to proceed.

'For me it's gotta be killing da bitch witch Pandora herself. She's why I love poppin' caps so much.'

Always the warrior, Prometheus smiled. *But drop the accent!* Why Ares admired rappers so much perplexed him no end. It seemed quite common for Destaurian guards to latch onto any language or an accent they fancied in an effort to reinvent themselves because their immortality easily gave rise to an eternity of boredom. One trip to the Otherworld and, according to the reports of the last Learned and Ares, like so many others, came back a changed guard. To look at him now one would never believe that the warrior rapper standing before him used to be a British Aristocrat in his mortal days.

'Well, Ares,' he continued, 'if you can find the Black Queen good luck to you. It's not like the Golden Age when she did much of the evil herself. These days she keeps pretty much hidden while her minions do her bidding. I have not personally seen her in over a thousand years.' He walked back to the head of the table, sat down, and gave a cursory glance in the direction of his eye candy, Artemis. She licked her lips and pouted seductively at him, as she had done all morn.

Then as if being looked at gave her permission to speak, she shouted out.

Again? Rude as well as insolent!

'Plus, dude, remember the hierarchy, white, grey, red and black. Kill the Black Witch Pandora and there's always another Red Witch waiting to step into her shoes.'

'Well, thank you for that Artemis, but did I say this was an open forum you rude and inconsiderate Learna?'

'Well, no,' she said, looking around, ensuring her audience's full attention, 'but one of us in this room, or in their bunks...' she giggled, 'doesn't have much time left to learn.'

The class laughed.

Prometheus was not amused. *Just keep pushing me and see what happens!* He turned to Samilious, their attaché and mechanicals gadget expert. To the casual observer he looked barely out of short trousers. To Destaurians, however, he was much older and wiser than the teenager of eighteen, perhaps nineteen years he appeared to be, and for which he could easily be mistaken for in the

Otherworld; Earth.

'I'd wager you can't wait to use one of your many newly created inventions, right, Samilious?'

'Absolutely, sir. It's all very well testing them out on each other, here at the Training Ground,' he pointed absently to a window, 'but to see them work out there in another time, or another planet, for a *meaningful* purpose, well, that's going to be the real test.' He grinned, excitement dancing in his brown, almost human looking, eyes.

'And your favourite is the TAG system, yes?'

'Absolutely! My Tracking Analysis Gadget system is the best. Considering Black Ice is technically not supposed to be powered by electricity or the modern amenities of the Otherworld, you did a pretty good job of smuggling in that nano microchip, sir.'

'Well, I wouldn't actually call it smuggling,' Prometheus said, with a growing sense of getting himself into trouble if he wasn't careful, 'but I certainly agree the TAG system is your best invention to date. How you got it to tag not only the wearer's location but precisely what they're doing I'll never know, but you can be sure it's going to get plenty of use very soon, Samilious.'

'Oh, dude, I'd much rather stay in touch with my Child of Destiny through her Destaurian Eyes,' Artemis said without raising her hand, or even waiting to be asked.

Interrupting again? Is there no end to her rudeness?

'Imagine being able to telepathically read all her dirty thoughts!' she giggled. 'I know I can read hearts, but it's just not the same.'

'Well, perhaps if you paid attention more,

Artemis, instead of interrupting so much, you'd remember that the ability to read the Child of Destiny's mind only works when you're in close proximity and cannot be relied on, like the TAG system, if you're on another planet or in a different period of time.' He scowled.

By the look on her face she didn't expect that, and he almost grinned. And then he noticed, really noticed, what she was trying to pass as her Guard's uniform.

'And what in Tartarus' name, may I ask, are you wearing, Learna?'

'Oh, don't you like it? I rustled it up myself.'

'That's not the required guard uniform. Only this morn I told you all this.' He studied her attire with amazement, wondering how he had not seen it before. Her standard issue tunic looked two sizes too small, and she'd unbuttoned it to an unbelievably risqué low level. No wonder he'd been having trouble seeing beyond her voluptuously deep cleavage all day. Not that he really minded that side of things. What bothered him most was his difficulty with exercising authority over her. She could do with a dose of what respect means. Was he really that rusty? This was his first time back teaching sessions as one of the Learned in a long while. For years he'd worked more closely with the Council, away from Black Ice, since his brother Epimetheus had gone AWOL. Surely things back on the Training Ground couldn't be this bad?

'I just modified it a bit,' she said, standing up to show everyone her tight top. Prometheus noticed the shape of her firm nipples pushed against the thin fabric of her tunic as she spoke. Permanently cold, or horny? He tried to concentrate on the matter in hand, but found himself praying to King Harsis das for the latter.

'See this shorter style skirt suits me so much better than the old-fashioned ankle-length type.' It barely covered her bottom and left nothing to the imagination, but just in case anyone missed it she did a quick twirl for all to see.

Despite the rules, and her uncharacteristic Destaurian behaviour, he could think of nothing but taking her there and then in front of the whole team. She had a definite problem with her need for attention, but what he needed to find out was whether or not it was just for show. All morn she'd been winding him up, and as much as he loved to watch this strange blonde-haired beauty he could not have this continue. She was making him look a fool.

She will not get away with this, even if she is the chosen one. What to do?

He could make up some story about how it was an unknown or perhaps a new ritual that you only get to hear about once you make it to the twelfth year of the DGU. And then, to his lewd delight, he'd fuck her in front of all the others, talking them through the sordid details of how to make her so wet and lusty, even prissy Hestia would be donning her pinny and baking cakes in his honour, in an effort to be next in line. Naked underneath the pinny, of course, and just for a second he smiled at that image.

He understood he was the oldest, wisest, most handsome guy in the room, and it was natural for Artemis to develop a crush on him so early on, but this was his session. Destaurians just didn't openly display their sexual needs like this. Not in public. Besides, he decided the rules, not her, and blatantly disobeying him in such a rude and undercut manner, however good she looked, was a punishable offence.

Sitting down, Artemis placed her forefinger on her glossed bottom lip and he watched as the tip of her tongue erotically roamed over her long, silver-painted nail, just like it would if she were licking the end of his cock. Feeling his dick throb Prometheus looked away, making another circuit around the room as he spoke, keeping Artemis under scrutiny from the corner of his eye. The way she flicked her long golden hair out of her eyes and leaned forward to push her breasts so tightly together did more than just excite him. He definitely wanted to take her there and then, in front of the class, and Tartarus to the rules!

As if to prove a point, and taunt him further, she swivelled her stool round so her whole body now faced him. Very slowly she separated her legs and revealed to him two things. One, she needed to be taught a lesson, very quickly and before he became the laughing stock of Black Ice. However much he liked what he saw. Clearly she had no respect for her elders.

And two, she wasn't wearing her regulation underwear either. In fact, she wasn't wearing any underwear.

Prometheus cleared his dry throat.

Artemis smiled and quickly crossed one long tanned bare leg over the other as if she knew her job was done.

'What da fuck? Attention seeker!' Ares growled under his breath. She turned and stuck her tongue out at him.

Right! That's it!

'Artemis, have you ever been spread wide open and fucked in front of your teammates, in public?'

Chapter Four

Immediately her spine straightened and she gasped aloud. 'Of course not! I've worked years to get where I am today. I'm named after the original daughter of Zeus, and Greek Goddess of the Hunt and Wild Animals.' She sucked in an angry deep breath and appeared to be quite embarrassed, but Theo wasn't so sure if it was all an act. 'To behave in such a manner is beneath me. I'm shocked. I... I... that sort of treatment is reserved for mere Children of Destiny!' she fumed.

'Then why do you insist on behaving like one?'

'I—'

'Stand up,' he said curtly. Should he? Shouldn't he? She certainly needed to be taken down a peg or two. Oh, to Tartarus with it. He might as well have some fun. If she was the one this could be the last chance.

Grudgingly she stood.

'Climb up on the table. Get down on your hands and knees. Crawl to me and then get out my cock and suck it.'

Shocked, her mouth fell open. The other Learna and Learner looked around the table, silently searched each others' faces for answers. Artemis hesitated. Prometheus cocked his head to one side and raised his eyebrows; an unsaid warning to not push him any further.

For a moment their eyes locked on, as though there was a secret battle of power between them. Maybe there was, but unwittingly she was about to walk, or rather crawl, straight into his trap. He crossed his arms and gave her a stern look. 'I'm waiting.'

'And I'm a Destaurian warrior. I don't have to do this.'

'True. But when you behave so outlandishly in my sessions, you will know in future there will be consequences. Act like a Child of Destiny and you will be treated as one. Now, obey me, or I will take you to the Punishment Tower, where I will really put you through your paces.'

She licked her lips and gulped. As usual, all eyes were on her. They all loved sex, but never before had they seen one of their own kind humiliated like a human host in public.

Just when Prometheus felt he could not stand the tension another moment Artemis climbed onto the black bench, got onto all fours and began to crawl across in a quick shuffling motion.

'No, no, no, that's lousy,' he chided. 'Go back and start again. This time with conviction. A Child of Destiny must be eager to please. Feeble attempts like that will get them whipped. Or is that what you want, Artemis?'

Her eyes widened with horror, yet she went back and started again. Red splotches of what looked like embarrassment, which Prometheus suspected was anger, crept up her neck and into her cheeks as she dropped to her knees and redoubled her efforts, slowly crawled towards him. This time more seductively, like a wild cat ready to pounce. In an instant his cock grew at the sight of her obeying like a lowly slut. On the surface Artemis could do the crawl perfectly, but when he looked into her eyes he could see her inner struggles. She may be abnormally flirtatious for a Destaurian, but a Child of Destiny she was not. She didn't have the inherent need to obey his sexual demands, to be used in whatever way he saw fit. This, like his cock, would come hard for her. He grinned. During his time spent in admin he'd forgotten how powerful the simple act of commanding another felt. And as she attached her lips to his swelling member he grabbed her golden hair and held her tight as he pumped into her warm wet mouth, watching her rosy face burn with such degrading treatment. What a sight for sore eyes. Her large breasts swayed to and fro, sending everyone, including Hestia, into a spellbound stupor as they watched her act like they had never seen any Destaurian do in public before. Now it was Prometheus' turn to lick his lips. Finally he'd got her where he wanted her.

'This, Learnas and Learners,' he said, as he pulled Artemis off his cock by her hair and then forced her lips up and down the side of his length until she got the idea to lick him, 'is what, as you must know by now, a Child of Destiny must do. Anything and everything I ask, with no doubts, complaints or care in the world other than to please me. Of course, this one fantasises of sexually pleasing me in public, but in practice it becomes difficult. Like all you sitting around the bench cringing, it does not come naturally to any Destaurian to obey in this manner. You are minus a host's genetic coding, for which I am sure you are all thankful. With the right match and the trust ingrained in her mind, however, you can imagine what pleasures await you.'

She pulled her mouth away from his cock to speak without asking permission. Another bad girl point. He may be the new Learned, their teacher, he pondered, but she was not a new Learna. She knew how one of Destiny's Children should act. He silently marked it up, pulled her mouth back onto his length and shoved it in deep before a word escaped her lips. Or so he thought.

'And once you earn that trust she will gladly do anything you ask,' Artemis' muffled voice mumbled, full of herself and his cock. Prometheus looked down at her on her hands and knees, looking every bit like she was beginning to enjoy her punishment.

'However,' Prometheus said with stern authority, removing her mouth from his cock to allow her to come up for air, 'when someone breaks that trust, say, they misbehave and refuse to honour their superior's request for full regimental uniform,' he paused, giving his words time to sink in, 'or perhaps they forget simple rules for putting hands up and only speaking when spoken to by their elders, then trust can invariably be broken.'

Artemis frowned.

'Therefore a punishment to regain that trust, which matches the extremity of the bad behaviour, must be given. Despite contrary belief, rules are *not* made to be broken.' He glared at Artemis. 'Stay on the table and stand up, Learna.'

She smiled. Nervously this time.

'To test my theory, let's see how much further Artemis will go to please me in front of you all.' Highly immoral on Destauria, but he was the Learned. They'd soon know not to mess with him!

In one quick swoop Prometheus clamped her wrists together with cuffs, threaded them with chains and looped them through a ceiling hoop she failed to see until it was too late. He pulled down hard on the chain, tugging her restrained wrists up high above her head. She yelped in surprise, and forced to stand on tiptoe in an uncomfortable position her legs wobbled. At this stage she was neither fully hanging, nor with her feet firmly in her high-heeled shoes. She wriggled and went to complain, but Prometheus noticed she quickly thought better of it.

'She will soon realise it is in her best interests to keep still and obey my commands as fast as possible, otherwise discomfort will turn into pain.' She stopped wriggling. 'This way trust is regained in a relatively short period of time, and the culprit is also quick to learn that her obedience will be rewarded when I am satisfied she trusts me enough to know that I make the rules and must be obeyed. Quite simple, yet very effective.' The rest of the team sat there, mouths open, lost for words and probably wondering what sort of torture Eros, Selene and Eos were in for, when they returned.

'Destaurians, do not forget; the severity of each punishment can depend on not only the severity of the crime, but how intense you need this period of her redemption to be. The more intense, the longer lasting. Pain is not always needed. It does however keep her focused.' He put his hand up her skirt and pinched her bottom. She cried out in pain. He grinned at the class and tied the chain against a hook on the wall behind him. 'Anyone know what else can be used to get the point across?' In his element he stepped to the side of Artemis. She had her eyes scrunched up, already embarrassed enough to not dare look into her teammates' eyes. Instantly Ares raised his hand.

'Yes, Ares, got a suggestion?'

'Humiliation,' he said, a little over keenly. 'Shame her and she'll feel so humble she'd never want to disobey you, for fear of going through the same experience again.'

'Very astute, Ares. Although it goes far deeper than inflicting fear you certainly have the correct gist. If she was a real Child of Destiny their fear would come from their own personal fear of not pleasing me. In an effort to redeem themselves they would take their punishment, however painful, since it's the knowledge that in doing so they are pleasing me. It's a complex business, but maybe Artemis will soon get the hang of it.' The team nodded, their shock fading. What an experience he was giving them. This was one lesson they wouldn't forget in a hurry.

'Now, I'm going to show you exactly how obedience can be enforced in this manner. Any suggestions for improving on what I have already done?' He looked around. No one dared to look him in the eye.

'Come, come. Let's not stand on ceremony. Artemis only has herself to blame here. She chose not to put up her hand and to disrespectfully shout the answers out. Why shouldn't you be allowed to? Permission is granted to shout out your answers for the rest of this session.' He looked at his wrist. According to his time-clock he didn't have much left.

'Take off her skirt!' Samilious shouted pushing his glasses back up on the bridge of his nose.

'Yes, let's see what she was trying to tempt me with.' Prometheus moved behind her, undid the clasp of her skirt, unwound it and threw it to the floor triumphantly. He heard a small whimper escape her lips. She was now officially breaking Destaurian law for the second time, and he was making her do it.

How good that felt! And to cap it all the room buzzed with excitement. The delight on Hestia's usually calm and collected face was extremely amusing. Priceless, in fact. Prometheus glanced at his time-clock again. Time was running out. He pressed on.

'Artemis may be happy to flaunt her sexuality, and you all know at the right time and the right place this would not normally be a problem for her. But if I were to take my index finger and place it here on her sex,' which he did, making her flinch, 'and slowly rub the hard nub of her surprisingly already wet clit, in front of all of you watching, I'm sure she'll soon be wishing she had obeyed my rules. Am I right, Artemis?'

She gasped as his finger slipped over her wet pussy and struggled to keep her balance as he began to explore her hole. She blinked with a confused look on her face, and all she could muster was an incoherent mumble for an answer.

'Artemis,' Prometheus scorned, 'I'm sorry but that's not good enough. Given the circumstances you find yourself in I would expect you to be a lot more willing to please me. If I ask you something, as I explained earlier this morn, I expect your replies to be clear and concise. You are all supposed to be master Destaurian Guards, and this elite unit does not have space for feeble mumblers.'

'I'm sorry, my Learned,' Artemis said much louder. 'I do regret my attitude and will not murmur again when you, sir...' she struggled to get her words out, '...when you, sir... speak... to... me.'

'Good girl. Now open your eyes and look at Samilious.' She did, and everyone watched her face turn a shade redder as her eyes fixed upon his. He beamed back at her, relishing every moment of her mental torture. The room was silent with anticipation of Prometheus' next move. They could have heard a pin drop if it were not for the squelching sounds Artemis' wet sex was making. Her breath grew more erratic and louder with every stroke.

'Ares, my desk drawer if you please. Get out the butt plug in the shape of a rocket.' Someone gasped. He hoped it was Artemis.

'Yo, sir!' Ares replied with a sense of eagerness Prometheus was proud of. It was the first time Prometheus had seen him looking anything but angry. Ares scraped back his stool and marched round to Prometheus' desk. All eyes, including those belonging to Artemis, were on him this time. 'The huge brown one?' he asked with a smirk, holding it up and waving it around for everyone to inspect. Artemis groaned. Everyone else laughed.

'Yes, that's the one.' Prometheus liked his style, and knew he would make a very good Destaurian Guard if chosen. Named after the God of Savagery and War he certainly had a sadist streak in him, a sign of a true Guard who would know exactly how to get what he wanted from his Child of Destiny, when his time came.

'Sir,' he said, handling the butt plug, 'I didn't think wood was allowed in Destauria.'

'Let's just say Samilious made some home improvements to it, and I think you'll find it's now classed as official equipment, so not a problem,' he lied.

'Here you go,' Ares said, handing it to Prometheus.

'No, you keep it. I wouldn't want to be accused of handling her too lightly.' He grinned, practically rubbing his hands together, but just then footsteps ran down the hallway outside. Eros burst in through the doors, his hair in disarray.

'What the…?' he exclaimed, the look of shock on his face quickly changing to one of bemusement as he eyed the naked body of Artemis and saw what their Learned was doing to her. Clearly he liked what he saw. He threw on his long coat, briskly walked to his stool and sat down. Keen to watch.

A moment later the twins, Selene and Eos, came running in, just as dishevelled and out of breath. Looking at Artemis, and not where they were going, they bumped into Eros' broad back, and stopped, rooted to the spot in disbelief.

'Ah, the lovers have decided to join us. Well as you can see we're busy, but mark my words you are not out of trouble, and your behaviour will be dealt with. Later. Now, Selene, Eos, come round here,' he commanded. 'Hold open her bottom cheeks.'

Giggling, they gladly obliged. Without wavering Selene took the left, Eos the right. They looked at each other, gripped her peachy flesh hard and dug their nails in. Artemis squealed. They grinned.

Payback time? Prometheus was pleasantly surprised by their initiative. He couldn't wait to dish out their punishment for skipping some of his session, but right now they looked like Eros had fucked them hard and fast. He'd get them later. When they least expected it. All three of them. First he'd take Selene. He just couldn't resist her long baby-blonde hair. So bright it almost shone like one of the moons, as if she were Goddess of the Moon herself.

Then, after red-haired sister Eos had warmed herself up watching them, he'd take her and make Selene watch. Of course he'd save Eros, the SEX Doctor, for dessert.

He glanced at the pale, freckled face of Eos. She really did look like the Goddess of Dawn. Still pulling Artemis' cheeks apart they looked back at their Learned for approval. 'Like this?' they asked together, their speech patterns as identical as they were.

'Good... good...' he mused encouragingly. 'Hold her still. Her ability to hold on is fading fast.'

Artemis groaned; pleasure now overcoming her need to fend them off.

Prometheus continued to stroke her wet pussy, and she thrust her hips forward and pushed against him for all she was worth.

'Samilious, you'd better come round here so you can see this.' He did. Fast. 'Now, Ares, insert the butt plug into her bottom-hole.' The class craned to watch what was happening. Even Hestia stood up and moved around to get a better look.

'Ooh... shouldn't she have some lube with that?' asked Hestia.

'What? This is a punishment,' Ares reminded

her.

'Quite right,' Samilious agreed. 'And as the attaché and mechanicals gadget expert I'd better come round and check you're inserting the butt plug correctly, Ares,' said Samilious, laughing. 'That's one expensive piece of equipment, comes with the TAG system included.' They all grinned.

Ares pushed the wooden plug into her. 'I call it Mr Rocket, because of its distinctive shape and size.'

Artemis whimpered, and standing in front of her Prometheus watched her eyes bulge as Ares pushed the smooth wooden plug into her rectum. Artemis' body stiffened, her chains chinked as they tightened, and Ares applied more pressure while Prometheus continued to work his fingers over her pussy. Then the large thick end of the plug slipped in with a slurp, and her mouth fell open.

'Aw, sweetheart, don't make such a fuss, my cock's bigger than that,' teased Eros, and then the whole team joined in.

Perfect!

Prometheus was just about to make his move and feed his cock into the one place that didn't annoy him, or call him dude, when a light rap at the door interrupted him, and Hermes the Messenger walked in.

Hermes passed him a scroll of royal blue, which Prometheus knew to be a summons from the High Council to their secret location in the Cloud Citadel-Kingdom, Nuvola. The location changed from day to day for security purposes.

He ripped open the seal, read the directions and dashed out of the room, cursing the Council for their bad timing, although he knew it to be more than that with the additional note they'd left at the bottom. *By punishing Artemis in public for not being able to control her urges in public, you have inadvertently broken a major rule yourself.*

Damn it! He'd overlooked how fast the gods above worked, but what he hadn't overlooked was how serious they took the matter of lawbreaking. He wished he could know what they had planned for him before he got there. He didn't like shocks, but unfortunately he received his biggest shock to date.

Prometheus did not yet know that this was the day after which his whole life would change. The day that, despite his protests he, not a Learna or Learner, had been chosen to become the Personal Destaurian Guard for the new Child of Destiny. The next time he would see his team would be twenty-two years and three months later; the day he brought his protected to the Black Ice Training Ground for her instruction. The day things went from bad to worse. The day the gods must have laughed at his misfortune, and this went down in Prometheus' diary as the worst day in his immortal life by far.

So much for tiny problems growing into opportunities!

He now had one major problem on his hands, but could not for the life of him see the opportunity within.

Heavens above, he trained Guards to do this job. The last thing he wanted was to do it himself!

Part Three - Twenty-two Years Later, the Otherworld; Earth, Cambridge

Chapter Five

The High Council, Prometheus thought, had excelled this time when dishing out his punishment. He lay waiting for his charge, upon her bed, invisible and horny, his arms folded behind his head and feet stretched out over the heavenly blue coverlet, ankles crossed, thinking of the torturous path he'd travelled since arriving on the Otherworld twenty-two years earlier.

For twenty-two years of invisibly protecting the girl while she lived her PreCent years on Earth – the Otherworld – he was automatically banned from leaving her side to do anything. Seeking sex being at the top of his list. Oh, but by the time she was of age he could watch her having sex with her boyfriends. Not that she had that many with her busy life, but the few she had were enough to increase his sexual frustration.

If she only knew how many times he watched her undress and slip between the cool cotton sheets of her bed, on which he invisibly lay waiting. To be so close yet hidden for all those years made him so deliriously high he feared that if he dared to touch her he might never be able to stop.

Soon he would take her back to Black Ice and fulfil that insatiable yearning to control her, do whatever he pleased, whenever he pleased and for however long he pleased. And nothing could stop him.

But when did his life ever go according to plan? He'd only taken his eyes off her for a few minutes to catch up on some CCTV footage on his mini-portable, and she'd gone and done a runner!

Sometimes the precarious slippery slope of life can, without warning and with a fierce velocity, crack once solid ground and plunge the unprepared into a gaping black hole filled with a stark, cold hopelessness, to flood even the strongest of minds with an inescapable darkness.

As Ronnie accelerated up the ramp and hit a patch of black ice she understood all too well how quickly life could change. She skidded to the left, smashed through a guardrail and knocked over a lamppost, which fell onto the roof of her Jeep. She screamed and shielded her face with both hands. The airbags inflated, and in her rear-view mirror she glimpsed a man staring at her. His face blurred, then melted into flashing pictures of her childhood, family, friends, buildings and strange landscapes – flickering like an old silent movie, powered by a higher force.

The airbags deflated and the car filled with a burning smell of the controlled explosion that deployed them. Trapped, shaking uncontrollably, she wanted to get out, but couldn't think straight. Had she lost control of the steering wheel? Did she imagine it ripped from her grasp by some unseen force, which appeared as if by magic to steer her out of the danger of the oncoming traffic? She must have.

Such things are impossible.
Best left for dreams.

Ronnie tried to sit up, but a strange heavy weakness overcame her and she started to lose consciousness.

Was she hurt? She didn't know, but something told her not to worry. Just relax. Everything would soon be fixed. Very odd.

On the floor she spotted a splash of red. Her beloved London bus broach, bought on a trip to London with her mother.

It's funny the things that go through your mind, said a voice inside her head as she listened to the strange noises around her. She could make out a few words. Police. Had someone called the police? Despite the pain in her head something told her she needed the police, and not the ambulance.

There were people everywhere. Some came over to help, others kept telling her that everything was going to be okay. But she didn't feel okay. Every bone in her body ached. Through her window, smashed by the force of the lamppost, she caught a glimpse of a strange man taking control of the situation. He stood at the side of the road, about three feet away, talking to a crowd of onlookers. Slipping in and out of consciousness she strained to hear what he had to say.

'It's all right, I'm a doctor and she's a friend of mine. I saw the whole thing, that's my car behind. I'll take her straight to hospital and then sort out everything.'

A friend?

Hospital? How bad was it?

She tried to check, but couldn't gather enough energy to even move. Snippets of conversations drifted through her mind. Insurance… terrible weather for the time of year… black ice…

In her semi-delirious state she felt a hand touch her forehead, her neck and then, before she could think what to do, the car seemed to spin and blackness enveloped her.

Am I dead?

No, you're dreaming, girl.

Who are you?

My name is Prometheus. Your Destaurian Guard. I have been waiting for this moment ever since I first saw you.

Destaurian? Guard? What do you want from me?

Do not fear me child, I've been watching over you, protecting you from harm since the day you first arrived into this world. You are safe with me, but there is a lot to explain and time is running out. You have much to learn. Relax and let this dream take you, for it is a journey you cannot avoid. The time to realise who you are has come. You must succumb to it. You cannot escape. You do not want to escape. Trust in me.

The day was hot. A high golden sun radiated warmth on her skin and the light reflected off the shimmering threads of gold woven into the oversized cushions, upon which she lay stretched out. Smiling, she looked across the temple gardens at the dancers at the bottom of the hill. The summer solstice celebrations were in full swing and the beautiful sound of panpipes soothed her busy mind. She loved her life. The long hot summer nights stayed as bright as her days, which were only distinguishable by the different food she was served for her morn, noon and night.

'My sweet Goddess of Hope, do you have everything you require?'

'Place another pillow underneath my head. I wish to watch the dancers as you pleasure me, boy.' The blond-haired Adonis did as he was told, and with a delicate touch he lifted her flower-decorated head, and propped her up with another soft pillow. A finger languidly swept across her olive-toned skin, sweeping a dark curl from her eyes and trailed down the contours of her cheek, under her chin and snaked its way down to her voluptuous cleavage.

In reaction to his seductive touch the Goddess Hope breathed in, sticking her breasts out further, up towards the startling green eyes of the young man, a mere boy, that was to pleasure her. Her perfect match for the day's festivities. The Gods were clearly smiling on her today. How thrilled she was to be honoured with the title of a Goddess herself. Being a mistress to Zeus definitely had its perks. And perky he was indeed; at times she could feel his hard cock nudging against her side.

Pupils dilated, the unknown courtesan stared deep into her sparkling steely-grey eyes as his finger continued its journey across her shapely breasts, and down her translucent white silk robe. With a gentle hand he smoothed the hem up over her knees and slid it slowly higher to reveal the trimmed softness of pubic hair, which glistened under the sun. She reached out a hand with a small moan and gulped at the sight of the boy's throbbing bulge, which threatened to burst from the restrictive material of the loincloth she'd insisted he, like her other courtesans, should wear. His fingers probed her moist opening with a teasing touch of lustful promises yet to be fulfilled – but only when she allowed.

Hope felt the tense muscles of his young body as

he laid gently between her spread legs, and her own desire increased tenfold. She slipped her arms around his shoulders and pulled him quickly down, grasping his hair and demanding his mouth she spread her legs for quick entry. His murmuring soothed her feverish mind even as his warm hand smoothed her heated flesh from her breasts to her hip. She couldn't hold back the moan as she felt him push inside her wetness. His slow possession only made her body burn all the hotter and each deep stroke brought her that much closer to the satisfaction she demanded.

The Goddess sighed inwardly. Because she was mistress to Zeus whenever she had sex with one of her courtesans it was taken for granted that she'd lead. No, expected of her. Why was that so? It didn't have to be that way. No one wanted to grab her roughly, throw her to the floor, lift up her skirts and harshly force their cock up deep inside her, for fear of upsetting the god to whom she belonged. But that is what she craved.

In her fantasy, which she knew well, this one courtesan took exactly what he wanted. His desire to satisfy himself at any cost took over. For with him, when they were together, something in the way he looked not just at her, but deep within, could not disguise the lust he desperately tried to contain. Which is why she found him so easy to fantasise about. He really did want more. She could tell. If only she could reveal that was what she wanted too. If only she wasn't the mistress to Zeus, the King of Gods, the ultimate God of Thunder and Lightning. If only…

As he moved gently in and out of her she imagined herself in the open field, lying on a blanket in the middle of the festivities, naked and waiting to have someone to please. Like a common slave. Their roles reversed. 'I've been watching you,' came a voice from behind. She gasped and tried to cover herself up with a large silk pillow. 'No! Get on your hands and knees for me!' he demanded.

She whimpered. 'Please have mercy on me,' she begged as she moved into position, her hands firmly on the floor, her bare bottom exposed. She dare not look around at her assailant's face. 'Please?'

He didn't listen. 'Raise your bottom higher, so we can all see your sex.'

We? All? The sick debasement of being forced to do such things in front of an audience made the blood rush to her pussy. A moistness tingled between her legs. The shame of knowing that this command horrified yet turned her on, disgusted her. She needed to submit to his needs, to be used. If that's how he wanted it, so be it. She would do anything for him. However humiliating. The goddess lowered herself on her elbows and pressed her forehead to the floor. Her bottom now raised so high she knew they could see all of her intimate parts. And her wetness.

'On display and ready to be used. Who's first?' he asked. Several male voices answered. Her juices trickled down her legs.

'Get in line. You shall all have your turn. This greedy girl will take you all.' Heat burned her face. Someone dropped to the floor and rubbed a wet cock over her bottom. His hands gripped the inside of her thighs, dug nails in and pulled her legs wider apart in one swift movement. She had no idea who it was. How many more did he intend to have use her? Was every man at the festival watching, just waiting for their turn? Were all her slaves demanding their sexual freedom back and going to take her however they pleased, and make her pay for what she'd done to them? What if…?

'What if what, my goddess?' Her eyes sprung open. She had not meant to say that aloud. She so wanted to ask him what if their worlds were reversed, would he be able to dominate and fuck her like a man possessed? But she knew in her position that was a fantasy she'd have to keep to herself. Nothing could ever become of it. Not if she valued his life. Which she did more than her own. It broke her heart not to be able to reveal how she truly felt about him. The yearning to have no choice in how *he* wanted *her* to please him. She may belong to Zeus but this courtesan was *her* king.

She wished he had the power to reduce her to nothing but a gutter servant. Was it just a fantasy? Was it possible that there could be anything more between them? If she could give up all the riches of the temple bestowed upon her when she became Zeus' mistress, in return for the use of her body whenever, and however he demanded, she would gladly be poor.

She did not know why, nor could she understand her feelings, but to her he had been put on this planet to protect her. As if he was her destiny. He just didn't know it yet. Or perhaps he did. If only she could confess to falling in love with him. The last thing in the world she expected.

'My goddess?' he said, prompting an answer from her.

Should she? Could she? She clung on tightly to him and pulled him closer. She gasped. With a swooping but graceful movement he covered her gaping mouth with his own trembling lips and kissed her deeply with a passion that made her body writhe beneath his muscular body. Together their orgasms caused stars to explode in her mind. His thick cock pulsated inside her.

'My goddess,' he whispered again as he pulled out of her, their bodies still quivering. 'If I may be so bold, your exquisite beauty burns in my heart. It is a sensation I have never felt before; one of love but also deep pain. One of joy yet overwhelming sorrow.'

She let out a contented sigh. 'I have not heard of this pain and sorrow before; it is not something the Gods talk about.'

'So what is causing this heavy feeling in my heart if it is not the pain and sorrow of being in your ardent company, feeling so close but so far away from you at the same time?'

'Maybe the Gods have gifted you with the talent of forewarning. Or the power to read your lover's mind.' For a moment they stared into each other's eyes as if they were alone and nothing else mattered. 'I as your goddess would like that very much. It is not uncommon for my kind to bestow such power on those that deserve it.' She shut her eyes and wished he could read her mind. 'Now, hush. Be thankful those words, pain and sorrow, do not exist in our world. Please me!' she demanded, getting back into her true role, as was necessary. 'For you are mine today, to do what I will, and my needs must be met. All of them!'

Somewhere in the Olympian temple behind them

came an ear-piercing howl that stopped not only the lustful couple dead in their tracks, but merrymaking at the bottom of the hill. The sound of music and singing abruptly stopped. Chatting, singing and laughter disappeared. Those that once danced now stood still like the statues of the Greek Gods that ruled them, which stood in the Royal Temple Hall. The skies above turned black, covering their world of paradise with an evil darkness never experienced before. Lightening flashed, thunder boomed all around them and the partygoers cried out in fear and surprise.

'I'll give you pain and the sorrow of death!' a threatening voice boomed out from the rapidly forming dark clouds above.

Those that could escape the deadly bolts scattered. Others ducked and dived out of the way of the jagged spears of light that appeared to chase their prey, threatening to pierce their victim's hearts, one by one. Helpless, the Goddess Hope and her beautiful male courtesan watched in horror. Members of her family, their friends and temple staff fell to the ground, writhing in pain until death claimed their souls and the lovers were the only two left alive.

'Who is this boy you have chosen to sin with?'

'He is nothing to me!' she lied. 'Just a courtesan like any other chosen to please, as was your wish. Lest you forget you granted me this pleasure.'

'This is no ordinary courtesan!' he boomed. 'With this one it is more than just sex. He feels something that no other has felt for you before. Love. I will not allow it. He must die!'

'No, Zeus!' she screamed, pushing the boy away for safety's sake. At the sight of her beloved's petrified face the goddess saw their future darken, as did the world around them. So he did love her? Her heart sank. If he should die now she would never have the chance to explain her true feelings for him.

'He doesn't mean me any harm. You cannot kill him for having a heart! I beg of you,' she pleaded, 'please let him go. It is I you should be angry with, and I alone.'

'Very well. As you wish. Along with the rest of your world. Everything you see before you will be shifted to another realm. I am bored. Clearly I have made mistakes with the rules of this world that are too late to correct. From now on,' his booming voice continued, 'everything you have now will be as it is in your new world, but with one difference.'

'Whatever you say, my lord,' she agreed, welcoming the onset of the end of her life as she knew it, as a way of escaping his wrath and the invisible chains he bound her with.

The boy scrambled across the ground towards the one he loved, to protect her. Fearing for his safety she held up her hand in a silent command to halt. Let him take me, she mouthed, then turned her eyes back up to the skies.

'What must I do to be forgiven, my Lord?' she asked, with her eyes cast down to her virginal white robe. 'Do I not deserve the granting of a chance to be forgiven before I move on?'

'Only a mortal fool asks for forgiveness! I would make you mortal if that did not cut your punishment short. Killing your lover would hurt you more!'

'I would rather die a thousand deaths than cause this young man's life to be cut short,' she almost whispered.

'Very well then,' boomed Zeus. 'Thy curse be upon you! You are *my* goddess and will do as *I* say. You will become the new Hope and I shall keep your spirit locked away in a Magic Box, where all the evils will live beside you. If anyone is dim-witted enough to open it your spirit will be freed. But with you will come all the evils that reside with you to unleash themselves into the world. A world where your immortal lover awaits you.'

'But, my king, I do not understand. How will I live as only a spirit?'

Zeus let out a cruel laugh. 'Your mortality will depend on a human host. Without a body your spirit will not survive.'

She gasped at the implications.

'Let's see if your immortal lover can sustain his love, whilst watching you live and die a thousand times in the bodies of humans!'

'But what will become of our people of the Golden Age if the box is opened to release me, surely evil will also be released?' she asked, mortified.

'From then on you, or rather your host, will be forced to wander this new Earth and become their keepers for eternity. How you both deal with the evils is up to the pair of you to decide. Now be gone.'

A short burst of lightening and a crash of thunder extinguished their lives as they once knew it.

Panting for breath, Ronnie's eyes sprung open. She felt as though she'd been held underwater until she could no longer breathe, and had just burst through the water's surface gasping for air. *What had become of her? Of Prometheus? Would she see her one true love again?*

A nightmare, that's all, she told herself. *Just a dream!* She blinked and sighed at the relief of knowing the nightmare had ended. She was back in her bed. Real life beckoned.

She then became aware of an unfamiliar musty smell and couldn't work out where it came from. She sensed someone moving around the room. With her heart still pumping her eyes began to focus and she took a look around. Pine panelling on the walls and ceiling surrounded her.

Where am I?

Then she remembered the car crash; felt her head ache. An icy chill surged through her. She was neither in hospital nor with a friend. At least she couldn't recall ever having a friend who insisted on tying her down in case she tried to escape.

Chapter Six

No longer did Tim Harris have a clear understanding of what was real and what festered inside his imagination. But since when did he ever do what he should? Lately his whole life was filled with things he should or shouldn't have done. He shouldn't have had that last drink. He shouldn't have left Ronnie to her own devices. Not while all this was going on. But he did. And now he was living with the consequences.

His eyes sprung open. He checked next to him on the bed. She wasn't there. Didn't come home. Was she even supposed to? Was she really his? Ever?

He honestly could not remember. But what was clear as the cold light of day was that the unwanted images of sexual suffering and torture, which floated in his unconscious mind, had leapt from his dreams and were with him every second of his waking day.

Some days were better than others, like he could almost control it. But it was the evenings that were worse. Lately that's when the urge to fuck appeared, and when it did nothing would sate his animalistic appetite except for coming. Whether it be by his own hand, up a whore's cunt, or in the mouth of a stranger through a hole in the wall, it didn't matter. When night fell the thirst came, so did he – inside the nearest handy victim.

Tim pulled a face, angry of even being able to think in that way. Something incomprehensible was happening to him and it was happening more often. A darkness he fought hard to control. Yet the first time the change gripped him it was so quick he hardly realised what happened until it was too late. Was it too late to get his old self back? He hoped to god it wasn't. But he needed answers and he wasn't going to get them wasting away lying in bed.

He thought of Ronnie and how from the first day they'd met she'd opened up her soul and told him all about her need to find out what had happened to her parents. What started out as him assisting her in some light research lead to the discovery that there was a lot more going on than at first appeared.

Along the way they'd met another man, Charles Leamington, who had a great deal of knowledge with regard to the help they sought. One thing led to another and the three of them became a tightly knit research team, all with one common goal: to decipher the mysteries of the unexplainable world around them, of which most people went happily through the course of their lives totally unaware.

What the fuck was he supposed to do now? After a day at the library where they both worked they were supposed to meet up with Charles to report back to him, with an update of the progress of their latest case. Tim expected Ronnie back by now. Damn it! She could be in trouble and all because of him.

He punched the snooze button, temporarily killing the alarm. The clock said 5:05am. Early. He used to hate the mornings. Not any more.

Fuck! How was he supposed to admit he'd drunk too much and let Ronnie go it alone? Since discovering new leads she wanted to dive in straight away. Shoot first and ask questions later. Like she always did. And with good reason too. He, on the other hand, wanted to talk with Charles – to bring him up to speed. Do things the right way. Safety first. One could never be too careful with the unscrupulous types they dealt with. But no, he had to let it get all out of control, didn't he? Instead of calmly discussing the situation the stress of what they'd gotten into started to show. The stress of walking around at work feeling like he had the word *freak* stamped on his forehead didn't help either. Did anyone suspect?

Anyway, Ronnie stormed out on her own, and he turned to the bottle.

Or was it the other way round?

He couldn't remember.

His head throbbed.

'*Why* did you run?'

Everyone knew how pigheaded and stubborn

Ronnie could be – one of many ways she reminded him of himself – but as the one person she confided in and really talked to, he had no excuse. He should never have let things between them go as far as they did.

The alarm blared again. Tim grunted, shut it up with his fist and climbed out of bed. First he needed to freshen up so he could think straight. No good barging in without sorting out what he was going to say. He'd only end up making the whole situation worse. So far nothing implied foul play. More than likely he was letting his imagination put obstacles in his way. There had to be a simple explanation for Ronnie's absence. One not connected to this case at all. Most probably he'd call her mobile and find she spent the night at work. It wouldn't be the first time he'd discover her asleep on her desk, being the workaholic she was.

Naked he padded out of the bedroom into the bathroom and switched on the shower. Instant heat and steam filled the room.

He thought of their current case, they'd been discussing last night. A seemingly normal middle-class family in their home town of Cambridge had gone out on a killing spree last week. Not together, but individually, and what made it absolutely ridiculous to believe was every member of the Marshall family had killed someone on the same day. The mother, Philippa, a housewife and regular charity fund-raiser, murdered a neighbour's sleeping child while babysitting for a friend who was out shopping for groceries. At the same time her accountant husband, Adam, was committing an armed robbery at a cash and carry a few miles away. He killed a shopkeeper with a sawn-off shotgun. Earlier, Callum, their fourteen-year-old son knifed another kid in the street while on his paper round, with fatal consequences. Finally, his little sister for some reason poisoned a teacher with rat poison. The reason she gave was the same reason the rest of the family gave. She said a demon made her do it. When the police came to her school and arrested her, little Clara was wearing a red and white gingham dress, with matching ribbons tying up her bunches. She was six years old.

Tim grabbed the shampoo, spurted a dollop into his hand and lathered up his short brown hair. He turned his back to the shower and let the power of the water massage his aching head and shoulders. He wished he could wash away his troubles as easily as the suds.

What he needed was a plan. To the general public the Marshall killings didn't make sense. All sorts of stories were circulating of some sort of evil illness sweeping England, and although they were not strictly true, or based on any evidence or reliable source, both Ronnie and Tim knew different. Among a few selective Institute members. The truth about what was really going on wasn't that far from the bizarre stories spreading, although that element of truth must never be allowed to become public knowledge. Neither should the fact that this so-called disease had spread a lot further than the tiny isle of Britain. Pandemic proportions. The world was rife with evil constantly being covered up by those already in the know. The best way for all involved, thought Tim. Especially now the full horror had arrived on his doorstep.

Tim turned, allowing the water to cascade down

his muscled chest. Who would believe an ancient evil which once resided in the mythical Magic Box of Destiny had been released into the world? He could hardly believe it himself, yet it's what they were meant to meet Charles for and discuss with him, before moving on to the next stage of their plan where these creatures were concerned.

Yesterday, when Tim typed up the information he was going to hand in to Charles it read more like a fantasy story than the fact-based report it was. Something he noticed more often these days, but struggled to accept. On his report he quoted some vital research information they gleaned from a few pages ripped out from an archaic book of some sort. Copy attached.

According to their research they'd stumbled across something big. Until the Marshall murders neither Tim nor Ronnie had realised quite how big. But the telltale signs – the creepy glint in their eyes, the flash of red just before they strike – are plain to see by the trained eye. Unlike the evil force they expel that hides inside the bodies of humans and feeds off their greed and envy as a source of power, the evil they cause is clear for all to see. To know more about what they were dealing with helped, but as yet they still did not have a clue how to stop them.

Tim towelled off and got dressed. He went downstairs, picked up his mobile phone from the top of the bread bin, where he always kept it overnight. He speed-dialled Ronnie's mobile. It rang, for what seemed like ages, and then switched over to answering machine. He left an awkward message and then hung up. He checked the kitchen clock. 6:00am. Before he started to panic he needed to check the Institute, but their switchboard wouldn't operate for another couple of hours. So if he wanted to make sure Ronnie was safe he was going to have to go and find out in person. He hoped he could keep his cool and not get into another fighting match with her.

Suddenly an image in his head shot into full view and startled him. He'd slapped Ronnie? Hard. He hadn't meant to hit her. In fact he couldn't really remember doing it, how it happened, or if it was a dream. But that image in his head shook him up. There was no other explanation, other than it must have happened for him to remember part of it. He sighed and shook his head sadly. Never before and never again would he stoop so low. How would she ever forgive him? He promised he'd never let anything happen to her. Despite the danger all around them, as long as they had each other they could survive all the monsters they came across. And looking in the hallway mirror at his own reflection, he wondered what sort of monster Ronnie saw in him now.

Picking up his car keys Tim noticed the empty bottle on the kitchen sink. Determined to put right the wrong he had caused he threw his keys on the kitchen table, raced through the house and gathered all the bottles of whiskey he had hidden from Ronnie. Twelve bottles in total, with varying amounts still left inside each one. Was his life really so bad that he couldn't face it without using alcohol as a security blanket? For a twenty-nine-year-old he was acting more like a spoilt child than he had realised. It had to stop. The last thing he wanted to do was lose Ronnie. It wasn't as if she didn't have enough to contend with already. Not after their newfound discovery.

With a deep breath Tim looked at the bottles on the kitchen sink. Before he could hesitate and change his mind he unscrewed the lids and poured the dark golden liquid down the plughole. Usually wasting it like this would have driven him to despair, but like being driven to drink by the nightmares that surrounded them on a daily basis, this had to stop. However hard it might be, he would not let the evil win.

Strangely, the distinctive smell of alcohol made him feel sick more than anything. Maybe the drink had served a purpose, but this sort of dependency went no further. From now on he would not allow another sip of alcohol to pass his lips, and he would prove to Ronnie he could be the friend she deserved. He vowed to apologise and make things right. All he had to do was find her first.

In many ways he hoped she had just stayed out of his hair until he cooled down, and was planning to return to him when he was sober, because the other option was too painful for him to contemplate.

He gathered the bottles and took them outside and dumped them in his recycling box. Heading for the car he thought of Ronnie and wished her safe. Ronnie Weaver, the only person who could heal him. The girl he'd let slip through his fingers because he couldn't hold his drink. The girl, who by now, as much as he tried to convince himself he'd find her at work, would be sharing another man's bed, in a completely different world of which he had no idea how to get to. But somehow he would. Somehow he had to.

Chapter Seven

'It's for your own good,' a deep voice said. 'I'm not going to hurt you, but it's the only way I can ensure you listen to what I have to say.'

What the—?

Under a blanket Ronnie struggled and tried to sit up, but her hands were tied with thick rope. Her legs, too. Not just playfully tied. Tightly restrained. For a moment her brain had trouble clicking in. Then it hit her. A rush of ice-cold terror slammed into her body, rushed through her veins and flooded her senses with despair. The crash. The man. Tied up. Kidnapped? Her worst nightmare and horror movie all rolled into one. Only this wasn't some crazy slasher film happening to some actress who screamed for England and got paid for it. This was happening to her. *She* was a mad man's next victim. With this thought her heart hammered against her ribs, threatening to explode with fear. Her eyes darted around the room, searching for something. What, she wasn't sure. Clues? Something familiar? A way out? Nothing helped. All she could see from her position was pine panelling, an empty wooden table in one corner and a large punch-bag hanging from a beam in the other. She wondered how many times a day he hit that to control his temper. Then she heard a whimper, and it took a second or two to realise the feeble mewing sound came from her. Suddenly she didn't care what the neighbours thought. Or if her kidnapper would kill her to shut her up. No longer thinking straight she didn't care about anything but someone knowing where she was, someone to save her. To break free. Get out alive!

Thrashing against her bonds she screamed. Loud, wild and for as long as she could, until her throat was raw.

'Finished?' the stranger asked with a hint of mockery, which turned her fear into anger.

'Why am I here?' Ronnie asked, moving her head from left to right in search of her captor, but it was no good. He stood out of her line of vision so she couldn't see him. *Do I really want to?*

'This isn't a hospital! What are you going to do to me? Please, let me go, I don't want to die!'

'Goodness gracious me. I'm not going to harm you. I pulled you out of the wreckage. I'll have you know I saved you!' he exclaimed, as though offended. 'Your car's in a bit of a mess, but we'll have that fixed in a jiffy, with a few additional improvements I must add. The main thing is you are safe. Now relax. Calm down. Then I'll untie you. Most young ladies in your position soon come to realise that I'm no danger to them—'

'You bastard! You've done this before?'

'Young lady, please do not use such language in my abode. Under the circumstances I think I have been very patient.'

Abode? That doesn't sound like the talk of a murderer. But why won't he tell me where I am? If she didn't know, how the hell would anyone be able to come to her rescue? The truth of this thought stunned her. She struggled against her bonds, but it was no use. Her ankles and wrists were firmly bound. Whether the man was unhinged or not she was not going anywhere fast.

'Now listen to me. Keep still. You'll only hurt yourself. If you do not do what you're told I can always bind your mouth, if that's what it takes to keep you from repeating such vile blasphemy. It is in your best interests to trust me. I. Will. Not. Harm. You,' the voice insisted.

'How can you say that when you won't let me go?'

Something creaked behind her. A chair. Was he going? Coming for her? About to make his killer move?

Changing tactics she bit her lip to prevent herself saying something she might later regret. Some killers thrived on the power of being in control, so much that they would never believe their victim would dare do anything except what they were told to do. By saying nothing else she believed she could stay one step ahead of him. Yes. Best not to infuriate him into killing. Bide a little time to escape. Find the nearest phone. Call for help. She took a deep breath and tried to force herself to relax.

Stay calm and think how to get out of this mess.

'Ronnie, please, the last thing I want is to harm you,' he insisted. Closer this time.

'You know my name?'

The chair creaked again. Behind her she heard the sound of bare feet padding across a hard floor. Pacing. What did that mean? Was he in a quandary? Did he not know what he was doing? Perhaps there was a chance for her after all. 'Tell me,' she demanded, trying to unnerve him. 'Do we *know* each other?'

There was a long pause.

'You don't know me, as such, but I know all about you.'

She gasped. She'd seen enough telly to know

only stalkers spoke that way. Shit! Not knowing what else to do she struggled against her bonds. Frantic. Crazed and desperate to be free.

'Will you please stop doing that?'

'Well let me go then!' she snapped, forgetting all about trying the psychological approach. Not caring that each time she wriggled to get free the friction of the rope burned the delicate skin of her wrists.

Footsteps drew closer.

'Please calm down, my child. You are making your wrists sore.'

'I don't want to calm down. I want to be free. Untie me,' she squealed, clenching her fists, trying to loosen her restraints. Frightened, but wanting so much to be brave, Ronnie shut her eyes, expecting her kidnapper to come into view. She dared not look at him. At least until she'd got her thoughts together and worked out what to do.

'I will untie you but you must listen to me and calm down first. It's the only way,' he said gently. His soft tone surprised her. 'Now, breathe deep and exhale slowly, as if you were meditating.'

She did. Even though his request was odd, given the circumstances, she didn't want to rile him any further. She needed time to think this all through. As any captive with a strong sense of survival she was more than willing to cooperate, especially with such a benign request. And the man's hypnotic tone, in spite of his position of power over her, gave off a magical ambiance that soothed and pacified, almost to the point that being near him felt familiar, like a connection between them she'd forgotten about.

'Good girl. That's right. Just relax.'

She heard him inhale through his nose and breathe out through his mouth and found herself doing the same.

'Praxis.'

Ronnie frowned. She knew what it meant, but the way he said it and nothing else almost sounded like a command. Her eyes grew heavy and she blinked. An overwhelming sense of exhaustion overcame her. At a time like this the last thing she wanted was to sleep, but she could hardly keep her eyes open.

'Aristotle once said if you desire a quality and you have it not, act in every respect as if you already have the quality you desire and you will have it.'

Now that did sound familiar. Where had she heard that before?

She stopped trying to fight the drowsiness and let her mind roam.

'What do you most want right now, Ronnie?' the voice urged.

Her eyelids fluttered and without truly thinking what she was going to say next the answer came to her in an instant. 'To have the courage to be able to trust you will not hurt me.'

'Then you shall have it, girl. All you have to do is act accordingly. Praxis.'

There it was again. That word and the accompanying feeling that everything was going to be okay. Her sense of danger and earlier fears seemed to slip away with just that one word. As if it had put her into a meditative state or cast a spell over her.

'To breathe correctly will centre your core, your inner more etheric world, and prepare you for the day ahead,' the stranger continued.

With this in mind she was pleased to be able to use this opportunity to calm herself, so that she could better concentrate on what to do next without panicking. It might even give her an advantage point over him. She took another deep breath and blew out and another wave of calm washed over her. No longer did she ache all over, which she thought unusual after what she'd been through. Not even her neck ached from the whiplash she must have received during the crash. In fact, restraints aside, she felt surprisingly fit and healthy. Even her headache from hell had dissipated. Her wrists and ankles didn't hurt as much either. A positive sign. Because at any moment, she warned herself, she would have to give in and take a peek at him. Come face to face with her kidnapper. A thought that should have terrified her, but didn't.

With a remarkable calmness that only meditation could bring, she told herself not to panic when she saw him. She had to keep her wits about her. Nothing would lose her advantage point more than her loss of control. Still filled with a floating sensation she focused her energies on listening to the sounds around her in the room. All was quiet, but for his gentle breathing. Too tired to worry about why that felt wrong she let the thought go. Inside her head a voice spoke to her.

Stay calm. Go with it. Let your troubles dissolve and relax.

Yes. Patience. Think logically. Assess the situation. Then act. It might save her life. She breathed in and exhaled again, slowly and deliberately. Her mind wandered. Won't there be people missing me? A boss wondering why I've not turned up yet? She tried to recall who she worked for, but she couldn't focus. It worried her that this was something she could not remember. Had she hit her head in the crash and lost her memory temporarily? Would it ever come back? She scrunched her eyes tightly shut and tried to force the answers to come to her, but what pictures formed in her mind seemed vague and unfamiliar, and that scared her. She bit her lip and willed herself to stay strong, something her job required of her. How she knew for sure she didn't know, but she had a strong sense that she was right.

It's why you meditate each morning, a soothing voice told her.

So what *did* she do for a living? She wondered if she was a writer. She liked the sound of that. Somehow she knew she was creative, and valued imagination and innovation over realism. A writer would fit right in with her trust for inspiration, and inference – her intuitive side.

Interrupting her thoughts, Ronnie heard the stranger breath in and out. Still meditating along with her. Hardly the actions of a killer. She inhaled.

Maybe she was an artist, or a potter. She fancied she might even be an astronomer or something totally bizarre like an intelligence specialist. Immediately something told her she was wrong and she'd be better off worrying less about her career and concentrating more about her current situation. She exhaled a long, deep breath and in her mind's eye saw all the negative energy and concerns for her safety carried out on her breath.

Whatever she did she hoped she wasn't a mathematician or an accountant. If there was one thing she was positive about, number crunching wasn't her idea of fun. But in truth nothing sounded right.

She thought back to the car crash. The details were blurry, yet she could remember parts of it. Again inhaling deeply through her nose and then exhaling slowly, without effort, she recalled the fear seizing her as she spun out of control, the relief upon the car finally coming to a standstill, the eerie numb quietness in her head followed by the uncontrollable shakes as her distressed body began to cope with the aftershock. She even remembered the kind people as they rallied around her car in an effort to help her. After that, nothing.

Then, as if the process of thinking was the cause of the pain and a warning to stop, her headache returned and thumped across her skull. She thought of her mother's warm smile, her own intuitive feeling that she was not in any real danger, and her belief that any feeling is valid, whether it makes sense or not. That she could remember some parts of her life, but not all, didn't feel right. She reassured herself with the thought that it would all come flooding back when the time was right. It had to.

Forever the optimist she hoped she would recover sooner rather than later. She might be missing some vital piece of information that could save her life. The feeling that this was indeed a crucial point to her survival entered her head, swam through, and disappeared as though never really there. As she sunk deeper beneath her physical world, passed layers of thoughts and emotions into the silent place within that is always calm, she sensed the man drawing closer. A rush of warmth waved over her like the soothing water of a bath. The tiny hairs on the back of her neck prickled as if her body was reacting to his presence. No longer afraid, she opened her eyes.

Deep-set, emerald eyes stared straight back into hers and she recognised them instantly. Ronnie gasped. 'You? But you... you can't be real!'

She swallowed and licked her dry lips, wondering how much damage the crash had done to her head. What she saw was impossible. Crazy-lunatic-lock-em-up-and-throw-away-the-key-mad.

'Prometheus?'

He smiled. Flecks of light danced in his penetrating eyes like tiny green jewels glinting in the sun.

'Please, my child, call me Theo.' He smiled. 'For now.'

Chapter Eight

'What with the accident, your dream, waking up somewhere you do not recognise, I know how overwhelming this can be. You are face to face with someone you think cannot possibly exist, and although in itself that is a lot to deal with there is much more. You must learn to get through this.'

'I'm listening,' she said, confused at how fast she believed him.

'May I remind you that if you ever doubt my words one thing you should hold close to your heart are those of Aristotle; to act with courage means you are courageous and the power to do so is already within you.'

Strangely calm. It all sounded so simple. *Act*

brave. Trust his words. She nodded.

'Good girl.'

Theo, the man she knew so well as Prometheus from her dream, reached a hand out towards her. For a second Ronnie flinched. *What is he going to do?* He touched her face and brushed a loose strand of hair out of her eyes and gently tucked it behind her ear. With a delicate lightness his searching fingertips traced the tiny shape of her ear. It tickled, forcing an undeniable tingle of pleasure to run down her spine. His tenderness surprised her. All she expected was for him to be rough with her. Like the way his goddess had wished. Maybe that would come later. She flushed at the thought.

'You are a strong woman, Ronnie; I know you can do this,' he said, as he continued to move his finger slowly down her neck and across her collar bone. His warm touch around her throat electrified her. A voice in her head told her this shouldn't be happening. This was dangerous territory. Tied, helpless and under his control, she lay at his mercy. He could do absolutely anything to her and she could do or say nothing to stop him. But that didn't frighten her. What frightened her was that she didn't want him to stop. She watched his concerned face as he studied hers. Contemplating his next move? Waiting for her to protest?

'Unfortunately, you may not like what you hear.'

Right now Ronnie didn't care. All she could concentrate on was his hand as it tightened around her throat and squeezed. A few too many seconds long. When he let go something flickered in the back of her mind.

Disappointment? Regret? Whatever it was, it wasn't fear. If that's what he wanted, she wanted it too. A baffling thought. Was it possible to trust him so much, so very quickly? Because she did. Without his touch an emptiness seeped through her pores. It crept through her body like a seeking black void threatening to destroy her; a yearning ache that only he could fill. Then as if to prove a point he touched her once more, making her shiver with excitement, and all was well again. His finger trailed further down her breast bone, then underneath the blanket into her cleavage, and this time he didn't stop.

'I am about to tell you something which is very important you believe. Understood?'

Ronnie shut her eyes and nodded as his fingertips moved further underneath the blanket and uncovered her breasts to the cool air. When she opened her eyes again they became fixed upon his lips as he spoke. Full, healthy pink lips, slightly curved in a reassuring smile. Very kissable.

'Good girl,' he said, circling a hard nipple. 'We are about to embark upon the path of the ovate, a path that leads from communication to understanding. Whatever happens know this my child; you are not to be alarmed, for what I say is of great importance, and the truth.'

He sat on the edge of the bed and studied her grey eyes for every reaction. 'I come from a time your world has long forgotten. I was sent to watch over you as your personal Destaurian Guard, in order to protect and guarantee that one day we would discover our fate. Today that time has come.' Suddenly he tweaked her nipple hard. Ronnie winced and bit her lip to force back a giggle. He took his hand away from her breast.

'What do you want from me?' she moaned, with

a desperation to do anything for him as long as he didn't stop touching her.

'I offer you peace, security and a spiritual centre. All I ask is for you to allow me the pleasure of continuing to be your guidance, only this time, not from afar.'

She nodded slowly, a little dazed by his powerful words. 'Good girl. Now, all we need to do is to restore your spirit and soon you'll be whole again... my dear, sweet goddess.'

Ronnie smiled and found herself drawn back to his magnetic eyes, flecked with emerald glitter and a sparkle she'd never seen before in anyone else. Magical, hypnotic and soothing. Every time those eyes fell upon her she floated away. Lulled into a spaced-out sensation which addled her thoughts. Just like in a dream where everything seemingly random eventually connects to the conscious mind when awake, if you know where to look.

Theo pinched her other nipple hard. She bucked and gasped. *This is no dream!* Instead of hiding behind her embarrassment she arched her back and pushed her breasts up as high as her restraints would allow and begged for more. But to her disappointment he stood up and walked to the end of the bed behind her.

Seconds later all was forgiven when he pulled his T-shirt off over his head, tossed it to the floor and bent down towards her, his hair tickling her face. Gently he planted a kiss on her forehead and warm tingles rippled throughout her body, spreading through her like wildfire. Hot juices trickled down her thighs.

So deep under the spell of his charm was she, it took a moment for her to realise he'd taken hold of the blanket and slowly, inch by inch, uncovered her trim stomach and the tops of her thighs. Ronnie watched his lust-filled eyes roam over her nakedness with a strange sense of floating, as if observing it happening to someone else.

Another wave of vulnerability mixed with an opposing wanton need for his touch overcame her. Followed by a flush of embarrassment to warm her face as he continued to pull down the blanket to reveal her spread and bound legs, and expose her wet sex to the cool air. To him. She looked down at herself. How could something so shameful excite her so much? Could something that felt so right be so wrong?

Pulled by the lure of being bound, defenceless and completely under another's control, she shut her eyes and welcomed the onset of the unknown. The bed shifted as he climbed on top to join her. The weight of his hands pressed down on the mattress on either side of her head. She didn't need to look to know he loomed above her and she was all his.

When Ronnie felt his lips skim hers she opened her eyes and studied his chiselled face as he pulled back from his teasing kiss. A strand of chocolate-brown hair flopped over his tanned skin. Underneath his long thick eyelashes his eyes gleamed with a roguish tinge, and yet they held her gaze with an intense and uncompromising dignity as though they were not merely eyes, but were instead cameras by which he could delve into the images of her mind and capture them to memory. Seeing into her soul.

Something about him intrigued her, like a dark mystery waiting to be revealed. Forbidden secrets.

Was she relying too much on that intuitive feeling again? Did it matter? Where did anyone ever get by staying in their comfort zone, never taking risks?

Indelibly she stamped on her mind a mental picture of this life-changing moment. For she was positive it would be. Whatever he wanted from her she would accept. It was the way. Expected of her. Somehow she knew that. Like she also knew she had waited for this moment for so long. Hadn't she?

'I'm going to eat you out and you are not going to come until I say. Understood?'

Although the harshness of his voice startled her, her pussy reacted differently. The corner of her mouth twitched into a smile. 'Yes, Theo, loud and clear,' she whispered.

His lips brushed down her throat, and continued their journey down towards her breasts. Here he stopped to nip and tease her flesh, lightly at first. He then progressed to tweaking her nipples with his thumb and forefinger, before giving them a pinch. Ronnie stiffened in response, her breath ragged.

He playfully began to use sharp teeth to tug and stretch her nipples, forcing her to writhe around underneath him and squeal with delight. Already she wanted to come, and from his intense green gaze he knew it. The same way he seemed to know exactly how far to bring her senses to a desperate, needy edge without even entering her.

His tongue trailed into the hollow of her stomach and circled around her bellybutton. Goosebumps prickled her skin. All the time his eyes flicked up to hers to make it clear he was checking her reactions, relishing her embarrassment; she could see it in his face. Feel it in his hard cock as it pressed against her leg. And then, just above her now dripping pussy lips his tongue stopped and hovered.

Allowing her to anticipate his next move it stretched out, not quite touching her wet slit. She clenched herself tightly and prayed he would let her come soon, because she wasn't sure if she could wait for his say so.

Then as if he heard her speak aloud he pulled away. For a few seconds, no more, but long enough for her to get her breath back and fully understand he had full control over her needy body.

He then wrapped his arms around the tops her thighs and held her tight as the tip of his tongue made contact with one slow, light lick along her moist opening. Her whole body jumped and prickled with the anticipation of her release.

Ronnie opened her mouth, pupils dilated, and a small groan escaped her lips.

A lewd need to push her tingling sex into his face and come all over it overwhelmed her. She clung to the rope that held her wrists tight to the bedposts, pushed down on her back and lifted her bottom into the air, acutely aware she wanted his tongue more than anything she had wanted before. No longer caring how unladylike she looked. Or how the ropes around her ankles pulled so tight they hurt.

His tongue returned to the nub of her clit and with a continuous sweeping motion he licked her up and down, forcing waves of pleasure to sweep through her body until she thought she would explode if he didn't let her come soon.

Not being able to hold back for much longer and starting not to care she rocked her hips, trying to push herself onto his tongue, desperate to have it inside her. If his tongue could do such things what would his cock feel like? She didn't know but was sure she was soon going to find out.

'Now, please…' Ronnie begged, panting hard.

'No, you are not allowed,' he admonished, his warm breath tickling her thighs.

She wished her hands were free so she could grab Theo's hair, hold his head firmly in place to direct his tongue to where she craved it. To come all over his face. No more teasing. But in reality not allowing her this option and controlling her orgasm not only thrilled her but drove her crazy with desire. And he wanted her too. She could tell by the craving lust in his eyes. If she didn't know better she would have thought he was having trouble confining something wild within the boundaries he'd set himself.

At the thought of him losing control and unleashing himself upon her the way his goddess craved, her body tensed. Reaffirming his position of power he gripped her thighs tighter and pinned her legs down onto the bed, taking back what little freedom he'd given her. The full use of her body was all his.

'Oh, please,' she squealed, now trying desperately to pull away from his tongue, fearing the very next lick might be the one to send her over the edge before he gave his permission. What then? What would he do?

Instead of replying his hot wet tongue lapped her wet pussy with loud slurps. Up and down, faster and faster his tongue moved, stopping only to use his fingers to flick unremittingly her swollen nub, to make her cry out in painful bliss.

'Come for me *now*, girl. Know that I own you. Your come. Your orgasm. *You!* You are my Child of Destiny; from now on everything you do is for me!'

With this she moaned loudly, thrust her hips against the pressure of his tight grip and bucked against his tongue, not caring about how painful the ropes around her wrists and ankles were. She squirmed under his masterful tongue and her orgasm peaked. She clenched her hands into tight fists and every muscle in her body tensed as her release came. She cried out as crashing waves of pleasure ripped through her convulsing body, and then at last, when the shudders of her orgasms subsided, she dropped back to the bed exhausted, her pussy still twitching.

It then took a moment during her blissful post-orgasmic haze to realise he'd started again.

'No, no, that's too much…' she pleaded and squirmed, in a half-hearted attempt to move her oversensitive pussy from his lapping tongue.

But stop he did not. Slowly but firmly he continued to work on her, drawing another orgasm from her aching sex. She wriggled and thrashed about as much as her bindings would allow, and just as she thought she was going to come without permission someone knocked on the door and broke the magic, bringing Ronnie to her senses.

A blonde woman with a ponytail, wearing a light-tan suede trouser-suit, strutted in without being asked and called Theo by his name. Immediately he left Ronnie on the bed, wiped her juices from his mouth with the back of his hand and walked determinedly to the woman. The moment he slammed her up against the wall, grabbed her ponytail and demanded her to bend over because he was going to take her up the arse, Ronnie knew that she and the newcomer were not going to get along.

Chapter Nine

Because of this woman and the way she spoke to her man, and about her as if she was a child, or invisible or just didn't matter, because she didn't even raise an eyebrow at Ronnie's obvious naked predicament even though she did indeed glance her way, and for a number of other reasons, Ronnie fumed. All the signs pointed to the fact that what she saw was commonplace. But if that was so, just how many times had Theo kidnapped other women and told them lies about being their protector? Ronnie felt used and dirty, displayed disrespectfully like a piece of cut-price meat in a butcher's shop. But worst of all, she had to watch them and their sordid reunion.

'About time,' Artemis said.

'Excuse me?' Theo responded, bemused, pushing against her back so her large breasts were squashed against the wall, his hard cock pressed into her bottom through her trousers.

'The last day you saw me exactly twenty-two years and three months ago?' said the woman, angrily.

Ronnie's grey eyes widened. *That's my age. But she looks younger than me!*

He grabbed her ponytail, wrapped her hair around his hand and pulled her head back. 'Artemis, I didn't know they were going to choose me for this damn mission,' he panted in her ear.

Oh, so I'm a damn mission now, am I?

Unbelievable! How quickly he changes his tune for this Artemis bitch!

His free hand grabbed the thin white material of her blouse and tugged it open. Ronnie heard it rip and buttons ping to the floor.

'Couldn't you have at least got in contact with me?' Artemis whined.

'And break the rules?'

'Since when have you, one of The Learned, been afraid of breaking the rules? Are you forgetting Mr Rocket and how you left me? In all my days I shall never forget…'

Ronnie watched the couple together, feeling decidedly left out as their banter continued. Okay, so what? They had a history. But to be so intimate in front of her as if she wasn't even in the room riled her, especially as she and Theo were already in the middle of something when the woman rudely interrupted. The pit of her stomach felt hollow. *Am I jealous? Maybe this is how they do things here. But dammit, I had him first!*

'Artemis, I think you're forgetting to whom you are speaking. Now, get on with your report and then let's get things moving. I've a Tartarus lot of catching up to do now I'm back.'

With no buttons left attached the woman's tattered blouse hung open, a white bra on view. 'Right, sir,' she looked over at Ronnie and gave her the once over, and turned back to Theo, who immediately shoved his hand down her bra and squeezed a full breast.

'I take it you've debriefed her, and not just removed her briefs?' she said with a smirk in Ronnie's direction.

What a cow! Ronnie gasped inwardly. *She's*

winding him up on purpose!

'Right, that's enough, young lady,' he said, taking a step back, placing his hands on his hips, legs apart. 'I don't care how long it's been, you cannot speak to your Learned in that fashion, nor can you just waltz in here without knocking. Now, undo your trousers and bend over. And from now on, unless you're out in the field you will wear a skirt in my presence.'

'Actually, I did knock,' the woman retorted airily, while she unbuttoned her trousers and smoothed them down silky thighs as if he'd just asked her to do nothing more banal than roll up her shirtsleeves ready for a jab.

'I meant at the *barrack* door at the front, not the door to my bedroom,' he said sternly.

'Did that too,' Artemis insisted, still facing the wall.

Theo grabbed a hip with one hand and pushed her head toward the floor. Her bottom stuck up in the air, the wall supporting her as he readied himself.

'So what is the current situation?' he prompted.

'Well, I'm here with her papers to sign, which I need to get back to head office tonight. You also need to sign for the equipment I've left in the assembly hall,' she prattled on, hardly taking a breath. 'I was supposed to be going out tonight. Fat chance of that now. As usual our beloved High Council has unexpectedly moved things up a notch,' she said excitedly. 'Our green light just turned amber. We've had some readings on the ART... oh, that's a new piece of technology Samilious has come up with during your absence; the Anomaly Reading Tracker? A, R, T? Kind of coolly named after me. *Anyway*, the movement is only small, but it means things are moving in the right direction, dude. It might only be a matter of hours before we see the red alert,' she said dramatically.

My papers to sign? The High Council?

'Theo? Are you listening to me?'

Although he didn't appear to be listening, Theo undid his trousers and delved into his pants to pull out what Ronnie could only describe as the chunkiest penis she had ever seen. Admittedly, she thought to herself, she didn't know how many she'd come across before – that was something else she couldn't remember. Nevertheless, what she watched slip into that girl's bottom hole was definitely not of a normal sized. Subconsciously she licked her lips at the sight.

'You've not stopped talking since you walked in,' Theo grumbled. 'Maybe this will silence you.'

'Just reporting in as I'm told—' she grunted as he thrust hard into her rear passage.

No easing it in or taking his care, Ronnie noted.

Artemis glanced over at her with a crafty smirk on her face. 'Oh, Theo!' she gasped, with a mock cry, her body jerking each time he drove into her. Rough, deep thrusts that threatened to send Artemis sprawling, but for the tight grip he had around her ponytail.

What the hell was going on here? Who is this rude woman? And why can't Theo keep his hands off her? Ronnie seethed. He's *my* protector, not *hers*.

Even though she was angry her heart pounded at the sight of them together, and she wished she could be where Artemis was right now.

After they'd finished Theo sent Artemis off to borrow a top from someone called Hestia. While she was away he untied Ronnie. He gave her a pair of new-looking white fluffy bed-socks, knickers and an old-fashioned, prickly nightie to wear, which looked like something out of the dark ages, and smelt like it too, but happy to be covered up once more Ronnie put them on anyway. Had this frumpish outfit been picked out by that woman to demean her further? Ronnie pursed her lips; even a sack would have given her more shape. But on the plus side Theo kept his top off like he always seemed to prefer, so she could admire his olive-skinned, muscled torso.

When Artemis returned she carried a stack of paper, some scrolls and ink pens. She dumped them on the floor and turned to look at Ronnie, purposely giving a long hard look at what Theo had made her wear. Unlike Ronnie Artemis liked what she saw, and grinned.

Someone rapped against the door.

'Enter,' Theo ordered. 'Oh, hello Hermes, what can I do for you? We're rather busy right now. This is my new Child of Destiny. Hermes the Messenger, meet Ronnie. Ronnie, Hermes.'

Hermes stood in the doorway wearing a tan suede outfit, and cloak with a matching flat cap. He smiled, tipped the peak of his cap, and nodded politely at the new female before him, looking away quickly before Ronnie had time to respond.

'I'm sorry for the interruption, sir, but this is rather a delicate matter and does need your urgent assistance, if you wouldn't mind. It shouldn't take long at all.' He turned back to Ronnie. 'Excuse me, milady. I'll bring him back as soon as this pressing detail has been cleared up.'

'Of course,' Ronnie smiled. 'And nice to meet you,' she called out as the man with the flat cap marched hurriedly out, followed by Theo, which left her alone with Artemis.

'Now, I don't know how much Theo has told you, so we're both going to go through this with you as quickly as possible. While we talk I'll be handing over various bits and pieces which require your signature. You can either spend time and read everything before you sign and delay this mission, or you can choose to sign them first, then take them away to read at your leisure. The choice is yours but I urge you to take into consideration the importance of this mission and the lack of valuable time we all have. Here's a few to be getting on with,' she added, passing Ronnie a stack of papers with crosses on them and an old-fashioned quill pen. 'Sign here, here, here and here,' she pointed. 'You get the idea.'

Confused at so much information being thrown at her all at once, and still trying to deal with everything she'd just witnessed, Ronnie took the pen and started signing. It all felt so surreal anyway, how important could it be?

'But if there is something I really don't agree with we can discuss it, yes?' she asked, as doubt crept in.

Artemis sucked in a breath. 'Tricky one. You don't really have much choice either way. Whatever happens you *are* a Child of Destiny, and you are here for a reason. That cannot be changed. I'm just offering you the nicest option first.'

'And what is my other option?'

Artemis grinned. 'We force you to sign the

papers required, and prepare you for the mission in other, less enjoyable, and shall we say, more frighteningly cruel ways which *guarantee* your acceptance. Of course that is also the much more painful option for all concerned. In more ways than one.' For a moment neither of them said a thing, and just stared daggers at each other. Although it was clear Artemis didn't like Ronnie and the feeling was mutual, Ronnie could not help but wonder why. If this carried on she was going to ask her, but then, she wouldn't be staying for any length of time, so what did it matter? *Let the bitch carry on wasting her breath.*

'I wouldn't put it quite like that,' Theo said, walking back in, throwing Artemis a stern look of disapproval. 'Treatment that harsh is rarely called for these days. Rest assured there's really nothing to worry about on that front. Artemis just likes to act tough. It's the huntress inside her.' He grinned, but Artemis was not amused.

Rarely, thought Ronnie, didn't mean *never*.

In a matter of seconds she looked away and something snapped around her neck. Artemis moved back, grinning with an unspoken 'gotcha' look. A black leather collar fitted tightly around Ronnie's throat. From it hung an 'O' ring with an amethyst stone in the centre. Annoyed, she gave the collar what she hoped looked like a casual tug and tried to loosen it, but as with all the bizarre things happening around her lately, she wasn't surprised when it wouldn't budge. She looked up at Theo for help, but he just studied the collar for a few seconds, as though temporarily distracted, and then shook his head as if to dispel his thoughts.

'Ah, yes, the Collar of Protection,' he said, as

though it were the most natural thing to say in the world. 'With that on no one can touch you without my permission. Now, where were we? Oh yes, first let me begin at the very best place, the beginning.' His torso glistened as he sat on the bed next to her. It was rather warm all of a sudden. The temperature in the panelled room seemed to fluctuate from warm to hot, as though the heating was up the spout.

'There is someone you need to be very wary of, and make no bones about it, she is one person you cannot underestimate and should be high on your radar,' Theo said in an authoritative tone. 'The High Priestess, Pandora, is not to be trusted. The last time my brother Epimetheus and I met her we'd been assigned the official positions of World Builders for the King of the Gods, Zeus.'

Now it was Ronnie's turn to inhale deeply. Okay, so somehow he had previously cast a spell over her where she not only believed every word he said, but allowed him to do all sorts of things to her, as if being together was so familiar to them. But this, on the other hand, was a little harder to believe. *World Builders for Zeus!* Still, she tried to avoid his eyes just in case he lured her into his dark fantasy world.

'To cover up for my brother's foolhardy and over-zealous use of gifts when populating the Earth, I became forced to conceal his tracks. Big mistake.'

'What did you do?' she asked, curious how he could lie about something so bizarre with such a straight face.

'What didn't he do,' Artemis butted in. 'Theus, that's Epimetheus' nickname, is a good for nothing—' Theo cleared his throat. 'I'm just saying, dude, he's the black sheep of the family. If anyone's going to get you into trouble it's him. And he did. All I can say is maybe it's not a bad thing he's gone AWOL. He's probably living it up in some foreign land shacked up with a tart and as happy as—'

'Artemis?'

She pulled up a chair and sat down. 'Sorry, sir, do carry on.'

'I stole fire for humankind to encourage their growth,' Theo continued. 'This angered Zeus. No one stole from him. But he planned to enslave humans like beasts, not for their development into civilised people.' He sighed. 'I couldn't let that happen.'

His empathic tone took Ronnie aback. But how could such a story be true? Her heart hammered against her ribs, but she indulged him. 'I'm sure you only did what you thought right at the time.'

He shook his head. 'I should never have interfered. In protecting my brother I put your world, and you, in danger.'

Despite such a tall story he didn't appear to be lying. Her gut instincts told her so. And to be honest, why would he lie? Hadn't he impressed upon her the idea of acting courageously in order to trust him?

'After several attempts to punish me Zeus tried another tactic. He came upon the idea that if I was untouchable he could get at me through my brother, which he did. He put his plan into action by sending him a gift in the form of Pandora, a human, bestowed with special powers and a box to hold them all in. The Magic Box of Destiny. The cause of all my strife.'

'He begged his brother to be wary and not accept anything from Zeus, but Pandora was created to seduce,' Artemis chipped in. 'Irresistible in every way.'

'We were doomed from the start,' Theo stated ruefully.

Ronnie blinked, not sure what to say or how to console him. His steady gaze made it impossible for her to look away. She hoped he wasn't bewitching her again with his charms. This was a time for answers. To get to grips with what was really going on.

'At first, when nothing happened, I wondered if I had read too much into our relationship with Zeus, and that maybe I had wrongly mistaken his generosity for the curse I originally expected. I would not have worried about my brother at all if it had not been for the fact that I could not shake that bad feeling whenever I thought of who actually gave my brother this marvellous, quite amazing gift.'

'A dude who tried to punish you in many ways, and was running out of ideas,' Artemis chipped in again.

Prometheus nodded. 'It didn't take long for Pandora to make her move, and she moved in with us. Hours changed into days. Days into weeks. Every second Theus and Pandora spent together their love for each other grew stronger. He became a changed man. Happy. Contented. They even married.'

'He married a witch?' The words slipped out of Ronnie's mouth before she fully thought them through, and despite the seriousness of the situation she almost laughed when she heard herself say them aloud.

'He didn't know at that stage,' he said through gritted teeth. 'Neither of us did. Heavens above! For a while their lives together seemed perfect. There was even talk of children. He loved her that much! There was nothing Theus would not do for her. That is, except allow her to open the box lest it held something to mess up the happiness they shared together.' Prometheus sighed and held his head in his hands.

Ronnie reached out and cautiously stroked the back of his neck in an effort to soothe him. He didn't tell her to stop. He looked up, their eyes met. She sensed his sadness, his anguish, but most of all his frustration. How could that be? *I don't even know this man, yet he always seems so familiar to me.*

'It was only a matter of time before Pandora's true self showed, but filled with an evil sent by Zeus, and with time on her side, her true character remained hidden. She lulled us both into a false sense of security that eventually got the better of us.'

'What happened?'

'One day, despite our warnings, Pandora's curiosity overwhelmed her. A curiosity so strong it overcame her natural fear of what might be inside, so when her husband was out she opened the Magic Box imagining eternal riches, glittering jewels and garments of silk woven with gold thread. How wrong she was, and we've been fighting her, her minions, and the evils that escaped the box ever since. Which brings me back to you, my child, and why you are here.'

Ronnie gulped. Not sure she wanted to know.

'There is no easy way to say this,' Theus went on regardless. 'Amidst every battalion of troubles there is always Hope. Many years ago when the Box first opened Hope, the one good spirit, flew free and in her search for a host found a woman named Hamira. And now, many years and hosts later, that Hope is you. Pandora will test your wits and cunning and try to destroy you, for without Hope your Earth will whither and die, making way for Chaos and Destruction—'

'Excuse me?' Ronnie gawked, stopping him in mid-flow. 'Did I hear you correctly? To test *my* wits and cunning…?'

'You, girl, have the tormented soul of the Goddess of Hope within you, which makes you a Child of Destiny, a Keeper of Hope; part of an Order to protect the time portal called The Magic Box.'

'Oh yes?' This man was unbelievable. 'But I'm not bloody superwoman!'

He gave her a look which instantly suppressed her need to fight him.

'No. You have no magical abilities at all. And if I have my way you definitely won't receive any. You are human, and that's how I want to keep you.'

Keep me?

'With all our magic abilities it is you that holds the greatest power.'

'I… I do?'

He nodded. 'As a Child of Destiny you have within you Courage, Humility, Integrity, Long Term Vision and a Dedication to your mission. Five of the greatest gifts a human can possess and that magic alone cannot penetrate. Your own powerful magic which comes from within gives you a true advantage.'

Artemis sat forward, hanging on his every word, Ronnie noticed.

'Although many Destaurian Guards like us are born with magic abilities it is not always the be and end of all our worries. Magic has complicated properties, which can cure, protect, and even fight battles, but that comes at a cost. The spellcrafter can only dish out so much before exhaustion sets in.'

Theo let out a gentle laugh, more to himself than anyone else. 'That's right. It would seem that our natural magical gift has some unnatural consequences in the aftermath. Nature has a way of compensating for what she deems deviant.'

'And what does all this make you?'

He smiled. 'I am many things. Official historian and genealogist, a keeper of records. In addition, I'm the founding member of an elite taskforce named the Destaurian Guard, your protector, your Guardian, and the man of your dreams.'

Yeah, right. *How conceited!* Yet she couldn't deny it; he was the man of her dreams, literally.

He looked at her. 'You don't believe me?'

'Well, you've got to admit the whole thing is rather farfetched, what with witches, the beginning of time, and me being some sort of Child of Destiny.'

He got up off the bed and walked to Artemis.

Ronnie stood to get a better look.

'The files, please.' He nodded.

'Oh Theo, please, the files can wait. Show her! It's the only way,' she urged, standing up and moving the chair to the edge of the room as if to make space.

'Show me what?' asked Ronnie, looking from one to the other for answers, but Theo moved to the centre of the room and turned his back to her. A sparkling, deep-blue light appeared around his body, as though she could not only see his aura, but reach out and touch it. Feel it. On his back she noticed two tiny stumps she swore were not there before. They grew in size, unfurled and fanned out in a feathery glow. Two enormous wings!

Is this really happening? Am I insane? Right now that's a clear possibility.

Rapt with amazement, shrouded in fear and uncertainty, Ronnie shuffled backwards, only stopping when she touched the wall behind her. Pinned. Nowhere to go. With her mouth agape she stared at him, filled with terror, but also an overwhelming curiosity. The span of his wings almost touched two sides of the room, beautiful but frighteningly dark and unearthly.

The oppressive silence in the room closed in on her and she had to force herself to breathe. Her mind, a whirling blizzard of confusion, kicked her fight or flight instinct into action. Aware she was trembling Ronnie glanced from Theo to the arched doors. With his back to her Theo began to rein in his wings, so seeing her chance she ran towards the door.

Chapter Ten

Fear pumped through Ronnie's veins as she gripped the door handle and yanked it open.

Beneath her fingertips the handle felt warm to the touch, as though alive. Shocked, she pushed it away with more strength than she realised she had. The door swung wide open and crashed against the wall. She lurched forward across the threshold, just before it bounced back and slammed shut behind her, making her jump as it did. The instant relief she felt knowing the door acted as a barrier between them was gone a second later, when the darkness she'd stepped into enveloped her. She stood stock still and scanned the black void for movement. Although she couldn't see anything she immediately felt ill at ease, with a strong sense that someone – or after what she'd just seen – *something* was there with her, watching. Hardly daring to breathe she listened to the faint voices of Theo and Artemis beyond the closed door.

'Aren't you going after her?'

'She won't get far. They never do.'

What does that mean?

She strained to hear any movement, but her heart pumped so fast she worried she wouldn't be able to hear anything but the pounding of her fear.

'That's not what I meant, Theo, and you know it,' came the voice of Artemis, annoyed. 'She needs you.'

I don't need anyone! Ronnie told herself angrily, taking a few defiant steps into the darkness, with her hands outstretched before her. Her fingers touched something rough, but warm, and she came to a startling halt. Like the door handle the wall radiated heat and seemed to throb beneath her fingertips as though it were... *alive?* She snatched her fingers away. Ridiculous! It was just some underground heating, that's all. *So why do I still feel uneasy? You've got the heebie-jeebies, that's all.* Ronnie told herself to calm down. She peered around, her eyes at last adjusting to the inky gloom. She was in some sort of corridor and could go only left or right, but neither option looked like fun.

The powerful sense of unease, of being watched, snaked down her spine. What if there were more like him, in their natural forms, waiting for her in the dark? As much as she wanted to escape, no way was she running anywhere until she knew what she might be running into. Or whom.

She squinted, forcing her eyes to focus, and slowly she made out a vague, shady outline of five, possibly six arches along one side of the narrow corridor to her left. Each one had a strange decorative lump above. The opposite wall was the same. Nothing to worry about; they were only arched doorways, like the one she'd just come out of, that's all. Yet still she couldn't shake off the feeling that someone or something was watching her.

Not daring to move she waited for more clarity of vision. Just to be sure. A misty fog, which seemed to be holding back the shapes in the shadows started to thin. One at a time blurry silhouettes drew steadily into view as if she'd discovered the power of night vision. With nerves drying her throat she swallowed. The fuzzy shapes took form. Perched above every archway sat a large black Raven, with disturbing, yellow, beady eyes following her every move. Her heart raced, and it took a moment to realise they were stuffed.

She shivered.

Dead things can't see.

So why does it feel like they're watching me?

The darkness returned and all she could see were their eyes, until they too faded into obscurity where anything could be lurking, waiting to pounce. For all she knew that corridor could go on forever, only stopping when she reached the mouth of Hell itself.

She heard a noise. She hoped it was from the other side of the closed door and not her imagination playing tricks on her, like the living, breathing walls she thought she felt. Her eyes flitted back to the door handle.

For a few unnerving moments she swore she aged ten years as she waited for the handle to move, forcing her deeper into the corridor of staring eyes. Nothing happened, but the creepiness never faltered.

She took a deep breath and quickly checked her other option. Going right led down an even narrower tunnel. Dark and creepy too, but as far as she could tell, no arches. No arches, good. Not knowing where the tunnel led, bad. Never before had she felt so trapped, or so vulnerable.

Another noise startled her.

Icy fear shot through her veins.

On tenterhooks Ronnie looked up above the door she'd just come through, positive the noise came from overhead. Two large yellow eyes stared back at her.

And blinked.

With her decision made for her Ronnie darted right and ran as quickly as she could, fumbling through the dark tunnel of nothingness. Trying to push from her mind all thoughts of what could be following and no longer caring why the walls appeared to pulse with life when touched.

After what seemed an age, but was probably only

minutes, she noticed the floor beneath her feet began to slope upward, and for some reason that excited her. Breathless, she forged on. At least she wasn't going further down into the depths of Hell. It must be the way out, she reasoned desperately, her panting loud and erratic. Up usually was, wasn't it?

Ahead she spotted a large door. An exit! She sprinted the last few yards, and upon reaching the door a tightness in her chest forced her to stop, hands on knees, to catch her breath before going any further. She leant against it, feeling its pulsating warmth enclose her, like a comforting hug. Exhausted, Ronnie flopped down to the floor to rest a little and wait for her breathing to calm, and as she did her eyes began to grow heavy and flicker. Then she heard another noise, which startled her to her senses. A scraping sound.

She sat perfectly still, trying to force her ragged breathing to quieten, and then she heard it again. And something else. Another noise, but different this time. It wasn't a rustle or a flap of a wing, it was breathing. And whatever it belonged to was so close she could feel its breath on her ear!

Ronnie jumped up and threw herself against the pulsating wall. She looked back the way she'd come. No way was she going back down there. Then something scuttled across her line of vision, and with a scream stuck in her throat she grabbed the door handle and tugged it open. It too throbbed beneath her touch, but she didn't care. She had no idea what was on the other side of the door, but whatever it was it couldn't be as bad as what might be inside the tunnel with her. Could it?

The door opened to a blinding white light and the

smell of fresh air filled her nostrils. Ronnie shielded her eyes until they became accustomed to the brightness and stepped through, but just as she was about to shut the door something inside the tunnel tugged the bottom of her nightie three times, and laughed.

Filled with panic and a desperate urge to release her scream she willed herself to stay calm. To slam the door would alert anyone this side of the tunnel of her presence. She snatched the material back and pushed the door shut with a quiet click and stood, pressed against the pulsating door, weeping quietly to herself, through exhaustion and relief to be out of that dank place.

As soon as she could think straight she would take a look around. She needed to know what she was up against, if she was going to have a fighting chance of getting out of there alive. What she needed was something like a sawn-off shotgun filled with rock salt bullets... where that bizarre thought come from she didn't know, but it made her head hurt.

Chapter Eleven

The first thing Ronnie noticed as her eyes adjusted to the brightness of the new room were the black walls all around her. Inside the tunnel they were rough, as though still in their natural form, whatever it was. But here the walls gleamed with a more cared for, polished appeal. Obviously looks mattered in this room. She reached out to touch the wall nearest her, wondering if it too felt alive under her fingertips, when something startled her.

Voices.

She peeked around a corner and saw another spacious room with a high apex ceiling. To her right was a long black bench and stools, which seemed to be made from the same material as the walls. Was it a dining hall?

More voices. They came from the left, from the other side of a large bookcase, which was blocking her view. Not daring to move in case they spotted her she strained to hear what they were saying.

'What da fuck? Aw, you know they freak me out, Selene. Why'd you tell me that? Creepy bug-eyed monsters shouldn't be allowed to skulk about gettin' up to no good.'

'But that's the whole point, they're not meant to be roaming around; they've escaped,' a female, most likely Selene, replied. 'Heavens above, it's not as if it's the first time. Little buggers are always escaping. Seems to be what they do. I just wanted to warn you, you know? So if you woke up in the middle of the night and one was standing at the bottom of your bed with a knife and a—'

'Will you quit that, Selene? What are you like?' He sighed. 'Look, little girl, do you want my cock or what? 'Cause I ain't gonna keep it up if you carry on like that!'

The female giggled. 'I'm sorry,' she said, not sounding sorry at all. 'It's just that you're a hulking great beast, a highly trained member of the Orders, and a warrior licensed to kill, and those things scare you witless!' More laughter erupted. 'I'm sorry but it just doesn't add up!'

Ronnie heard a scuffle, something being knocked over, grunts, groans and a weird slurping sound.

Obviously fed up with waiting he was now taking the matter into his own hands. 'Ooh, yes… now that's good. Just a little bit higher… hmmm, a bit more? Ah…' the girl sighed, 'that hits the spot.'

'Oh yeah, babe. Like that?'

'I love it…' she squealed, as the sound of something rocking backwards and forwards picked up tempo. 'So do you think the PreCent will be added to the rota this time?' she panted.

'Well I don't know,' he said breathlessly. 'Not all of them are allowed.'

'Do you want her to be?' she pressed.

'Hell yeah. A PreCent is new meat, babe… for all of us,' his husky voice added, with a long groan.

Ronnie wondered if the thought of fucking both girls at the same time had just entered his head at that point. Absentmindedly her hand slipped to her crotch; there was something very horny about hearing others having sex, especially when they were not aware someone was listening… and that someone was getting off at their expense.

Although she could hear her own voice scream it was all too risky, another voice told her that was part of the fun, and before she knew what she was doing she'd lifted up the hem of her nightie and stepped out of her knickers. For a while she shut her eyes and listened intently to the sounds of ecstasy they were making as they enjoyed each other, and the anticipation of what she was about to do was turning her on before she even touched herself. She didn't know what was happening to her, and she didn't care as long she sated her sudden, inexplicable need.

She leaned back against the wall, thrust her hips forward and started to rub between her legs, not allowing any fingers to enter... yet.

She pushed her nightie up further with her free hand and tweaked her nipples, at the same time picturing herself being caught in such a position, and how they would force her to finish herself off with them watching as a punishment. She imagined how ashamed she would feel for being such a dirty girl, and although horribly embarrassed with what they were making her do in front of them, she'd enjoy seeing the look in their eyes as they watched her bring herself off at their request. As she obeyed.

She finally allowed her index finger to slip between her sex lips, her mouth opening as she felt how wet she was; all she needed was a little encouragement.

Still listening to their sounds of sexual pleasure, turning her on even more, Ronnie eased her hips further forward and fingered her sensitive clit in tiny circles.

'Well, yes, but you know how I feel about not being able to make my own choices around here,' Selene panted. 'Always waiting for my chance to be bonded, and even then it's not of my own choosing.' Feeling very close already Ronnie's fingers moved faster. 'It wouldn't hurt if they could keep their hands to themselves sometimes,' Selene continued. 'Their presence can actually destroy the rota balance.'

'Aw, babe, that's so sweet.'

'What is?'

'You're so jealous.'

'I am not. You know what the rota's like. It's the same old repetitive thing; hundreds of years in, hundreds of years out. Bar for a new PreCent we all get to use, every few hundred years or so.'

Interrupted by whatever he was doing to her, she moaned with pleasure and Ronnie found herself doing the same as she worked more fingers in and out of her pussy, feeling he orgasm rise.

'I'm telling you, I agree with Art,' the girl went on, her voice somewhat distant, clearly distracted by whatever was being done to her. 'She might be a workaholic who thinks she's higher than everyone else... oh, that's good...'

Sure is, thought Ronnie, looking down at what her own fingers were doing.

'But she knows her stuff. The rota sucks. Give me the Otherworld and their unlimited freedom of choice any day.'

The Otherworld? Ronnie wondered, feeling too far gone to worry about it now. Her body tensed. So close now. So unbelievably fucking horny she wondered how she could come silently, when all she wanted to do was scream out and tell the world how good it felt.

'What, and risk falling in love with someone who'll leave you?'

'They're mortal. Humans die; we don't. Face up to it.'

They're immortal? Ronnie's eyes snapped open. *Do they all have wings like Theo?* She let go of her nightie and clamped a hand over her mouth, not sure if she gasped aloud or not. Who were these people? Where the hell was she? Feeling her orgasm temporarily ebb away she rubbed harder. Whoever they were, she thought to herself angrily, they were not going to stop her having fun. She needed this like she'd never known before.

'I know it's not ideal to watch the ones you love

grow old and die, but it's something we have to deal with...' licking and kissing sounds drifted around the room.

'But love's not allowed. It's a bad thing. Theo is very strict about that and you know it. How can you advocate love anyway, when it caused your sister, Eos, a nightmare when she fell in love with that mortal Tithonus? The Prince of Troy,' he added, mimicking a posh voice. 'Do you really want all that misery to happen, Selene? Quick, turn round, I'm going to fuck you doggy style now...'

That's more like it, Ronnie thought, wanking herself eagerly, her orgasm close again.

'At least my sister had time she says was well spent with the human of her choosing...' She gasped as he must have entered her from behind. 'Time she treasured long after he broke the bond and died. I would gladly give up my immortality for a love like that with the right human.'

'You'd better not be visiting the Otherworld for mortals to fuck, Selene.'

Ronnie heard the sound of a palm smacking flesh, and the girl squealed.

At the thought of being on all fours next to the girl Selene with both their bottoms in the air wet and ready, and him taking it in turns to fuck them one at a time from behind while administering a large amount of spanking pain, Ronnie nearly came.

'Ouch! We're not all like Art!' Selene puffed.

Ronnie blinked. The part where Art fucked humans hardly registered. What interested her was that Artemis must know how to get back to Earth, and if Artemis knew, there was still a chance she could escape after all.

'All I'm saying,' the girl continued, breathing hard, 'is that PreCent has the best of both worlds, and it's just not fair.'

With all the talk about humans, immortality and Earth being another planet that she was no longer on, Ronnie felt her head spin. But her need to come surged on. She went back to her fantasy of this stranger being behind them both, taking it in turns to dip his cock in and out of first one, then the other. After swapping over several times, exchanging juices, he'd enjoy himself so much eventually he'd have to make a decision and choose one of them to ejaculate into.

Of course that would be her, the filthiest slut of them all, but she, like Selene, wouldn't be allowed to come. Being told no and fighting the urge to come was equally as exciting as coming; that delectable sense of being controlled by someone else. She thought of Theo and wondered what he'd make her do if he caught her secretly masturbating whilst hiding from two of his guards, and before she had time to contemplate an answer she bit her lip, desperate not to make a sound, and came. Her body convulsed and she reached out to use the bookcase for support. It wobbled. She froze, picturing herself looking like a startled deer caught in headlights.

'What was that?' asked the girl. 'I thought I heard something. You know Theo's back with his slut, yes? If he catches us having it away in the main hall rather than the Sex Temple we're in big trouble. And there's no way I'm having him treat me like he did Art that day. That was so embarrassing to watch.'

Still feeling her pussy pulsing, Ronnie grabbed

her knickers and quickly stepped into them, ready to run.

'Hush, babe. You're with me now. Everything's all right. I understand. Honest I do, I feel it right here.'

Temporarily distracted Ronnie moaned in ecstasy at where he probably touched her.

'I know inevitably a bonding will happen...' the girl said, trailing off, her ragged breath growing louder. 'But it's like waiting forever.'

'So a PreCent's just light relief until then, right?' he asked.

'Oh, heavens, I'm so close to coming...'

'Me too, babe.'

Suddenly they cried out in unison as they came together, and now sated herself, and not sure what happened, Ronnie felt awkward for eavesdropping on a couple being so intimate with each other. She turned to look for another way out and took a step back – right into the bookshelves.

'Shush! There *is* someone there! Shit! Get off me! Where's my skirt? Where are my panties?'

'Hey chill, baby. Wait here. I'll go and check it out. Hey, who goes there?'

Ronnie looked around, desperate for somewhere to hide. The last thing she wanted to do was go back into the corridor of eyes and the tunnel of nothingness.

'Aren't you going to get dressed first?' the girl asked.

'Nah, it ain't gonna be Theo at this time of the morn,' the male voice said, drawing closer. 'I was hoping I might get a chance to start poppin' caps if it's the bugs making all that...'

A naked black man walked into view. Prong first,

Ronnie couldn't help but notice, and although an inopportune moment, an image of Theo's cock flashed through her head. Was it possible that this man's was even bigger?

The six and a half, maybe seven foot tall naked man increased his pace and advanced towards her, and in his hand, pointing at her, he held a gun.

'Well, well, well, little lady. Where did you spring from?' He lowered the weapon.

'Who is it?' called the girl.

'Well, it ain't no bug,' he leered, and tried to grab Ronnie with his free hand.

Chapter Twelve

Tim sat on the living room floor, which even he had to admit was a complete mess, but he didn't care. Every piece of information they'd gathered during the hunt to track down the killers of Ronnie's parents now lay around him in a circle as though he were building a nest from piles of paper.

Last night, Sunday, something strange happened when his lust-filled urge returned. He was sure he hadn't had a drink because there wasn't any in the house, but he woke up with the equivalent of a raging hangover and every bone in his body ached like he'd been thrown down a flight of stairs. On top of that, he was on the floor of a derelict house he'd never seen before, with no recollection of how he got there or what had happened in between.

Whilst recovering he'd spent the day off work in the same spot on his living room floor studying the paperwork, desperate to find a missing clue or a shred of insight that both he and Charles could have missed, that would help pinpoint Ronnie's exact location. If anyone other than Charles got hold of the files they would lock him up and certify him as clinically insane. Maybe even slap on a murder charge, too.

Earlier, in his desperation to trace Ronnie, he raced to the library where they worked. All the while in the back of his mind he knew he wouldn't find her there, or at any of her favourite haunts, but he checked anyway just in case. To his dismay both her and her car were nowhere to be found and the shred of hope he clung to, vanished.

Two days had now passed since she raced off in her car. On Monday morning he'd managed to make excuses for her at work, and booked time off for both of them, saying he'd run into the chance of a holiday of a lifetime when a friend had given him first refusal on two tickets for a six month trip around the world for free.

Obviously it now meant both he and Ronnie were out of work and soon to be penniless, but in the long run it was for the best. No one was any the wiser. She didn't make friends easily at the library and chose to keep to herself on account of knowing what she did, and not trusting anyone because of it. He'd officially cut her off from anyone who could have had a hold over her. So with no employer and no interfering friends he had at least safeguarded them both from suspicion and possibly someone getting the police involved. But with that huge problem out of the way he now had a bigger one to contend with. Right now Ronnie was officially missing and only he and Charles knew it. What frustrated him most was that he knew where she was but how to get there had him stumped. There was someone he could go to for help, but she was hard to reach. And if they did make contact she might not give him what he wanted. Well, she would, but at a price, which as a last resort may be his only option. Time was running out and if he didn't act fast he might never get Ronnie back.

Chapter Thirteen

'Leave me alone!' Ronnie shouted, her mind racing with the horrors of what he might do to her. She ducked under his arm and gave him the slip. Ahead she saw an open archway which led outside, and ran for it.

A strangled cry of dismay flew from her throat as she stopped dead in her tracks and surveyed the view outside with frightened eyes. Thick, crisp white snow covered the ground, trees and shrubs as far as the eye could see. To her consternation a howling wind rang in her ears, cold mist sprayed her face and barely had one foot stepped over the threshold when a sharp chill rendered her numb with cold. From behind a calloused hand grabbed her arm and held her back.

'Ain't no use running out there in these conditions,' the man chuckled.

In the distance huge mountains loomed and encircled the land. She spotted a sparkling pillar of ice, once a cascading waterfall, now a curtain of dazzling blue-white where the water and icy cold had formed a coalition. It clung magnificently to a glacier-carved canyon wall; still and silent as though frozen in time. A gigantic dark bird, much bigger than any raven, flew across the white sky, swooped down as if showing off, and then soared out of sight. Close to the mountain border a whisper of smoke rose and disappeared into nothingness. A sign of civilisation? Even one tiny cottage in the middle of nowhere seemed hopeful. The whole breathtaking scene looked like a spectacular Christmas card, but in reality the terrain looked dangerous and inhospitable. Ronnie felt utterly trapped, bewildered and lost.

'Without specialist equipment, food and protective clothing, chances of surviving in the subzero temperatures of Black Ice are slim,' he said, reading her thoughts and confirming what she feared.

She stepped back inside, and although no door or glass window was evident, in an instant the frozen air vanished as if there were a barrier keeping the warmth in and the cold out, in some magical way.

'But, that doesn't look very black to me...' she offered feebly.

'Black Ice in its natural form looks like the rougher more unkempt rocky walls of this building. Outdoors, in its most magical form, it can give the illusion of a changing scenery. The icy weather and snow you see now may all be gone tomorrow. Some say the magical properties of Black Ice have a mind of their own, almost like someone is using them to suit their needs. Who that is and why they do it, we can only speculate.'

'But where does the Black Ice come from?'

'It erupts from the depths of the only remaining volcanic glacier in the area, and like a living entity it spreads and moulds itself to form everything from the mountains in the Wildlands at the borders, to the plants and trees in the Sterile Forest which surrounds this building.'

Transfixed, Ronnie tilted her head. 'But what's the point? What good does it do?'

'What you see before you is an ancient magic, and even Destaurians cannot begin to understand all its workings. The mountains in the Wildlands protect us from unlawful visitors, as they are filled with wild creatures and the terrain is particularly precarious. We don't know why, although most of the time the land appears to work with us. One thing we are certain of though, and eternally grateful for, is that the magical properties of Black Ice form a shield across the lands protecting us from the prying foresight of the Pandora witches. Without it we would have nowhere to keep you safe.'

'He's right, my dear, you do not want to go out there,' a female assured her, but still mesmerised Ronnie didn't fully acknowledge her presence. 'If the weather doesn't kill, the creatures in the Sterile Forest will. The winds from the North have blown down the Cahnnox fence, and believe me there's nothing worse than being stomped on by a house-sized bewildered Cahnnox.'

'But that's impossible; nothing's that big!' Ronnie exclaimed, whirling around, expecting to see the female called Selene for the first time.

'My dear, a Cahnnox can feed all of us here for a month, and we're big eaters. Why do you think most of this building is underground?' With a smile she wiped her floury hands on her apron before offering one to shake. 'I'm Hestia, the cook around here.'

Speechless, Ronnie shook with her. Hestia sounded so much older than the small plump twenty-something girl she looked. Others gathered around, from somewhere, and sensing Ronnie's unease Hestia quickly introduced them. The infamous Selene was the first to step forward, with a narrow-eyed look of suspicion that made Ronnie wonder if she knew she'd been listening a few minutes ago. What Selene lacked in manners she more than made up for in beauty, particularly her baby-blonde hair, which shone as though made from the moon itself; definitely not human. They shook hands lightly, without conviction, and Ronnie couldn't help wonder how well Selene got on with Artemis, after overhearing how she spoke about her behind her back. One to keep an eye on, that was for sure.

Surprisingly, Selene's equally pale twin sister Eos turned out to be identical in every way except for her shockingly red hair, parted in the centre, a splattering of freckles and a smile that suggested she was genuinely pleased to meet her, as was the third new face, a man dressed in a white coat with a stethoscope around his neck.

'Doctor Eros, at your service, sweetheart,' he said with an irresistible American drawl. Ronnie smiled; crowned with a lovely head of short blond curls he reminded her of a cupid, which was quite appropriate for someone named after the God of Love.

The twins wandered away and sat together, deep in conversation, already bored of the new arrival. Were they so used to having girls, complete strangers like her, just turn up? How many more like her had Theo kidnapped?

Doctor Eros lingered a little longer, explaining that he was the one to come to should she not feel well. As he spoke Ronnie noticed Selene looking decidedly put out over the length of time the doctor spent with her. With a harsh scowl she called him over. He bowed to Ronnie politely, and with a look of reluctance joined the two girls. How many men had Selene her hooks into? Which reminded her; the coloured man she'd encountered before wasn't there any more.

'Please may I introduce you to Samilious, our attaché and mechanicals expert,' Hestia continued, and waved a hand to another tall, dark-haired man in a long fur-lined suede cloak with matching boots. With a boyish grin he took her hand and kissed it. 'Oh, and what he doesn't know about gadgets is not worth knowing, my dear.'

'Gadgets?'

'Bugging devices.'

'And if you need to know anything about String Theory, Relativity Theory, Multi-Universe Theory or travel through space and time, I'm your man!'

Ronnie gawked. 'Sorry, did you say time travel?'

'Yeah, hopping around from planet to planet, backwards and forwards in time,' Samilious confirmed with a wink.

Ronnie frowned. Was he being serious?

Then the coloured man appeared again, towering over her. Now he wore a tanned suede cape of his own, but looking at his bare legs poking out from underneath like large tree trunks, still not a lot else. No longer scared of him, Ronnie suppressed a giggle.

'Yo, babe, allow me to officially introduce myself,' he said, grabbing her hand in a vicelike grip and shaking it vigorously. 'Ares. And I must apologise for scaring you earlier. I thought you were, well, what matters is that you're here now. Safe and sound.'

'I'm Ronnie.'

'Oh, we all know who you are, my dear,' Hestia said with a patient smile. 'You have no idea how long we've been waiting for you to turn up here.'

'You have? Well I'm sorry to be rude, but I just don't get it. One minute I'm in a car crash, the next I wake up with such a bad head I'm hallucinating. Not to mention amnesia. Where the hell am I? Can't someone just explain, please?'

Ares bowed and then backed away, leaving her alone with Hestia.

'My dear, I do apologise. Hasn't anyone filled you in? Please brace yourself for a shock. You are no longer in the Otherworld, the world you call Earth.' Suddenly Ronnie came over all dizzy, her legs trembled and she felt sick. Hestia directed her to a stool and sat her down.

'A different planet? But that's absurd!'

'Have you seen your Learned, Theo, in his true form, my dear?'

Ronnie nodded, close to tears. She blinked them away.

'Then you will know that you are special enough to be brought here to start your training as Child of Destiny. It is your true calling, my dear—'

'I know all that!' she snapped. 'I've already told Theo I'm not Superwoman. Yet he insists I have this weird goddess addling my brain, which if you ask me is going to cause all sorts of hoodoo mojo in my head...'

A woman nearby laughed, and it wasn't until

Ronnie had said that out loud that she realised what she'd done whilst listening to the two guards fucking. Although she was aware of enjoying the experience at the time, it didn't feel like she was in full control of her own body.

'It's true, and she will show herself to you soon and when she does, I can promise you, her guidance will improve your life here in Destauria. She's a sorceress of Mindlust, and will lure you into a new dimension where submission to your Guardian will dominate your thoughts.'

So that was the Spirit of Hope!

'You can't fight it forever. Both you and Theo, your Destaurian Guard, are part of an Order originally dedicated to the protection of the Magic Box of Destiny, and there is nothing you or anyone else can do to take that fact away.'

'Sorry; originally? What do you mean?' Ronnie frowned nervously.

'Although you can never stop searching for it, over time the box has become so well hidden that...' she paused as if having trouble telling her, 'and this is somewhat embarrassing for all involved, but... no one seems to know where it is any more,' she said quickly, and almost inaudibly.

'Oh, good,' Ronnie laughed, raising her eyebrows and standing up. 'So I won't waste any more of your time. I'll say goodbye and thanks for your kind hospitality and noodle off home then.'

'Dear child,' Hestia said with a sad shake of her head. She reached out and clasped Ronnie's hands in hers and gave her a heartfelt squeeze. Ronnie sat back down. People only ever did that when they were about to break bad news. As if she hadn't already had enough.

'So what does this Order I'm supposed to belong to protect now?' she asked, not really wanting to know the answer, yet needing to.

'You cannot protect the box, but you can prevent it from falling into the wrong hands if it is ever discovered. And once unearthed we will know about it. Mark my words. You will, however, be able to protect the Otherworld from the dangers that already escaped from the box when it was first opened.'

'Yeah, yeah, yeah, once owned by an ancient family of witches called the Pandoras—'

'Listen, Ronnie,' Hestia said brusquely. 'I don't want to sound harsh, but for your safety and your sanity I need to get through to you once and for all. The quicker you do what's expected of you and start serving your Learned as a true Child of Destiny should, which I repeat, is what you are, the easier your life will be, for without the blessing of your Learned,' she paused, shaking her head, 'you can never go back home.'

Chapter Fourteen

'And what if I still refuse?' asked Ronnie, aware of a warm prickling sensation running down her spine as she could sense something, or someone, drawing closer.

'Oh believe me, Ronnie,' a male voice butted in from behind, making her jump. Ronnie scrambled to her feet, knocking over the stool she was sitting on. Before he even spoke she knew it was him!

'We have ways of forcing you to do this if we

have to. But let's just say, for argument's sake, we let you walk out of here right now and say no more about it.' Ronnie nodded eagerly. 'Then you will not only put yourself, and all of us who are trying to help you, in danger, but the Otherworld, your world as you know it, will sink into the oblivion of Chaos and Destruction, as ruled by the Pandora witches. And before you say it,' Theo continued sternly, holding up a finger to Ronnie's mouth to hush her, 'no, you are not Superwoman and you never will be. But you are central to our plans and the survival of Hope. Believe me, there are a lot more people dependant upon you completing your training than just us.'

He turned to Artemis. 'Take the girl to her room now,' he ordered.

'Yes, my Learned,' she said, walking towards Ronnie, who took a defensive step back.

'My room? I'm staying here?'

Theo did not respond. He didn't need to. His silence said it all.

'But I can't stay here. I must go home. My parents will be wondering where I am. They'll be—'

Artemis opened her mouth to speak and then shut it again, obviously thinking better of it.

'Do as you're told and go with Artemis!' Theo admonished.

'No, I demand you take me home!' Ronnie refused defiantly. 'At least let me pop back and tell them I'm all right.'

He frowned and cocked his head to one side. 'Are you disobeying me, your Guardian?'

'Disobeying?' she said incredulously, pulling a face of disgust. 'What is this? I have rights. I can help you out with this stupid mission of yours, but you can't make me obey you. I didn't ask for any of this to happen. Please, just let me go home, at least for a quick visit.'

'Your obstinacy displeases me. I can see you have a lot to learn. So, know this. You are a Child of Destiny, and whether you like it or not you *will* obey me. It's what I demand, and what is expected of you. Now, I will take you there personally and teach you a lesson. Come.' He turned and started to walk away, expecting her to follow. 'Now!'

Ronnie stood rooted to the spot. 'No,' she said, less confidently than she had hoped. He stopped, turning slowly to her again. She folded her arms and stamped her foot with one last show of rebellion. 'You. Can't. Make. Me!' she screamed, her eyes full of hatred.

Theo strode towards her. Ronnie swallowed. By the look on his face it didn't take a genius to know she was in trouble, as if things could get any worse. Not knowing what he was going to do panic coursed through her veins, and before she had time to think of a plan of action he grabbed her around the waist, his free hand raising her arm and wrapped it around his neck. Then with an alarming speed he bent at the knees, tilted his body forward and heaved her up, throwing her over his shoulder as if she was nothing but a rag doll.

Not wanting to be carried off without a fight she struggled and punched him anywhere she could reach with her free hand, like a demon possessed. 'For God's sake put me down you arsehole!' she screamed at him. But without a word he calmly grabbed both wrists and held them together in one fist. At the same time his other hand crept under the nightie, and with a firm grip he clutched her thigh and held her close, lessening the impact of her kicks. Once held securely he marched forward at a fast pace, with Artemis running behind. He took her back down the dark passage, past his door, and deeper into the gloomy depths where all the ugly ravens perched. It was the last place she wanted to see again. In a sense she feared what was in the corridor more than what he was going to do to her, so in case he decided to dump her there she stopped fighting and went obediently limp. As she did she noticed the words *Raven Passage, Beware!* painted high up on the wall in a faded shade of red, and wished she hadn't.

When they came to a halt at an archway Ronnie was surprised to see an iron gate that looked like a portcullis. Artemis pressed a button, which looked surprisingly hi-tech considering most of the building was more like a medieval underground cave. The winch creaked into action, rotating the rattling chains and hoisted the iron grille up into the ceiling until it disappeared.

'Steam powered,' Theo mused proudly. 'We don't have electricity here. Everything in this building will be propelled by steam, clockwork, Cahnnox or the energy from the lightning conductor on the roof. Genius really,' he added, more to himself than anyone else.

He carried her into the room, and when she expected to be deposited onto a bed and left for the night to dwell on her predicament, he surprised her by dropping her to the hard flagstone floor. The cell was dingy and depressing, and nothing but gloom-filled shadows surrounded her. She shuddered.

For some reason there was a pile of books on the

floor beside her, and he eyed her looking at them.

'When you are not serving me the books will be your pastime. The History of Destauria, particularly the chapters on Black Ice and its surrounding areas, should be concentrated on initially. To be in control of your own destiny you first need to learn the ways of Destauria, where you now live.'

Dumfounded she looked up at his magnetic eyes, and nodded, hardly believing this was the same man who had turned into some sort of monster, a winged beast, before her very eyes. But although she couldn't deny the danger he exuded, she no longer feared him. It was as if since showing her his true form she'd been given some sort of passkey to move on. He had trusted her enough to share his real self, and here he was instructing her of books to study, without a hint of alien life form about him.

'When you have grasped the concept of our world, please take your time over the volume entitled Disciples of the Destaurian Council. In it you will discover the ways of The Orders, of which you are now one.' He stooped and picked the biggest and heaviest book out of the pile. There was a large golden sword on the spine, the colour of which matched the ancient lettering on the cover. 'You may read all of it, but the Laws, Duties and Code of Honour of the Order of the Children of Destiny will be particularly beneficial to you. And there are several volumes.' He passed her the heavy book. With both hands she held it tightly to her chest, as if somehow knowing that the words on its pages would be more than just beneficial. They could be her ticket out of here. 'It explains how to behave, our customs, and what I will expect from you. During your time here several fellow Destaurian guards will assist you in their specialised skills, but Artemis will be the one to whom you will ask questions if anyone you need is not available.'

She wanted to shout and scream at him. What the fuck was going on? Didn't what they did together earlier, before Artemis rudely interrupted, mean anything to him? How could he change so quickly from the caring lover she thought he was to this cold, heartless creature she saw before her now? Was she just a means to an end in his eyes? It seemed that way. But instead she listened without resistance as he told her the last book she should read was the *Malleus Maleficarum; A Destaurian Guide to Witches*. How to spot and prosecute them, and how to stay clear of their demonic temptations and not end up one of their latest recruits.

'Some of it is a little out of date but the basics are still very much part of our world today. Now, put the book down and turn around.'

She did so, and before her was a large cage, within it another pile of books and a blanket.

'How long am I going to remain your prisoner?' she asked, alarmed, spotting behind him an old-fashioned room divider covered with a patterned fabric, screening a wall.

'If that's how you see it, then maybe that will help improve your behaviour faster. Your cage is not meant to frighten you. This is your safe haven, where you will be sleeping, as all Children of Destiny have done before you. They say it makes them feel safe and secure.' He pushed her towards the open door of the cage, and unable to find the words that would make this all go away she looked down to the cold floor, somehow feeling silly for making such a fuss when over and over again they all seemed to be saying the same thing. He was her Learned, her protector, and ultimately wanted what was best for her in the long run.

'Don't I even get a pillow?' she asked, rather stupidly.

'I'll send Artemis with one. They're not something I use myself, so I rarely think of them.'

Ronnie shrugged. 'Thanks, but at least you have a bed to lie on.'

'Oh, I don't sleep on beds. It's years since my circadian clock worked. Guards never sleep. I do rest, but that's to relax my thoughts more than anything. While I rest I like to keep my ear to the ground, metaphorically and literally; if something's sneaking around I want to know it's there before it's too late.'

She scratched her head. It was on the tip of her tongue to ask what sort of a *thing* might be sneaking around, and if it was something she should be wary of, when he completely changed the subject.

With one word he managed to physically jolt her with a force so strong it stung like a slap in the face, and that one word changed everything.

'Undress…'

Chapter Fifteen

'Undress, I said,' he repeated. 'You have much to learn about the ways of Destauria, especially what is expected from you. You still need to understand I cannot let you get away with your previous disrespect towards me. Such outbursts as earlier will not be tolerated.'

Ronnie turned, looking for Artemis for some sort of support. Surely even Artemis wouldn't have left her alone with this madman, but as she suspected, Artemis had vanished.

'Neither will I tolerate you saying our gods' names in vain. Remember, the gods above are an almighty, all seeing power. As long as we behave correctly they leave the High Council and the monarchy to their own devices, and only step in if things get out of control.' He paused to take a walk around her as if appraising what he saw from all angles. 'Know this; you do not want the gods to take matters into their own hands. And before you say it,' he added, coming to a halt in front of her, 'yes, there are many myths surrounding our Greek origins, and that's exactly what they are. Myths taught to the universe as a disguise for what is really going on. Because if mankind knew what was going on around them, well, it doesn't bear thinking about the mess they'll make. Myths are clues to treasures of a forgotten past and you, a human more privileged than most, will learn the truth from the manuscripts I've left for you to educate yourself with.' He nodded to the pile of books on the floor of her cage.

'How do you keep doing that?' Ronnie asked.

'Doing what?'

'You seem to know what I'm thinking. I'm positive I never said anything out loud about you being a myth.' She narrowed her eyes. 'That's just plain spooky.'

'That, my child, is what we call here Destaurian

Eyes. I have the ability to read your mind when you're nearby, and if that has started it means Hope is also close. And I can't begin to say how much better that makes me feel.'

Shocked at the thought of anyone reading her mind, she snorted. *So you have eyes in the back of your head now?*

'Stop stalling for time or I'll undress you myself. And yes, I did hear that, but will put it down to you testing me. A once in a lifetime offer.'

So you really can read my mind?

'When I want to, yes,' he replied, and her eyes widened with amazement. 'Now, this is the last time I am going to tell you. Undress.'

When she still didn't move he gave her a scolding look of disapproval. 'Now!' he snapped, making her jump, so quickly she removed the socks. Without saying a word he held out his hand, and Ronnie passed them to him.

'Nightie next,' he ordered, and although her vision blurred with tears she refused to let herself cry in front of him. Instead she picked a spot in the darkness just over his shoulder to stare at, while she took a deep breath and slowly pulled the nightie up, revealing the knickers, her trim stomach, and then her firm breasts. Yes, she knew he'd seen it all before, but that didn't ease her feelings of solitude and vulnerability. She wondered what he thought when he looked at her body, and sighed inwardly. Why was she finding this so difficult?

Reluctantly she pulled the nightie off over her head, and for a moment stood hugging it protectively to her breasts; a hopeless effort to cover up her nakedness and growing sense of humiliation.

'Good girl,' he mused. 'Now give it to me and take off the panties.'

She blinked. Tears she'd forgotten she was trying to hold back trickled down her face. Leaving one arm crossed over her breasts to conceal them she passed him the nightie, but he dropped it dismissively to the floor and appraised her body, tapping her arm away from her breasts.

To avoid dragging this out further than she needed to she hooked her fingers into her knickers and pushed them down with a wriggle, and then dropped them into his waiting hand, avoiding his gaze.

He took them from her, and in the most cocky way possible held them to his nose and took a long, deep lungful of her scent.

She shifted awkwardly, wondering if he could tell she'd not long orgasmed. After acting such a slut earlier why did she feel so humble and shy? Where was her inner Goddess when she needed her most?

Oh, I will always be here as long as you serve our Guardian.

Hope?

'Tis I, and now is a time for me to step back and allow you to truly feel your connection with your Learned. All Children of Destiny need to learn to occasionally rid themselves of their own inhibitions without my interference.

'You should feel honoured—' Theo started, but although she knew she was supposed to hold her tongue and do her best to serve she couldn't hold back.

'Quit telling me how to feel!' she snapped. 'How am I supposed to know how to feel when I don't even know who I am any more?' She pouted and promptly crossed her arms over her breasts, trying to cover the fact that for some reason her nipples were stiffening, which she shamefully dismissed as being to do with the damp chill in the dingy cell. He could be so damned infuriating at times, yet those sparkling green eyes were so hard to resist.

He arched an eyebrow. He stepped forward and uncrossed her arms, uncovering her breasts. He placed her hands down by her sides, signalling for her to keep them there.

'Young lady, you are a Child of Destiny and you will start acting like one immediately,' he said sternly. 'Don't you dare stand before me like that again. You should never be ashamed of your body; it's beautiful. There is a reason you are naked, and your misplaced modesty is not one of them.'

She gulped. The look on his face was deadly serious as the tone of his voice sent delicious shivers of arousal rushing through her body.

'You need structure in your life, girl. You've been without it for far too long. From now on I am issuing you with three new protocols, to which I expect you to abide; low, medium and high. Low Protocol Situation, LPS, will be called for during times when we wish to temporarily fit in among the Otherworld, or any place where we must remain undercover to avoid detection and exposure of our mission. Understood?'

'Yes, Theo,' she said, feeling like a naughty schoolgirl.

'When a Medium Protocol Situation is required, the ability to speak fairly freely whilst being mindful and respectful to anyone you come into contact with at all times is granted. MPS will also include periods of training with others when I am not about. Clear?'

'Clear.'

'In HPS, the High Protocol Situation dictates a set of strict rules of conduct and custom where the Guardian requires complete focus, with no interaction with anyone else, unless directed. Here you will present yourself before me with your hands clasped behind your back and your head held high. Back straight. Shoulders back. Chest out. Do it now.'

She nodded and obediently moved her hands into the required position, her pert breasts thrusting towards him. Once again heat flushed her face.

'Legs apart.'

She shuffled her feet a little wider, evenly distributing her weight, feeling herself stand taller as she completed the stance.

'When I'm sitting you will automatically present yourself in the *knaala* position. If you don't know it already, ask Artemis to show you. If at any time I am unable to tell you which protocol the situation calls for, I expect you to take the initiative and decide for yourself. But choose wisely.'

She nodded, unsure what to say.

'In addition, when I say "eyes" you will immediately look into my eyes, so I know I have your full attention. This is particularly important.' He paused a moment, blatantly appraising her body.

'For further reading every rule you need is detailed thoroughly within book one of A Child of Destiny's Guide to Serving her Guardian; Protocol and Etiquette. Tell me now if you do not understand anything I have said so far.'

'I understand everything,' she said clearly.

'Good girl.' He nodded his approval. 'Then there will be no excuses for getting anything wrong, unless you like to be punished…'

A strange shiver of excitement spasmed through her body.

'I can imagine HPS may be extremely hard for you to cope with at first. It requires absolute and instantaneous obedient response, without delay, hesitation or question. Above all, during this mode you are relieved from all decision making and responsibility, focusing only on your diligent service to me. No matter what else is going on, who you are with, or what you are doing, in this mode you must come to me and place yourself in the correct position and await further instructions. You do not talk unless I permit it. Is that clear? You may answer.'

'Yes, Theo, *crystal* clear.'

'For that cheeky tone, my girl, you are no longer permitted to address me as Theo. You will speak my name with the proper respect due to me. I am your "Learned", not some spotty-faced Herbert of a boyfriend you can boss around. Am I making myself clear?'

Though nervous and anxious she resisted the urge to giggle. Had she ever dated a spotty Herbert? Maybe the fact she couldn't remember some things was more of a bonus than she thought. She bit her lip and nodded.

'Pardon?'

'Yes, my Learned.'

He seemed to pick up on her urge to giggle, and brought her mind back into focus with one last gem.

'Remember, your nakedness is a mark of your status and part of your training. Unless I give you orders to clothe yourself, or you need to go outside, you shall remain naked at all times.'

Ronnie blushed at the embarrassing thought of exposing herself to everyone at the Training Ground in such a demeaning manner. But as she stood there on display with her legs slightly apart, shamefully aware of her nakedness and the power he had over her, a moistness coated her pussy lips. She tried very hard to keep still and not think about what that might mean.

'Now we come to your management. I will devise a menu of healthy nourishment meals you can eat three times a day, every day. No more skipping breakfast as you did in the Otherworld, and no more liquid lunches.'

He really was watching me!

'When you are not doing my bidding, or training, you have my permission to leave your cage, roam the Training Ground and talk freely to any member of the Destaurian Guard. Use that time wisely. Learn how things work, and where important items such as food, tools and weapons are kept. I will get Hestia to show you how to clean, sew, gather and cook food and magical herbs for potions and wards. Samilious, our attaché and mechanicals expert, will teach you all things technical. He is also our librarian, and you will find him in the Book Tower most days. With Ares, our master Black Ice-smith and Warrior, you'll learn survival; how to both make and use weapons to defend yourself and fight. You will train with him, and the DGU members, in the Killing House every morn before breakfast.'

'The Killing House?' Ronnie repeated, not sure she liked the sound of that.

'It's a separate building which you can get to through the Assembly Hall. With two floors and five rooms on each level it's built like a normal house you'd find in the Otherworld, except for the special rubber-coated walls and high-tech equipment. It's not for living in, it's for training in.'

'Training?'

'Yes, you can't be expected to join in without being aware of the dangers. The Killing House is aimed at teaching the Destaurian Guard, in their guerrilla roles, how to enter any building inconspicuously and take down any threats inside using CQB; Close Quarter Battle skills combined with various weapon techniques, including pistols, submachine guns, knives and swords.'

Never having even seen a real gun, Ronnie wished she hadn't asked.

'And in your search for understanding of what is hunt and what is prey, and anything else, speak to Artemis. I want hands on. Experience how we live. This is a crucial aspect of your training; to understand and survive your new role.

'Yes, my Learned. May I ask a question?'

'You may.'

'I forget, what do the others do around here?'

'The twins, Selene and Eos, are the Spellcrafter experts of Black Ice.'

Oh, not what she expected.

'The Magic Boffs, I believe Artemis calls them. They have a comprehensive and authoritative knowledge of the herbs and potions Hestia gathers and cooks. Both girls study and experiment with new ways to create or enhance spells, wards, and other magical techniques. Think of them as scientists of magic. Absolute wizards in The Den, which is just as well, as they practically live down there.'

'Down there?'

'Under your basement cell there's another level. That's where our royal-sized laboratory, The Den, is hidden. Do not go there. They do not like being disturbed.

'And Eros, he's the doctor, yes?' Although as far as she could tell he didn't do anything.

'Eros? Oh, he's the busiest of all. Our Sexual Extra-Curricular Xtasy Doctor. He also sorts out all the entertainment and the social side of our lives. The SEX rota is an important part of this. All Solitaire and humans go to Eros for anything from check-ups, additional sessions of SEX, right through to the practice and theory of SEX as laid down by Destaurian law. He also specialises in love, and can give you several suggestions of how to avoid it.'

'But why try to avoid love? Isn't that what makes the world go round? My Learned,' she added hastily, nearly forgetting one of the many new rules.

'Your world, maybe. Not ours.'

She was just about to ask if he was being sarcastic when Selene and Eos appeared. He held up a finger and halted them, and they waited patiently.

'On the morrow after your training and morn nourishment meal, I am taking you to the Sensual Tower for your first visit to the Temple of SEX,' he told her. 'It's time I put you on the SEX rota.'

Ronnie gasped. They put so much emphasis on

sex, but without love.

'You'll be fine. You'll soon get the hang of it. It's perfectly natural for a Child of Destiny to want to be fucked and used by others for my pleasure.' He turned to Selene and Eos, clicked his fingers and walked out. They followed him obediently, two paces behind.

Clearly the Children of Destiny weren't the only ones to be used at his majesty's pleasure, she thought with a pout.

Chapter Sixteen

In the morning Ronnie had spent her first gruelling training session in the Killing House learning how to draw, hold and fire a pistol quickly and accurately while stun grenades were being thrown around. Afterwards she found herself in the centre of a cylindrical room, reclining on a large round mattress, lying just as Theo had left her, ready for the SEX Temple training; naked except for her black leather collar. When he promised to come back in an hour she nearly cried. Until then she was to be his good girl and do anything her visitors requested of her, because that was what he demanded from his obedient Children of Destiny; women not afraid of being used by a whole village, if that's what he required. Still in shock she waited as she kept a nervous eye on the archway, the only means by which her visitors could enter. Would anyone turn up, and if they did how many would she be required to serve?

It had crossed her mind to flee, but to get out of

the temple she must go along another dark corridor, which linked to the tunnel of eyes. Alone. It was a creepy labyrinth of dark tunnels in which she could easily get lost, and who knew what lurked within. Besides, even if she was brave enough to venture there, to where would she run?

After several minutes passed and no wicked beasts, winged demons or denounced angels turned up to ravish her naked body, Ronnie found herself relaxing slightly. And feeling a little bit… annoyed? Disappointed, even? Maybe it was all a mind-fuck, and Theo had no intention of having her used as he'd led her to believe. Perhaps he got off on watching her reactions as he told her of his plans for making her his guards' fuck doll.

While she waited she scanned the cylindrical room, finally taking time to absorb the temple's beauty, quite impressed with the richness of the decoration. The exquisite intricacy of the lustrous blood-red patterned floor tiles matched the luxuriously covered dark-red silk mattress. Now, if this was her bedroom instead of that gross dungeon, she might start liking it here, she mused. The walls, like everywhere, were made from pure polished Black Ice, which glittered with thousands of tiny gold-coloured stones. When she looked up to see the source of the gems' reflections she was bedazzled by the vaulted tower ceiling and its stained-glass panes depicting scenes from Destaurian history. So much so she almost forgot why she was in the temple, until a male voice disturbed her.

'This is your first time, is it not, sweetheart?' the kind-looking Doctor Eros asked, hands clasped behind his back. In his white coat even without his stethoscope he still looked every part the physician. Ronnie went to answer but her mouth was so dry only a croak escaped, and she had to clear her throat and try again.

'Yes, Eros,' she struggled. He held out a hand and helped her off the mattress onto her feet.

'When in the Temple of SEX you must always address all males as sir,' he said, looking sternly into her eyes. He pulled out a clipboard and made some notes with a pen attached by string. He looked at her every now and then, using only his eyes as if writing about her in the most serious fashion. It embarrassed her that he seemed to find so much to write about her.

'This won't take long, sweetheart, and then we can get to the meat of the action.' He threw the clipboard on the bed and then reached into a pocket and pulled out a pair of latex gloves. How strange it was, Ronnie noticed, they surrounded themselves with a mishmash of modern, ancient and totally futuristic objects. Only earlier she'd signed scrolls with a scratchy quill pen, and here Eros was easing his fingers into tight-fitting gloves made of latex, which he pinged once firmly in place. Then his next smile no longer made him look like the cherub she thought he did when they first met. This one had a vulture's appeal and announced her impending exploitation.

'Stand on the bed and turn around,' he demanded, and as she obeyed Ares and Samilious came in.

'Yo, my sex doc, we're not too late then? Oh good, an inspection!' They both laughed and walked around to join Eros, facing Ronnie's shapely bottom.

'Bend over, girl,' Eros ordered, and tentatively she did, her face burning with shame, and when a latex-covered finger pressed its way into her bottom and wriggled around she nearly died.

As far as she could remember she'd never been touched there before, and it was surprisingly sensitive. And she was sure she'd never before been at the mercy of three men, either. Could she cope if they went too far? Would Theo come back and stop them before it got out of control?

'Samilious, check how wet her cunt is,' the Doc crudely ordered, making her blush furiously while mixed emotions ripped through her body. Eager to oblige, the youngest looking of the trio undid his trousers, took them off and climbed onto the bed to join her. He grabbed Ronnie's hair, bringing her face up to his so she could not avoid his dark eyes as his free hand probed the folds of her sex. To her horror his finger just slipped in she was so slick with juices of excitement, and shame. He added another, and then a third, and used his fingers to pump inside her while his thumb rubbed her clitoris in tiny circular motions. Despite the age Samilious looked this was no naive, fumbling youth. He knew what he was doing and how to humiliate her further. And as if to prove it he pulled his fingers out of her pussy and held them up for the other two to see them glistening.

'She's gagging for it,' he announced proudly, and before she had time to protest Eros withdrew his finger from her rectum, Samilious lay on his back and she was forced down onto elbows and knees with a hand on her head pressing her face onto a standing, pulsing cock.

'Suck it, girl,' Samilious commanded. 'And do it

good.'

Reluctantly but obediently Ronnie opened her mouth and took the tip lightly between her lips, thinking it was so big she should take it into her mouth slowly, but the two crowding over her had other ideas and forced her mouth down the whole throbbing column until it nudged the back of her throat, making it hard for her to breathe. Then using her hair one of the men pulled her head up and pressed it down again until she almost gagged. He did it again, and again, and Ronnie quickly learned to suppress the urge to gag by angling her head slightly, managing to take the stalk of demanding flesh deep within her throat.

One of the men moved her thighs just slightly and she felt a stiff cock nudge against her wet pussy. Then with two big hands firmly gripping her waist the cock moved up a little, pressed against the tight ring of her rear opening, and one of them fed it slowly into her bottom. She squealed around the column of flesh plugging her mouth and her nostrils flared as she inhaled deeply through her nose. But oddly happy to be a horny little slut she rubbed her own nub, desperately needing to come, and she was just about to get her release when one of the men slapped her hand away.

'You don't have permission to touch yourself, slut.'

Strangely, being told she couldn't have something she desperately wanted thrilled her. So being a good girl she concentrated on savouring the pleasure of the men using her body for their own gratification. She tensed, and sensing her nearing the edge they thrust deep inside her with increasing intensity. Then Samilious grabbed her head in a vicelike grip and grunted as his glutinous seed spurted down her throat, forcing her to swallow several times in order to breathe. Fingers toyed with her wet slit, but again just as she was about to come they moved away. Other fingers pinched engorged nipples, and a gruff voice whispered crudely in her ear that he was about to come in her arse, and he did, erupting deep in her rear passage.

Exhausted she flopped, her face resting on Samilious' thighs, her flushed cheek nestled against his sticky, wilting, spent cock. But they weren't finished with her, and no sooner had the spent stalk slipped from her bottom than another shunted into the warm snugness of her cunt. Its owner fucked her rapidly and came quickly, and at last Ronnie came with him, wearily, whimpering quietly in rhythmic unison with the sound of his groin slapping against her buttocks.

She had given what they demanded without a fuss, as Theo had told her she must, and that made her acutely aware of the incredible power he held over her. And she felt strangely proud of herself. She'd obediently done something she didn't think she ever could. Whether her inner goddess had helped in any way could not be a certainty, but it didn't feel as though she had interfered with any Mindlust control this time. What an empowering experience. She only wished Theo could have witnessed it.

As they collapsed on the mattress, exhausted and sated, something cold and hard pushed into her anus. She looked up to see Eros standing on the tiled floor with his white coat hanging open, busy scribbling something down on his clipboard and ticking boxes. His large cock hung replete between his thighs.

'Theo wants you to wear the butt plug,' he told her, as though prescribing nothing more than a drug for a minor ailment. 'To take it out for anything other than going to the toilet you'll need his permission. Without it you'll be in trouble. All guards are under strict orders to regularly check it's still in position. Is that clear?'

'Yes, sir,' she whispered.

Having used her for their own gratification the trio walked to the door, leaving her naked and exhausted on the mattress. Then just before leaving her alone Eros turned.

'Oh, I nearly forgot. Your Learned wanted to plug you himself, but it looks like Princess Liavara took up too much of his time. Still, I'll report to him and confirm it's in place.'

She felt a horrible and unexpected pang of jealousy. Who was Princess Liavara, and why was he with her and not with Ronnie?

The shrill alarm bludgeoned his skull, forcing the unshaven man out of a gruesome nightmare into an equally disturbing reality. His eyes snapped open. He tried so hard to push those dark thoughts out of his head, to stop the depraved images of his mind, which like her face, haunted him everywhere he went. But each day the strength of the images increased, as did his yearning for her. The violence. The horror. And hearing her agonising cries in his head when she realises what he is about to do will change her life forever. Annoyed, Tim punched the off button on the alarm.

He reached under his pillow and with trembling hands pulled out the large knife. Never before had he felt an attraction so strong. Never before had he needed to rein back his feelings so hard, and for so long. But now the little prick tease had his attention he couldn't let go. Was he so out of control? Could he stop this if he wanted to? Right now he didn't care. But like any addict he was sure he could stop, if he really wanted to. Which was his problem. He was, as he prided himself, unstoppable. He didn't want to stop taking his drug. Her. Especially not now he was so close to the end. Everything he wanted within his reach. And this time he wouldn't fail. He was inches away from success. He could feel it. Smell it. And soon he would taste her. Oh, not much longer to wait at all, he reassured himself with a smile. Soon he'd unleash himself upon her and nothing would ever be able to stand in their way again. But how long had he had to wait for the moment? All that planning and admiring her from afar, and for what? To have that inhuman creep step right in and take his prize from him, just before he was going to make his move. Complete the deal. But not this time. Quietly patient, outwardly calm, wins the day. And the girl, of course.

Chapter Seventeen

All night something had gripped Ronnie's heart and squeezed it so tight it ached. The hand of jealousy. Eating her morn meal she sighed as a sadness welled up inside her, followed by a surge of anger, which she couldn't hold back.

'Why have I not heard of this woman called

Liavara before?' she demanded.

'This is not just any woman. Liavara is one of the true daughters of King Harsis Das, and Queen Perranda Ras.' Artemis smiled, looking as smitten as she sounded. Then she frowned and folded her arms. 'She is a beautiful Royal Princess and you do not speak of her, or any royals for that matter, in that tone. Am I understood?'

Ronnie pouted, determined not to be shut up this time. If this woman, Princess or not, was another threat she would tell her all she knew. Nothing was going to stand in her way. Nothing! Not now she'd just started to see sense and accept her role, even if it was a means to getting out quicker; a get out of jail free card. At least she was trying for once.

She placed her bowl on the floor and went to where Artemis was standing, and looked at her through the cage bars. With each step she felt the uncomfortable presence of Theo's plug. It acted as a constant reminder of his control over her, which she was rapidly liking, since he wasn't around in person that much.

'But what does she want… with Theo?'

He's mine!

'That's hardly a matter for your concern, child. The Learned may own *you*, but you have no say in what he does, where he goes, and especially not whom he sees.' She stepped forward and leaned closer to Ronnie's face. Through the bars their noses almost touched. 'You seem to have trouble remembering that you are only a Child of Destiny. Yes, you do play an important role as the spirit of Hope's body host, but you are not so special you can't be replaced and it's time you faced that fact.'

'And you are not my Personal Destaurian Body

Guard. You cannot tell me what to do!'

'No? Well my orders come directly from Theo so we'll see about that. If you refuse to do as I say you are effectively disobeying your Learned.' She straightened up and pointed to the floor at her feet. 'Get out of the cage this instant. It's unlocked. *Knaala*, right there!'

Ronnie frowned, pretending she didn't understand.

'Oh, don't you know anything?' asked Artemis, getting frustrated. '*Knaala*, that's kneel. If you refuse me I'll go back to Theo and tell him how jealous you are of Princess Liavara and he will surely be displeased and punish you. Much more severely than I would. Now do it!'

At the thought of pissing off Theo at such a crucial stage, Ronnie went to the cage door and pushed it open.

'Come on, Ronnie, you can humiliate yourself better than that. Heavens above, it's not far. Get on your knees and crawl. That's what Theo likes, and so do I.'

Ronnie shuffled to Artemis' feet, purposely trying not to be seductive with her crawl. She looked up defiantly. 'For your information I am not jealous.'

'Next time I say *knaala* you'd better do it with some enthusiasm or you'll be in big trouble. Now, kneel. Knees apart and hands behind your back. Obey me, girl, or do you want me to send for Hermes to message Theo? After I've punished you first, of course.'

'But I'm not jealous!' Ronnie argued.

'Look. You seem to be forgetting a lot of things. But you're not going to get anywhere if you forget this.' She sighed. 'We're immortal, Ronnie. We each have a special gift. I have the ability to look inside human hearts and see things you cannot. It's what I do. Right now your heart is hurting. You are jealous of the thought of your Learned being with another, but Princess Liavara is only the tip of the iceberg. You're not keen on his participation in the sex rota and to cap it all, my relationship with your Learned scares you, too. But jealousy has no place in a Child of Destiny's heart.' Ronnie turned her head away, but Artemis pulled it back. 'Look, I know we don't see eye to eye, but it's the truth. As is the fact that your Learned can choose whether to share you with others or keep you for himself, as you have already found out.' She placed a finger under Ronnie's chin and lifted her head up, so they were facing each other again. 'He's free to fuck anyone he pleases, and there is absolutely nothing you can do about it but obey. Now, *knaala* properly.'

Ronnie shifted back onto her heels, feeling her buttocks press tightly against the plug in her rectum. She spread her naked thighs apart and clasped her hands behind her back. Not once did she remove her eyes from Artemis'.

'Now, I have the power to allow you to repent for your jealousy. Do you want that?'

'Yes, Artemis, I do.'

'Good girl.' She pushed the wall-divider to one side, and Ronnie gawped at the high-backed gothic-style armchair Artemis perched herself upon. Elaborately gilded with gold it occupied a fancy embrasure and looked like a royal throne.

'Come lay yourself over my lap. You need to be punished.'

'What? Are you going to spank me now?' Ronnie said somewhat dismissively, her voice full of sarcasm, but before she had a chance to defend herself Artemis quickly reached out, grabbed her and flipped her over her bare thighs in one swift motion, and gave her succulent heart-shaped bottom one hard smack she'd never forget.

'How's that for a taster?' Artemis smirked.

Ronnie squealed indignantly and tried to get back up, but Artemis held her down and admired the instant red handprint that appeared on her exposed bottom. 'Do you not want to repent, girl?'

'Well yes, but like this?' she panted. 'With a spanking? There must be some other way. I'm not a child—' another smack, another squeal.

Artemis grinned, relishing the site of a grown female struggling to cope with being treated like a naughty child. Especially a human girl, of which she was particularly partial.

'Not a child in the Otherworld sense, no, but you are a Child of Destiny and that means offering yourself fully, without reservation and vacating all limits.'

'To Theo, yes,' Ronnie protested. 'But not to you.'

Artemis pursed her lips. That much was true, but Tartarus, if she was doing all the groundwork, laying the foundations for the girl's training on Theo's behalf, she figured she at least earned the right to take a bit of the fun too. It's all training, she reasoned, in case she was being watched. Walls had eyes as well as ears, although they hardly bothered to open these days. She raised her hand high in the air and brought it down so hard both females were stung – one's palm, the other's buttock.

'Stop struggling, and rest your hands on the floor; it's better that way,' Artemis ordered, unable to stop herself from squirming on her seat as tender flesh lay across her bare thighs.

'For you, maybe,' Ronnie snorted.

Spank! Spank! Spank! Spank!

Human girls were, after all, her preferred taste, and she adored the power of having one whimpering at her mercy. 'Repent, girl!'

'No!'

The Dryads were always so partial to a good bottom warming but nothing could replace the feel of a human girl against her skin. Nor could it beat the way even the most obedient of Destiny's Children fought against a good spanking.

'You *will* repent!'

'No I fucking won't! Not like this!'

Fortunate to be bestowed the special gift of reading hearts, Artemis connected so much better to human girls; such complex creatures who under a firm hand threw out so many mixed emotions; shame, guilt, regret, remorse and best of all, Mindlust. Pure bliss. Senses overload, and it could make her come without being touched, which she loved – loved almost as much as watching them squirm under her harsh hand. Not that she couldn't be gentle when she wanted to be, when it mattered.

Relentless, Artemis spanked her again. 'What do you think the word repent means?'

'Why, don't you know?' Ronnie retorted cheekily, but Artemis responded with another slap to her burning bottom.

'Don't answer my question with another question in the middle of me enforcing your discipline,' she scolded, aghast at the girl's nerve. 'What. Does.

Repent. Mean?' Artemis asked again, spanking the words out rhythmically.

Why should I care? She's not my Child.

'T-to request forgiveness for one's actions,' Ronnie stammered, conceding to the question.

But I do. Perhaps too much.

'Well, repent then,' Artemis insisted, giving her another spank.

Is that why I've given her such a hard time lately? Have I yearned so long for a Child of Destiny of my own to train and play with, that when I get one I like it's not mine to keep and therefore so annoying?

'You think a spanking is the answer?' Ronnie protested. 'I'm not a child. You can't treat me this way.'

'So say you're sorry!'

Smack!

'No!'

Smack!

'Say it!'

Smack! Smack! Smack! Smack!

'No, I won't!'

'Why not?'

'Because I'm not,' Ronnie stated adamantly through her tears. 'Princess Liavara gets more attention from my Learned than I do. It's not fair! *I'm* his Child of Destiny.'

Artemis was pleasantly surprised by Ronnie's first true acceptance of her ultimate destiny. Perhaps some progress was being made.

'Well then, start behaving like one and perhaps he'll take more notice of you.'

Immediately the words slipped out Artemis knew she shouldn't have said them. Yes, the girl did seem more difficult to manipulate than others; too feisty, too quick to argue, and just plain hard work at times, but Theo pulled her out of the car crash to save her life. Perhaps it was too early. Perhaps she wasn't fully ready. It wasn't her fault.

'Okay! Okay!' a runny-nosed Ronnie cried, tears dripping to the floor.

'So submit fully and say you repent your jealousy.' As she continued spanking the rosy buttocks before her, her fingers accidently slipped over Ronnie's wet sex lips and she knew she wanted the girl, if only she was hers. But this was no sex rota orgy and making her orgasm now would be unacceptable and only incur Theo's wrath and the sting of his whip.

'I do, I'm sorry!' sobbed the girl, bringing Artemis to her senses.

'Not good enough,' she said, punctuating each syllable with a smack. 'You must beg forgiveness. Make us truly believe you mean it. Your Learned will expect no less.'

'I'm sorry for being jealous, and for fighting against you all,' Ronnie sobbed. 'Really, please forgive me. I'll do anything, just forgive me.'

'And that's all you have to do girl, anything. Do you promise?' Finally Artemis sensed a true desperate need for forgiveness.

'Yes,' Ronnie sobbed, her face red with embarrassment, wet with tears of shame. Artemis clenched her pussy lips together. The sorry sight of the snivelling wreck begging forgiveness turned her on. She held back. A trip to the Otherworld later this nigh would sort her out. Right now this was all about Ronnie, and she needed to stay in control.

'There, there,' Artemis said, pulling Ronnie's

limp body up and sitting the girl on her lap, hugging her tightly. 'It's all right now. I've forgiven you. It's all over,' she cooed, gently stroking a loose strand of wet hair out of Ronnie's eyes. She wanted to make the girl come. Give her a true release, but without Theo's permission she could not. Not without dire consequences.

'But I can't stop crying,' Ronnie sniffed, laying her head on Artemis' chest.

'It's perfectly normal. Your inner Goddess is working you hard. Darker desires are driven by a need to resolve themselves and Children of Destiny do that through emotional release. It's the way of our world, but you'll feel better for it. Just as you would if you stopped fighting against us and make it your business to listen and learn to how you can better serve us, without jealously rearing its ugly head.'

Ronnie sniffed, nodded her head and looked up at Artemis. A stray tear trickled down her cheek. 'Thank you, Artemis. I do feel better now. But may I ask you something about Theo, please?'

'Of course, child. If I can help I will.'

She shuddered, her tears subsiding. 'You mean that?'

'It's the least I can do,' she sighed. 'I think I've been a little unfair to you lately, but that's all going to change now. So, what is it?'

'If this is my training and Theo is my Learned, why do I get the feeling he's avoiding me?'

'Hmm….' Artemis mused, pretending to be deep in thought. *Right, that's it! He's not going to get away with his behaviour any more. It's time he faced up to his responsibilities once and for all, or I'm going to the High Council and requesting to take her as my own, and when I give the reasons why, it will be the last we see of him.*

Harsh? Maybe. But someone needs to help this poor girl. What use will she be to the mission if her own Guardian is too busy struggling to deal with his own issues?

'It's okay; this is how it always goes,' she lied. 'Now I can report back to your Learned with details of how I think you're ready for the next step, and from thereon you will be working together much closer. Now, I'm going to the Sterile Forest to hunt. You stay and rest. Catch up on some reading. I'll be back later to see how you are when I bring your eve nourishment meal before I go out. Okay?'

'Yes, thanks, Artemis.'

And now I've built up her hopes I only hope I can convince him to do what's right by her or this whole damn mission is going to shatter to pieces, which we may never be able to pick up. And we all have so much at stake here. Something's got to budge.

Chapter Eighteen

Ronnie put down her empty dinner plate. 'You're going to do what? No you are not, Artemis!'

'You can scream and shout at me all you want, but it's not going to change the fact that Theo has ordered me to shave your head. C'mon, be a good girl like you said you would.'

'But this? I happen to like my hair. Shaving it all off is a big thing.' Ronnie looked at Artemis' straight, hip-length blonde hair. 'Surely with lovely hair like yours you can understand that? Haven't I been punished enough?'

'It's not the same for me; I'm not a Child of Destiny. And it's not a punishment. Removing your hair at his request is the most empowering thing you could do for your Guardian, a sign of finally surrendering your will unto him and accepting you are his property to do what he wants with. Don't you want to please him?'

'Yes, of course I do, but this is just so hard for me to do.'

'That's the whole point. Nothing in life that's worth doing is easy. It's a traditional ritual to mark a new beginning for both of you, and Theo finds the look extremely sexy.'

'I bet you're just saying that to make me do it.'

'Listen, child, I'm supposed to be going out this nigh, and I thought our earlier talk meant you were willing to start obeying more.'

Ronnie sighed and looked away, and before she knew it Artemis grabbed her by the hair and pulled her to the floor. Adamant she wasn't going to have her head shaved she struggled and broke away. Both panting they stood up facing each other, neither certain what to do next. Artemis was a trained huntress. She'd never outrun her. What's more, in the basement there was nowhere to run.

'You do realise that if you don't hold still it will hurt?' Artemis said, coming for her with a shaver that looked like something out of the dark ages, and as sharp as hell. 'Look, you're making this much harder on yourself than you need to. I don't like to see you upset or wish you any physical harm, so let's just get this over with, shall we? I know it can't be easy—'

'What do you know? You still have all your hair. It's beautiful. Why does this have to happen to me? Why can't I keep mine? Since I was a little girl I've never wanted my hair cut, not even an inch. I'd...' she stopped short of finishing her sentence.

'What did you just say? You remembered something?'

Forgetting the razor Ronnie nodded with excitement.

'Yes... yes! My memory's coming back! I remembered being about six years old and arguing with my mother about going to the hairdressers. I said I wanted it long like Rapunzel's, so my prince could climb up my hair and rescue me...' Ronnie's face dropped. The irony of the cage being like Rapunzel's tall tower in which she was imprisoned was too close for comfort. Was this Theo's way of making sure that no prince would ever come to her rescue? The end of all her thoughts of escaping to see her mother?

Artemis cocked her head to one side, and if Ronnie didn't know any better she would have sworn she saw pity in her eyes.

'What did your mother say to you in response?' asked Artemis.

'Sorry?'

'When you said you wanted to keep your hair long? Did she let you?'

'Oh...' She shut her eyes and saw her mother's smile. She smiled back. She opened her eyes and glanced between Artemis and the horrid razor in her hand. 'She said my prince would love me even if I had no hair, because that's how she felt herself. If he didn't it meant he wasn't good enough for me.

Besides, it was only a couple of inches, it would grow back.'

'Wise words,' Artemis smiled. A genuine smile full of warmth, Ronnie noticed. 'It is only hair, you *are* pretty, and it will grow back.'

'But that was only a couple of inches; you want to shave it all off,' Ronnie said, much calmer than she thought possible.

'Look, Ronnie, as much as I'd love to stand here chatting to you all night in this lovely dark basement, I need to get this done. I can't leave until you agree to it. So I'll make you a deal, okay?'

'A deal? How about you shave my head and I go home, right now?'

Artemis grinned. 'I need to put an end to this and go out tonight, but I have a few more jobs to do here before I'm done, and I'm rapidly running out of time. How about you let me shave your head and in return I'll tell you something about your past life.'

'What? You know something?'

'Enough to make an exchange.'

'You'd do that for me?'

'What can I say? I'm desperate?'

The fact that she couldn't fathom if Artemis was telling the truth or joking no longer mattered. Bigger things were going down here. Losing all her hair was a humongous thing to deal with, yet given a choice of that or getting her memory back it really was no contest. She heard her mother's voice in her head. *It will grow back, darling.*

'But by the time my hair grows again my memory might be back too. So I could perhaps ask for something different?'

Artemis shook her head. 'No, it won't.

Apparently I only need to discuss a few specific things and if you're allowed access it will trigger a response in your brain and start the PLMR process.'

Ronnie frowned.

'That's Past Life Memory Recall to you, and it works extremely fast so we have to be careful not to overload you with too much in one go. I don't entirely know how the memory recognition, in this instance, works, as Theo's never done a full memory wipe before, so I've not had to deal with this—'

'A full memory wipe? But I lost my memory in a car crash. You make it sound like Theo had something to do with it. He couldn't do that to me, could he? Could he? *Did* he?' she demanded, her voice rising in anger, fed up with feeling so lost, not knowing who she was any more.

Realising she'd said too much Artemis looked uncomfortable, but it was too late.

Ronnie sighed. No longer wanting to fight, she lowered her voice. 'Please tell me he didn't.'

'I'm sorry, Ronnie, I have to go.' She fumbled through the fob for the right key.

She's locking me in?

'No, don't leave me down here. Not like this. You've got to explain. You can't go like this. Please? You said—'

'I know what I said, Ronnie, but I've changed my mind. Destaurians do that, you know,' she added spitefully, and turned around and walked out of the cage, closing the door in her face.

Ronnie gripped the iron bars tightly, and spoke through the grille. 'Please, Artemis, stay. Let's talk.' Artemis avoided her gaze, placed the key in the lock and turned it. 'But you were going to tell me a memory. Shave my hair; at least stay and do that.'

'No, I can't,' she said, twice flickering her eyes awkwardly to the right, like she had developed a sudden tick. Then she gave her a sympathetic look, checked the cage was locked, and turned round and left the basement.

'Come back!' Ronnie cried. 'Come back, please!' But Artemis didn't, and Ronnie let out a high-pitched wail. Not out of the fear of dark, rats, or anything she had worried about previously, but out of frustration for not getting things right.

Maybe if she'd only tried better in the first place things wouldn't have gone this far. Maybe if she'd just had her head shaved, she'd be sitting quietly and subserviently in her cage glowing with warm memories of her mother, friends, where she lived, what she did for a living. Answers to all her questions. Maybe Theo was just a liar and a cheat. Maybe. So many maybes.

Tears of anger and frustration streamed down her face. She stood up and gripped the bars of the cage and shook them with all her might. Like Rapunzel she was locked away, and soon she would have no one to rescue her. But one thing was sure; it was time Theo started to tell her some truths. She wanted her life back, and one way or another he was going to give it to her, along with all her memories, if it was the last thing she did. Which may well be the case. But at that point she didn't care.

Despondent, she slumped to the bottom of the cage and sobbed. And when the tears could fall no more and the mist in her eyes cleared, she saw the razor lying on the floor where Artemis had dropped it in her hurry to leave. For a moment she just stared at it. Then, tentatively, she picked it up and studied the cold contraption in her hand. With clenched fist she gathered her hair into a ponytail and through numbed emotions, like a whiteout after a spore storm, and her erased memory, she used the sharp blade to saw through her hair from side to side. The cold air crept around her neck as large hanks fell away, tickled her back, and fell to the floor. Until the ponytail was no more. Then she raised the blade to her forehead and diligently scraped, from front to back, with a cautious sweeping movement. First down the centre, then the sides, above her ears, and then around the back. Every now and then she stopped to feel the unfamiliar clean-shaven skin beneath. Finally, when it was all gone she placed the razor on the floor near her feet. It clicked as the gleaming blade made contact with the black ice floor. Wearily she crawled over to her blanket and laid down, her knees up against her chest, her arms hugging her legs and her head tucked in. Drained, her eyes grew heavy, and she blinked away one last silent tear unable to fight the onset of sleep. After all, tomorrow was just another day.

Hold hope close to your heart and your soul will grow with a new-found strength.

Just like my hair.

She didn't know where that thought came from, but it stayed with her as she drifted into a deep, unworldly slumber.

Unbeknown to Ronnie, the slow vibrations of the black iced floor silently wrapped around her body while she slept curled in the foetal position among clumps of neglected and useless hair. It allowed her to sink within its comforting gentle beat. Warm, cocooning and protective.

From his private chamber, Archangel Theo also kept guard through one of the many miniscule high-tech surveillance cameras dotted throughout the basement. Cameras always watching, never sleeping, allowing no privacy.

Chapter Nineteen

Beyond a secret doorway hidden behind the throne in Ronnie's basement cell, Theo sat in the Surveillance Tower control room observing her battle with inner demons. How he longed for his guardian angel invisibility from the Otherworld when he was able to watch over Ronnie with intimate closeness. Now the secret was revealed this could no longer be, hence the reliance on so many gadgets. Unfortunately, each tiny miracle had a darker purpose, a flip side.

In the morrow she would realise to remove her identity in that manner is a cleansing experience and very humbling. With a little mystical help he had the power to minimise her pain and inner turmoil, without erasing the recollection of this new chapter in her life, for which she needed ingrained in her memory to keep her humbled. However, his power over her would not stop there.

For a few days every time she went to habitually push her hair out of her eyes it would remind her that she cannot, because of him. He will allow her to grow it back straight away, and although she is unaware of the increased speed he can make that happen, it meant that she wouldn't be without hair for long for which she will be grateful. But this was not a pointless exercise, he mused.

She would be told that he would allow her to grow her hair back to act as a reminder that it was his right to do so, not hers. She, as a Child of Destiny, has no rights of her own because she belongs to him. Usually this is something Destiny's Children accepted without question, as it is their way. But then, he should have known Ronnie was always so very different to the other girls they brought to Black Ice. The words 'should have been there for her' swam round his head, haunting him as Artemis sat on all fours between his legs and rubbed his cock through his trousers.

'What are you watching?' she asked.

'None of your business,' he replied, undoing his trousers and getting his throbbing dick out for her to lick.

For twenty-two years and three months he had watched over this girl, Ronnie. Always protecting and keeping her under surveillance in order to anticipate her movements, plan ahead to keep abreast of where she might go next. To foresee, as much as it was possible, any hazards she may encounter was no easy task, but paramount for her protection.

He groaned as Artemis squeezed the base of his cock, making it grow harder and bigger.

Looking back he never thought guarding another Child of Destiny would be easy. From a young age this one had an incurable fascination for proving herself to the best of her abilities, in whatever she turned her hand to. He often wondered why. It wasn't as if she needed to fight for the love of her parents; as their only child they adored her. Yet even from a young age she always had to be at the top of everything she did; sport days, spelling tests and even her dancing classes. Maybe that had something to do with it? Maybe, unconsciously she felt stifled by their love and she wasn't proving anything to them at all, but to herself to prove she could do things on her own, be self-sufficient on her own merits. Until now he'd never given that much thought.

Artemis slowly worked her other hand up the shaft of his cock, pulling his foreskin up over his bell-end, and then slowly pulled back down until both her hands met.

No doubt the death of Ronnie's parents played a big part in her perfectness. Within hours the happy ten year old he knew so well hardened before his very eyes and withdrew into herself. Despite this, her fighting spirit and keenness for perfection never faltered. In some ways that proved beneficial.

Out of necessity to pay her own way, she'd claimed her first and only job at sixteen as a librarian for her local library, without any help from anyone. Not even him. He could have helped her more if he'd wanted to, but she didn't seem to need it, and he liked that in a PreCent. In the face of adversity she could stand on her own two feet and look after herself.

He liked that, he thought, as Artemis rhythmically worked his shaft up and down, drawing his need to come up to the surface. He grabbed her hair with both hands and lowered her head so her mouth was just above his cock.

Ronnie, he thought, quite often remained to the outside world as the shy, quiet librarian, who had a tendency to obsess about things. For instance in the gym, which she joined in an effort to make more friends with people who didn't know her background, she obsessed about her weight and stamina, always pushing herself that one step further. Obsessions, he knew, were dangerous. Like her need, as she grew older, to track down her parents' killers. The whole reason she'd been brought to Black Ice before she was officially due.

Artemis stretched out her tongue and tried to lick the tip of Theo's cock. He lifted her head up, trying to prolong her agony, but she managed a quick lick before he could get her tongue away. He shut his eyes and groaned with ecstasy, then looked at the screen again.

At Ronnie.

For the first time since she'd arrived he admitted to himself that for a human, she was beautiful. He could quite easily push Artemis to the floor and storm in next door to fuck Ronnie, to take her like he should have done ages ago. But like her, he too could be stubborn. In the same way she'd taken her search for justice too far, forcing the King Harsis Das to demand he put a stop to it.

For that reason Theo felt he had no choice but to use the car crash as his opportunity, and plausible excuse to wipe all that she'd discovered from her mind, the perfect cover up for when she started asking questions about her previous life.

That said, he worked hard on bringing out the best in her, in spite of her flaws, no one, not even a PreCent, was perfect. Although Artemis was doing a pretty good job on his cock, the way she flicked

161

the tip when he lowered her head just enough so she could reach it when she really stretched out her tongue. He loved making women work for his cock. His cock was the only one true way of making the naughtiest girls behave. But he couldn't do that to Ronnie while she still lived in the Otherworld, which was why he turned to the use of subliminal messages to try to smooth her out around the edges. Was that so wrong?

It was his duty to protect her; he had to find a way of preparing her for what was to come. For her sake, and for his goddess. A twinge of guilt tingled down his spine when he thought of what he had done.

Over the years during her time on the Otherworld he'd implanted subliminal messages into her subconscious brain, by various methods, either while she slept, watched telly or read alone in her flat. Using the word 'praxis' was one way to start the procedure. It was his job to prepare her for this moment, and her quest ahead. It was he who gave her the key need to learn meditation, so along with additional methods he could persuade her in his own special way to participate in the calming of her mind at times, under normal human circumstances, may not be possible. She needed to be perceptive to his magic so when the time came for them to finally meet she'd be halfway there, more pliable, hence making his job easier.

He watched Ronnie as large hanks of hair fell to the floor of her cage. It turned him on to see her do that for him, to witness the sacrifice she would make to please him. To know that this moment he too would treasure, and not just because he was watching Ronnie while Artemis was desperately trying to suck his cock. To think that would be a mistake, which reminded him of the one big mistake he'd made with Ronnie, which was too late to turn back by the power of magic. Too dangerous for her.

Of course, he hadn't done this job for so many years he made the mistake of completely erasing her memory. Not thinking through the full implications of what he'd done until it was too late. In doing so he never changed the person she was, he reasoned to himself, just removed a few selective memories, which could jeopardise the mission. He'd return them when she had accomplished what was required of her. It wouldn't be forever. Unfortunately the removal of her parents and her boyfriend Tim from her memory was perhaps overkill, and in hindsight a bit of a mistake. But they all played a huge part in the events which led up to the accident, he couldn't take that risk. Plus he couldn't bear to watch Tim fucking her.

Fed up with teasing not only Artemis but himself, Theo loosened his grip around her head and seeing her chance she instantly plunged her mouth down the length of his cock, taking it in as deep as she could, just the way she knew he liked it.

She should be doing this, Theo thought, looking at Ronnie through the screen as Artemis slurped and choked on his huge cock. Why did Ronnie always fight against her true destiny and who she really was? She was a Child of Destiny, her one true inherent need should be to serve him however he wanted.

Maybe the fault was his, Theo wondered. Maybe she sensed his closeness when there was never anyone there? The way he always lurked invisibly in the shadows following her every move, bar for the times she needed to be alone for her privacy until she grew to the age of maturity, eighteen. Since then he had never left her side, whatever she did, wherever she went, and whoever she was with. Could this have affected her in any way?

He gripped Artemis' head again and showed her how fast he wanted her lips to go up and down the length of his stiff member.

He thought back to Ronnie and how he was with her when she interviewed for her very first job, met her first boyfriend, ate her first kebab – so many firsts – all of them she thought she'd done alone. Yet he never left her side. It gave him great pleasure to see her mature into a feisty headstrong woman, a good quality for a Child of Destiny who would need that kind of energy when facing the foes of her future, although it made her difficult to monitor. He'd never had a girl quite like her. He was proud of her. So what had changed, in him? As far as he could see since returning to Black Ice to train her, he delegated all the work he was supposed to be doing himself.

Why?

Why did he feel something for her that he hadn't felt since he was with Hamira?

Was there more to the feelings he felt for her than he cared to admit? He hoped not. What would the High Council have to say if they found out? It went against the grain, his whole teaching methods, but this girl was different and he couldn't deny the effect she had over him. Was she more than just a job? There was no way in the Heavens she could be.

He studied her slim body and small frame, and wondered if that cute mouth of hers would be able to take the girth of his cock, and groaned. Why had he not used her mouth yet as he was entitled?

In the great big scheme of his very long immortal life had he lost touch with what it was like to be human? Had he turned into some heartless demon? Was he neglecting his Child? If he was he could not but help be so busy.

Hermes was constantly popping in with news of the Paraphanites' latest shenanigans. It seemed there were far more than originally anticipated roaming the Otherworld and the King was demanding more to be done, but how? There were only seven of the Destaurian Guard, and thousands of them. Never had it been such a problem before. Every spare minute of the day he worked on his plan to improve the situation without the help from anyone else.

His brother, Theus, was still AWOL and that worried him. Not to mention that he was behind with his genealogy records and he knew the sex rota was no longer working the way it was originally intended to, yet to say anything would be to reveal his hidden cameras which only he and Artemis, sworn to secrecy, knew about.

Then there was Artemis happily sucking away at his cock, despite the fact that he knew she preferred girls. But as long as the sex rota was in place he could fuck whoever he wanted, and use them to fit his needs. He was the almighty Learned after all, and even the Guards had to fall to their knees and serve him, with thanks to the rota. He smiled, feeling his climax nearing its peak. Artemis had started to notice that not once had the rota fallen the correct way to put her and Ronnie together, because he had made it so. Only moments ago she'd moaned about it again, so he gave her this job to keep her mind off it.

Most distracting though was Princess Liavara demanding more of his time, and he could not upset her because in doing so it would upset his relationship with her father, King Harsis Das, and he needed to keep his connections with the monarchy strong, especially since the Destaurian Guard were not performing as well as they should.

Princess Liavara had a penchant for sex, but not being a Guard she was not on the rota. But if he could change that he would, because despite her constant summons to her private quarters on Nuvola at the Royal Palace, she was one horny, delectable little fuck and he liked nothing more than imagining getting both Liavara and Ronnie together so they could fuck each other in front of him. He nearly came at the thought, and reined his lust in as his eyes fixed back on Ronnie's and he could imagine she was the one sucking his cock.

Ronnie. His girl, his servant, his property, and since they'd returned from the Otherworld, her world, Earth, he'd hardly had time for her. Had his ambiguous immortal life misshaped his thoughts? If only he had not written that damn rule number one. Show no emotion. But he had, and there was no way on Tartarus he could ever take it back. Not without a price.

He'd just have to hold off until the Bonding Ceremony, and see how he felt then, but that too would be hard. Something else he had to contend with; all those years avoiding love to finally throw all that hard work away and allow it? How could he change the person he was after just one ceremony? It was something he struggled with time and time again.

He looked at Ronnie through the monitor on the wall, and hoped the very humbling act of shaving her head would finally be the answer he was looking for and not only would she change, so would he. To cut off her hair was akin to cutting off her past life and sealing her fate with him, and that pleased him immensely. So much he held even tighter around Artemis' head and forced her to pump his cock faster, while all the time he watched Ronnie and then spurted his seed into Artemis' mouth.

Without a word he switched off the monitor and sent Artemis out of the room, and decided to cheer himself with a film. He had so many choosing one proved difficult, so in the end he decided to watch two, but which one first? Space Cowboys of the Otherworld, or Ronnie playing with herself as Selene and Ares fucked around the corner? Theo opted for the latter, and watched it twice.

Chapter Twenty

When Ronnie awoke the first thing she remembered was the shaving of her hair. She rubbed her head to check, but instead of feeling shocked and hurt at her loss she surprised herself and smiled. Somehow she did feel different, just as Artemis said she would. Like her acceptance of her role brought with her a new, energised feeling of starting afresh.

What's done is done. Nothing would bring it back, other than patience. Something she suspected she would soon be an expert at by the time they were through with her.

Her head felt cool, and weightless. It reminded her of a layer of unspoiled, freshly fallen snow just waiting for that first footprint to lead the way towards her new, unmarked life.

She yawned, stretched herself awake, and cast a glance at the hair on the floor that once belonged to her. She felt nothing for it. It was just hair. It didn't matter. What mattered was what Theo thought now he could see how serious she was, and the sacrifice she'd made, her gift of submission. Without hair she had nothing to hide behind, could not disguise her true feelings. Never before had she felt even more naked than she already was and she liked the effect it had on her, which she didn't expect. Now she had a clean slate perhaps they could start building a proper life together, as was his original wish.

She stood and wound the clockwork light, which hung from the centre of her cage, and then walked over to the pile of books Artemis had given her, and began to read some more, as she was told to do for Theo, her Learned.

When she'd finished she didn't know what she had expected to gain from the texts, but it wasn't to feel like she had a connection to her new surroundings. But she did. She learnt a lot. Even after reaching the last page of the book she couldn't quite close it. With aching eyes she re-read the introduction and before she knew it she was skim-reading most of the book again, picking out what she thought to be the most important bits. Setting as much off as she could to memory. 'Easy when you've got a lot of space to fill.' She almost laughed.

Destauria was discovered by a man called Andrastus. No one knew where Andrastus came from, nor indeed where he went, but he became the founder of a growing community of travellers who helped make the land named Black Ice what it is today, habitable and safe from the Pandora family of witches, and the secret location for what is now the Black Ice Destaurian Guard Training Ground.

She skipped a few paragraphs and found the section she wanted.

Andrastus, later became known as the God of Artisans, and Black Ice-smiths throughout the land. Only officially he wasn't a god, but a wizard who could mould and carve the frozen magical Black Ice into any form – furniture, shields, armour, weapons. [See Appendix 52]. She did. Weapons: most notably The Andrastus Dagger. The elusive silver-bladed dagger of Black Ice, with a handle made of white gold. The only weapon that can kill a Black Witch, the highest rank of witch of their Order, the High Priestess Pandora. It is believed that the Black Ice Magic is an entity of its own, held together by the Spirit of Hope, once a Goddess cursed and confined to a Magic Box [See Appendix 218] by the almighty Zeus, for falling in love with a courtesan at the same time as she was his official mistress. This boy was no courtesan, but had been sent by the gods to protect Hope. His name was Prometheus. [See Appendix 253]

She blew out a breath. It didn't seem to matter how much she read that paragraph back, she still came to the same conclusion. She'd dreamt of that

Hope, felt her heartache and the love for that courtesan, as if it wasn't just a dream and that somehow she was really there experiencing it. Although the man was blond then, she recognised his eyes instantly. Hope had fallen in love with Theo. He had loved her, too. The pain came from both their hearts. She felt it. But because of whom Hope belonged to, and her protector Theo's need to keep himself disguised, there was nothing either of them could do, but to play the games of the gods.

For the umpteenth time she visited the appendices, and found appendix 253, reading it as if it were the first time she had ever come across it.

Prometheus: Denounced God/Titan, now Destauria's official historian and genealogist, Keeper of Records and Fallen Angel. Leader of the elite task force Destaurian Guard arranging protection to all the women borne from the Goddess of Hope's bloodline, who are chosen to shield the Hope's spirit within their own bodies, until each one dies, and a new host is born. Hosts are now called Children of Destiny, for they hold the future of Hope in their hands. Although these humans are of great importance, they are expendable. New rules state Children of Destiny should live and die by their guardian's SWORD; Serve. Worship. Obey. Respect. Defend.

What amazed her was where the Black Ice came from and what it was capable of. It spews from the depths of the only remaining volcanic glacier in the area – pushing up to form, not only the mountains which encircle the Sterile Forest, but all the trees, shrubs and plants within. Which is why it is so aptly named, sterile, as not one inch of the forest includes real plants and trees within. Not real in the sense that she knew plants and trees to be, and as far as she was concerned the trees she knew where never magical like these.

One thing she was certain. She had found herself in a totally different world full of witches, magic, gods and people who were once in her dreams and now stood as large as life insisting that because of her bloodline she was a Child of Destiny with a mission only she, or people of her kind, could complete, with the help of the Destaurian Guard; a guardian angel. Whatever her mission held before her, it was big. Far bigger than anything she'd ever had to deal with before. She was sure of it.

Hestia came in and unlocked Ronnie's cage and then left, saying she had to go and check the pie she had in the oven before the morn's training session.

'I'll meet you there,' Hestia said brightly.

A short while later Ronnie put her book down.

Okay, time to go.

She opened the portcullis, braced herself, and ran through Raven Passage towards The Killing House for more combat training. As she fled past the stuffed birds she could have sworn there was one missing.

The Killing House training was particularly challenging. Ares tested their mental strength, determination and endurance by making them run miles with a 15lb backpack through the snowy Sterile Forest, which Ronnie found hellishly difficult, but like everyone else in the DGU, she made it. Even though she came last. Unlike everyone else, this was her first time and she was the only mortal. Everyone except Artemis, who had somehow gotten out of this gruesome training session.

Relieved to be back in her cage, feeling safer than when in the tunnels, Ronnie settled down with another book. She heard someone enter the basement, and it wasn't until her stomach rumbled that she realised it was Artemis with her breakfast nourishment meal. As regular as clockwork, she mused, going back to her book.

'Artemis, if the Sterile Forest is magical, and not made from real flora and fauna, then how am I able to breath?' she asked, not looking up. 'Everyone knows green plants extract carbon from carbon dioxide via photosynthesis to give us oxygen. Well, they do from where I come from. But how can they here, if they're not real?' Not getting any response she looked up. Artemis was staring at her, her mouth agape, her eyes wide.

'The air round here, if you can call it that,' Artemis answered with suspicious eyes, 'can be whatever you need it to be. It doesn't prejudice against any of the creatures on land.'

'Creatures?'

'Yeah, man, beast, good or evil. Anything can live here.' She frowned.

'Which is also why…' Ronnie paused to find the page, '…why the mountain borders and the areas beyond called the WildLands protect us from visits of the Pandora family, by not allowing the higher Order witches to have foresight within Black Ice. What exactly is foresight? I mean, what does it mean to you living here?'

'All witches can, to a certain extent, see things going on in the present, but only the high priestess can see things in the future, and then only a flicker, more of a shadow, of what is to come, not actual events because events can change depending on present day actions. It's complicated stuff, but you'll soon get the hang of it. So what made you cut your hair?' she added.

Ronnie looked up. 'You didn't think I was strong enough to do it?'

Artemis spluttered. 'I, er, well, after all that fuss you made, that hissy fit of yours, I didn't really expect to come down here and find it all gone. So, why the sudden change of heart?'

'Honestly?'

'I'm interested. You've obviously decided to get into your training.' She looked at the books strewn around the floor. 'Why now, after all this time?'

'Well, you're not going to suddenly give me back my memories and send me home with an apology for messing up my life, are you?'

'Fair enough. No, we're not. You're a Child of Destiny. This *is* your life now.'

'Just as I expected. So while I'm here, if it gets me out of this Hellhole quicker, I'll do what you all ask of me. Hopefully you, Theo, or someone from the Council will let me out for good behaviour, once this mission is complete. I mean, what else can I do?'

Artemis bit her lip.

'Besides, it's quite an invigorating experience. I feel like a new woman, a blank canvas on which only Theo can paint what he wants.'

'You do? I mean, well, that's great! I'm really pleased for you,' she grinned.

'So bearing this new me in mind, obviously you'll be wanting to help me even more, now I have finally come to terms with who I am.'

'Absolutely!'

'So please tell me one thing, Artemis. I just need to be sure of one thing about my previous life and I'll never ask anything about it again. I have moved on, and I'm not going to dwell on your answer. I just need, for the sake of my sanity, to know this one small thing. Surely I've earned it?' she said, rubbing her freshly shaved head.

Artemis sighed. 'Go on then, what is it?'

'Lately I've been remembering, no, more just sensing, that my parents are no longer with me. I just couldn't remember at the time, but now I know about the memory wipe that feeling is so much stronger. Please tell me if I'm right. I haven't got any family left, have I? I'm actually all alone.'

'That's not one small thing, Ronnie, but you do deserve to have your question answered.' Artemis nodded. 'I am forbidden to say more, but that. I'm sorry, child. Look, I'd stay with you but I'm due on the damn SEX rota, and I can't miss it. And I'm going out later this aft and won't be back until late this nigh. But in the morrow I'll stay with you all day and help you get through the rest of your training. Has Theo seen your hair yet?'

Ronnie shook her head. It felt strange not having to brush her hair from her eyes. 'Not yet, but I can't wait to see his face when he does.'

'He's been very busy lately,' she lied, 'but as soon as he knows what you've done he'll take more notice of you, I just know it.' Artemis stepped into the cage and gave Ronnie a hug.

Tears escaped Ronnie's eyes, but she held back crying. She'd done plenty of that, and now it was time to let go of the past and move on. Her mother and father, Hazel and Henry Weaver, would always hold a place in her heart and nothing could ever take that away.

'I must go, see you in the morrow,' Artemis said with a smile, and off she went.

Tomorrow is ages away, thought Ronnie, first she needed to get through today; the first day of her new life as a Child of Destiny. She smiled. From now on she would do whatever it took to please Theo, and not for the reason of escaping. That reason no longer existed. Theo now was her one and only reason for wanting to please. Theo was all she had. Finally Hope had arrived. For a while everything seemed to be going well.

'What's this I hear that you've been struck by jealousy?' asked Theo, with a look of concern. 'The truth this time.'

Artemis! She said she wouldn't tell him. Ronnie was horrified at her betrayal.

'I'm sorry, my Learned, it is true.' *Shit! If he listens in now, he'll be able to tell when I lie. How embarrassing!*

'I... I've come to realise I care for you more than I thought. It's hard for me to see you with another.'

You are all I have, I can't lose you to someone else.

He stood before her and studied her. Searching for the truth?

'Girl, listen to me, for this is paramount to your health and learning. Jealousy can consume the soul until there is nothing left but hatred and evil. I will not let that happen to you. I *will* make you control it.'

His tone instantly made her pussy sit up and listen. It seems he only turned up when she needed reprimanding. If she always misbehaved he'd have to stay by her side to correct her. She tested her theory.

'But—'

'No buts. You will learn there is no place for jealousy in a Child of Destiny's heart.'

Ronnie recalled Artemis saying a similar thing. But the original issue was no longer the point any more. *Think! How would Artemis wind him up to get what she wanted?*

'You must understand I am older than I look,' he said, obviously taking her silence for obedience. Not what she wanted. 'I've got years of experience behind me, so trust me when I say I've seen this before.'

'Where?' she snapped rudely.

'Most prominently, in King Zeus' wife, Queen Hera.'

Ronnie swallowed hard. *How old is this guy?*

'Zeus had a habit of marrying other wives, as was the tradition in the early days. When he married Io Queen Hera became filled with jealousy – an evil that escaped Pandora's Magic Box of Destiny. It visited her day and night until she almost let it destroy her.' He shut his eyes and rubbed his hands over his temples, as if the memory was still fresh in his mind.

'May I ask what happened to Io?'

'All you need to know is that I managed to save her, as I plan to with you. This nigh you will prepare yourself for a royal visit.'

'A royal visit? But I'm not ready for that. You know I'm not!'

He raised an eyebrow. 'Are you questioning my decision?'

'I'm sorry, my Learned, I won't do it again.'

'No you won't.' His tone of voice startled her. 'I will send Hermes to the royal palace with a message requesting the presence of the company of Princess Liavara this week.'

Ronnie's heart froze.

'You will entertain us as it is my will. Failure to do so will result in a trip to the Punishment Tower. Not to mention, displease me.'

Oh! How could my plan backfire so badly?

'Think of this as your own personal mission,' he added, and turned to go.

Quick! Think of something to keep him here!

'Oh yes, my mission, how could I forget?' she said sarcastically. 'I'm to single-handedly fight a war against the wicked witch Pandora and her *minions*,' she said, making her hands into claw shapes, 'in order to save the world from destruction and chaos just in time to pop back home for tea!'

Despite her insolence a flicker of a smile appeared for an instant upon his face. But Ronnie didn't see it; she was too busy thinking of how best to get a reaction out of him next.

'Obviously something is still amiss. I think tripling your SEX Temple duties should deal with that, don't you?'

This time Ronnie was indeed too shocked to answer. And then she thought about the benefits of what he'd just said.

God he's good at this! Once again her hands were tied, and she lowered her head to look at the floor, so he couldn't see her smile.

Princess Liavara, bring it on!

Chapter Twenty-One

Theo lay stretched out on his back with Artemis by his side. She snuggled up beside him, placing her head in the crook of his neck, twirling his chest hairs with her finger in a slow, delicate movement. He shuddered.

'Theo?'

'Hmm?'

'I've been thinking. Something's bothering me. So, you know me, I'll come right out and say it. This is not right.' She pressed her naked body against his, and squashed her breasts into his side. Her finger trailed down the centre of his chest towards his pubic hairs and his twitching cock. 'You of all people should know we shouldn't be doing this.'

'I'm sure the gods will overlook us,' he said, dragging the tips of his fingers down her spine, making her gasp. 'I'm one of the Learned. They can't punish me more than they already have. They need me.'

Artemis arched her back as his finger both scratched and tickled her spine. 'Maybe they don't need to, if you fail this mission there'll be punishment enough. They could be testing you. Having fun, with you as their entertainment.'

'They wouldn't do that to me,' he said, with an edge of annoyance in his voice. 'Besides, I won't fail,' he added, more interested in what her hands were doing than the conversation.

Artemis sighed and stopped her finger just above where his growing cock lay. He reached over with his free hand and pinched her nipple. A silent signal for her to carry on teasing him the way he liked it. She yelped and removed her hand. 'We're with each other alone and far too often, which goes against the rota, and...' he turned his head to look down at her. Her eyes met his.

'Why bring this up now? It's not been an issue with you before?'

'Ronnie?'

He sucked in a breath and blew it out sharply. 'She'll cope without me for a few more minutes.'

'But that's just it. You're with me all the time. It's upsetting the balance of the rota, yes, but more importantly she is your Child of Destiny. It's her you should be with more often. Not me,' she stressed. 'When's the last time you trained her, Theo?'

'You know that's your job. I can't do everything. I have far more important things to do. Do you know one of the Birds of Doom has flown from Raven Passage?'

'And you *still* believe that's an impending doom message from the gods?' Artemis said, rolling her eyes.

Theo snorted. 'And there are half-lings running loose in our tunnels making the staff feel ill at ease? I'd say that's pretty important, wouldn't you?'

'More important than your Child of Destiny?' she asked, scrunching her nose up and frowning. He rolled her over onto her stomach and held her down by the back of the neck. The palm of his other hand slid over her back, down her spine to the curves of her bottom, where he rubbed and squeezed.

'Are you saying you don't want any more of this?' he asked, pinching a buttock hard.

'No, you're putting words into my mouth,' came her muffled reply, then under the grip of her neck she forced her head around so she could speak more clearly, although Theo still had her pinned down and his hand was now making its way towards her sex. She shut her eyes and gritted her teeth, determined to not let him put her off from what he needed to be told. Not easy.

'It's just, you should be doing more. When you're with me her level of protection from you is lowered considerably,' she blurted out, cringing at how he would react. He pushed three fingers between her moist pussy lips and forced them deep inside. Her mouth fell open, a moan she tried to keep from escaping burst out. If he carried on this way she'd never get her point across in time. And time is what they had very little of. She'd heard him say that often enough. How could he deny he was going against everything he was teaching his guards?

'If there is one thing in all my training I will never forget is the line written in the Book of the Orders, authored by Prometheus in the days when he not only believed in what he did, he believed in himself: *To have a successful destiny you must nurture your child; Courage, Humility, Integrity, Long term vision, and Dedication to their mission*. I'm sorry, but how in Tartarus do you expect Ronnie to be dedicated to her mission if you avoid what is in fact the very mission itself – her?'

'You do not question the motives of your Learned.'

'That may be,' she said cautiously, as his fingers now pumped inside her. She gulped. 'But as much as I love being with you, I'm no Child of Destiny.

Unlike Ronnie I only play at pleasing you like a Slut Child.' His fingers stopped moving and she felt the grip on her neck loosen. As much as she hated him to stop she wriggled out from underneath his clutches, scrambled up to the top of the bed, and sat up next to him.

Mortified, he sat up too.

Before he had the chance to reprimand her she carried on. The softly, softly approach was just not getting through to him, and he made it so hard for her to concentrate.

'No, you're forgetting something here, Theo. And I don't just mean your duties as Ronnie's Guardian.' He looked at her incredulously. 'Don't look at me like that. You know very well, when we're on a mission I am perfectly entitled to tell you what I think, if I'm not happy with the situation. Right now is one of those times. Remember, out in the field on a job I am equal to you, whatever your position at the training ground. So listen up, dude.' Speaking slowly as if to a child she bravely said, 'I. Think. *You*. Are. Jeopardising. This. Mission!'

Aghast, he frowned at her. Speechless.

She jumped off the mattress, grabbed her clothes and got dressed.

'How very dare you!'

'Oh, I dare all right, dude! Since you've been away these past twenty-two years and three months I've changed a lot, grown up! I take my work very seriously indeed. Which is more than I can say for you,' she shouted, thrusting her feet into her boots. 'Someone needs to tell you. You're neglecting your duties. I know you've been hurt, but don't you think we're all in the same boat? Especially with this rota nonsense you've put in place to prevent any of us getting too attached to one person. It doesn't work. It's crap. It just frustrates us all and we're bored with the same old people to fuck! But no one else dare say anything in case they piss *you* off.' She took a deep breath and then mimicked his voice with a disapproving shake of the head. 'Because this is the way it's always been!'

'If you don't like the way I run things maybe you should put in for a transfer. I can help you with that,' he sniped. 'Perhaps the Fire or Water kingdom will have you.'

She stood with her hands on her hips and glared at him. 'If you transfer me to Hydrodom or Pyredom, then I'll be forced to take this higher,' she said, raising a finger to her chin, and her eyes to the ceiling as if contemplating her next move. 'The High Council, maybe? The Floating Kingdom of Nuvola is pretty high. I'll tell them you're getting lazy.'

'You wouldn't dare!'

'Try me!' she snapped, marching to the door, slamming it behind her.

'Buck up your ideas, dude!' he heard her shout from beyond the closed portal. 'Things are surely not right when your own Child of Destiny comes to me about your lack of power over her!'

Theo turned his eyes back to his naked body and glanced at his cock, now chilly and limp. He shot out of bed, intending to chase her, but as he passed his punch bag that hung from the ceiling he took a heavy swing at it, and once he started, he couldn't stop.

Chapter Twenty-Two

Ares had trained Ronnie in attacking a multi-storey building by abseiling in a full body harness using fast roping and hands, so fake wooden swords in place of the real thing seemed absolutely pathetic.

'That's a toy sword,' Ronnie complained, screwing her nose up at what he'd given her to practice with. To try it out she brandished it about in the air aimlessly.

'All in good time, girl,' Ares laughed. 'Do you think we'd issue you with something so sharp when you're practically naked?'

'I'm not nearly naked,' she laughed. 'I've never worn so many clothes than when I'm in The Killing House. In fact I can't wait to get back and take these off; clothes just don't feel right any more,' she said, and tugged at her tanned shorts as though they were too tight. On top she wore a matching long-sleeve shirt, standard issue protective indoor sparring gear.

It made a change from being naked, but lately she'd noticed how quickly she became used to being around others wearing nothing but her magically locked black leather collar, which she loved. Now clothes just felt restrictive.

On top of that, to Ronnie's amazement, in only a few days after shaving her head her mousey hair had already grown back two inches at an incredibly magical speed, and blonde. Although she loved her new spiky style and vibrant colour, these things no longer felt as important as they once had. What was important, and necessary, she now realised, was how the small trauma she'd endured in losing her hair at Theo's wish emphasised her submission and his power and ownership over her, an incredible feeling of both exhilaration and comfort.

Being shared like a fuck doll during her SEX Temple training also helped release her inhibitions. There wasn't a part of her body they hadn't explored.

'How am I going to protect myself with this thing?' Ronnie laughed, holding up the wooden sword.

'This is a basic sparring weapon used for training purposes only. Remember, Hope already knows how to use weapons, so with a bit of a refresher with each one you'll get the hang of it very quickly indeed. Did Theo tell you that?'

She thought about lying, but being around immortals with their special magical gifts, they always saw straight through her. 'No, he didn't. To be honest, I still don't know that much about him, but since it's not my place to ask such questions I guess I'll have to accept I will never know some things about him.'

She lunged forward and tried to take him by surprise, feeling silly with a stick of wood. With one swift movement he blocked her immediately. She went for his midriff and he belted her sword away before she had the chance to finish her move.

'What would you like to know?' Ares asked, placing one hand on his hip and slowly stretching out his sword-holding arm.

Ronnie matched his movements.

'Maybe I can help, babe?' He winked. 'We can quite easily spar without paying attention too much, because your inner goddess can already fight, you just have to build the confidence to allow it to happen. So, girl, watcha wanna know?'

He stayed pointing the tip of the sword at her chest. She held her own at his chest, wary and waiting for his next move. Their eyes never left each others.

'About Hamira, the first host for the goddess. I get the feeling he really loved her. What was she like?' she asked tentatively, unsure as to whether she should be talking about such things.

She decided to take the initiative and lunged forward towards the warrior's shoulder. His defensive move was fast and just seemed to flick her away as if she was nothing but a feeble fly.

'Yes, she was a lovely woman; so kind, caring and gentle. Perhaps too much. It was a very sad time for us here when Pandora struck her down, but it's not quite seen the same up there,' Ares said, pointing towards the skies.

'Up there?' she asked, looking up. 'The gods? Nuvola?'

He nodded. 'So you've heard of where the High Council live? The Cloud Kingdom, or as we call it the Floating Kingdom of Nuvola. Your Learned was not always as experienced as he is now, which I'm sure you can understand. We all have to start somewhere, yeah?'

Ronnie nodded, eager to hear more about the man who had become such an important part of her life, but of whom she had absolutely no knowledge. He knew all about her, but she knew nothing of him. How unfair was that?

Seeing his chance when Ronnie had taken her eyes off him for just a second, Ares made his move, but when she blocked him and knocked his sword out of his hand they both gasped.

Wow!

There could be no disguising the fact that Hope's fighting training had returned, within Ronnie. A liberating experience!

'Well, after Hamira died he almost destroyed himself in pity. She was his first host for Hope. He loved her so much.'

Although she knew this a twinge of jealously shot through Ronnie's heart, but she kept quiet and watched Ares walk over to his sword and pick it up. They both stepped back into position, one hand on hip, the other stretched out straight with the tips of their swords almost touching. Ronnie got the feeling he was no longer going to take it easy on her, and that made her smile. She was dying for a fight. For some fun. She felt invincible!

'Of course none of us blamed Theo, yet he knew he couldn't take back his mistake, so the Council brought in a new state of thinking; the Cleaving Festival. The word festival is of course misleading,' he added, poking Ronnie's arm playfully.

She narrowed her eyes, anticipating his next move.

'Festivals are supposed to be celebrations full of cheer, as I'm sure you are quite aware. During the Cleaving Festival we are persuaded, or depending on which way you look at it, ordered to have fun. They encourage this by giving us a day off.'

Ares moved closer, his voice now nothing but a whisper, as if he was wary of someone overhearing.

'But it doesn't hide the fact that while we are all enjoying our day off, which we do, despite the seriousness of it all, the person this is in honour of is going through the embarrassment of proclaiming they have failed and we all know it.'

They pushed together and their swords ended high in the air, where they stayed for a few seconds. They crisscrossed a few times, always managing to stave the blade from stabbing their bodies.

'Only in not so many words.'

Then with a burst of energy they both pushed back and walked around, eyeing each other up.

'Exactly!' Ares said.

'But if it were not their fault, as in Theo's case, how can he consider himself to be a failure? That's not fair,' she spat angrily.

'Aside from the fact that he loved her, and felt he had personally failed her?'

Ronnie nodded in agreement, even though the thought of him loving someone else, when he seemed so cold towards her, hurt. 'That I can understand, but the Council? The stigma attached?'

They burst forward, wooden swords banging and thudding in thrusts and counter moves. Just as quickly both retreated unscathed and breathing hard.

'When a guard becomes a bonded it is a big issue. And you'll need to know this too. When I say a big issue I'm talking of another huge celebration. The all important Bonding Ceremony, which all us solitaires aim for.'

'Solitaires?'

She nearly lost her concentration…

'Single Guards, without their Child of Destiny. When you make it to the Destaurian Guard you are guaranteed a child of your own, it's when that's the problem. Being immortal getting to the Bonded stage can take a very long time. Once you, as a guard, are bonded, other Destaurians look upon you differently.'

Ronnie pondered that thought.

'But come unbound? That's pretty serious.'

'Unbound?'

Ronnie feinted to Ares' left then spun to the right, lunging past his defences, poking him in the side, causing a grunt and her to smile with newfound confidence. A look of combined surprise and pride flickered over Ares' face as he saw this Child of Destiny growing before his eyes.

'If a Child dies before their time the guard responsible is considered by the gods and the High Council to have not done their job very well. It's shameful when one has been honoured with the job of being a designated guard and protector of a Child of Destiny who dies. They have failed. Big time, babe! Of course, other Destaurian guards know the importance and dedication put into our roles when we become officially Bonded, and we appreciate they get a full week off to recover and we only get a day, but we've been trained to succeed.

'If I'm honest I'm sympathetic with Theo's situation, but like the rest of us I can't help thinking what I've had drummed into me for all these years; when you become a solitaire again, after being bonded, it's the lowest of the low. Yes, a week's holiday for them does help them mourn and heal, but it's never enough. You see, they never really get over it. Especially when we all know the Council are basically hiding the problem from the gods until it blows over.'

They both parried sword thrusts.

'But can't the gods see and hear everything,

Ares?'

He shook his head. 'Oh, they're far too busy for that. We're taught to believe that gods are the ever-knowing eye, but to be honest I think we're much too amusing for them to stop us in our tracks. It would ruin their entertainment.'

Ronnie lunged forward, only to be blocked by Ares.

'Yet we are all led to believe the Cleaving Festival sounds like fun?'

'Yeah, when in reality the Cleaving Festival is an excuse to hide the numerous sins of the failed guard. By removing an unbonded from the scene they are basically keeping the embarrassment out of the public eye. And the Bonding Ceremony, believe me, is very public.'

Ares scored a hit on Ronnie's wrist which dislodged her sword.

'The Cleaving Festival is supposed to be the complete opposite, but it's not. No one guard wants to be a bonded and then have that privilege taken away only to be made a solitaire once more. It's not good. In fact, you could say it's the total pits. And your Learned has had to deal with that. Now can you see how important you are to Theo?'

She could. And although she felt an enormous amount of responsibility to do what was right by her Learned she also realised that Theo was not being as true to himself as she imagined him to be. Her next question scared the hell out of her, but she had to ask.

'Do you think he put that "no love" rule in place I read about in one of my training books because of all this? Of being hurt before?'

Disarmed, Ronnie instinctively kicked at Ares'

groin only to have him brush her aside and smack her bum with the flat of the sword.

'Hey girl, yes! It's still very much part of our culture today. Maybe you're not as stupid as you make yourself out to be!'

Under normal circumstances Ronnie knew she would have kicked his butt to kingdom-come for a comment like that, but these were no ordinary circumstances, especially as they were sparing. He was trying to get her angry as part of the training.

If Ares hadn't been so talkative she would never have gleaned so much about Theo. Instead of being angry, she thought herself very lucky to have such helpful friends around. A strange feeling where Ares the warmonger was concerned, but nevertheless a good one.

Ares pointed his sword tip at Ronnie's throat and backed her into a corner, where he suddenly dropped his weapon and kissed her deeply. Her nipples hardened beneath her shirt. His hand slid down the front of her shorts, stroking her dampening pussy.

Everyone's plaything!

'I hate that rota,' Ares added. 'The "no two people should be with each other more than any others" is a total waste of time. Utopia, my arse! As much as it pains me to say this,' he said, not looking in the least bit pained, 'if you ever get the chance to change this ruling, being his bonded and all that, please know you have my blessing.

'In fact, we all feel the same. I can understand it being your job to be on the rota, because basically, when you're not out in the field saving all our lives,' he said sardonically, 'your job primarily is to be used by all of us. But for Destaurians? The same old people can get a bit boring. Repetition does that, you know. But there is something unsettling about the whole thing. Destaurian guards are supposed to be highly regarded people, so why do most of us, save Eros who can't keep his cock in if he tried, feel like we have no choice in this rota? Because I'm telling you, babe, we don't. And believe me when I say this, unlike you, we do not like feeling like slaves ourselves. So, people like you make us feel so much better. Now get down on your knees and make *me* feel better. Suck my cock.'

Ronnie did, feeling eternally grateful for what she had learned about Theo. Clearly she was becoming more of a Child of Destiny than the person she once was. Did that worry her? No. If she wasn't allowed all her memory back it was for a good reason, and she'd accept that without argument. For once.

She fell to her knees and took his huge hard cock in her mouth. The way he rammed it in with no regard for her turned her on immensely. He was using her, and that was what she was for, and she'd been told she was good at it too. She knew some people would be shocked by this, but as she took his spunk down her throat, and her pussy yearned to come but was not allowed, she knew better.

'You know, we used to worry about cutting diseased monsters with our swords,' Ares said, tucking his cock away after she'd licked it clean for him as she'd been taught.

'Why?' she asked, licking the remnants of his spunk off her lips.

'Because it would make the pure sword unclean. Nowadays be can't be so fussy, but it does warp the blade's soul.'

He raised the sword towards her and this time she immediately blocked him without getting off her knees. They both looked at each other, impressed.

'Fast Learner! Have you ever thought of a life with immortal archangels, witches *and* their minions?' he laughed. 'You could really get some weapons' practice in then! Oh, shit, I'm supposed to be on the rota five minutes ago. I've gotta rush, Ronnie, see you later. And keep practising!' he shouted, disappearing into the tunnel.

Behind her someone started to clap. 'You used to use your guns against people like him, Ronnie.'

Upon hearing her name she turned to see a stranger clad in layers upon layers of clothes, dusted with snow, and one look at the balaclava covering his face was enough for her fight or flight instinct to kick in.

She snatched a knife from a nearby counter and pointed it threateningly. 'Who the fuck are you?'

Chapter Twenty-Three

The strange man frowned, yet continued to walk towards her, his arms open wide. 'It's me, Ron. God, they've butchered your hair! Never mind, it'll grow back,' he sighed. 'But, boy oh boy, am I pleased to see you!' the man said, with smiling eyes. 'Come, give me a hug. It's taken me days to get here. Almost didn't think I'd find you.'

'I asked you a question! Who the fuck are you and what are you doing here?'

'Hey, Ron, calm down, it's okay,' he said,

holding both palms in the air. 'Everything's going to be all right now.' He stepped closer, then hesitated.

Ronnie backed away.

'You really don't remember me, do you?' he asked in a genuinely surprised tone. 'Back at the institute they said this would happen, but I didn't believe it.' He shook his head. 'Well, you're gonna be all right now, darling. I've come to take you home.' He pulled off his balaclava. 'It's me. Tim?'

Tim? The name did sound kind of familiar, but she couldn't recall his face anywhere. A pain pounded against her head. Should she know him? She had no idea. To so easily believe he was a friend was questionable after what she had experienced over the last few days. As she found out so painfully in The Killing House, to lower her guard might be a fatal mistake.

Could she trust him? Should she?

If this was a friend honestly coming to save her what did that make Theo? The Guardian Angel she thought he was, or something darker, more demonic, who had twisted her mind into believing this false truth? That she'd not really thought of this before shocked her. Had a magical veil lifted from her eyes? But as Ares said, evil exists so goodness can be known, but which is which?

Determined not to back down she held the knife higher, and he reached into the inside of his jacket pocket.

'Keep your hands were I can see them!' she shouted, and his hands sprung into the air, palms facing her

'It's okay, darling, I'm not going to hurt you,' he said defensively.

'What do you mean; I used to use the guns on things like him? *Angels?*' When she said it suddenly it all sounded so wrong.

'Okay, so you don't remember me. Back at the institute they warned me this might happen, so I brought a photograph of us, to prove who I am. Let me get it out, okay? No tricks, honest. I'm here to convince you to come back with me. Not to hurt you. The last thing I want to do is harm you. Okay? God knows, you must have been through enough of that already.' Without waiting for an answer he slipped his hand in a pocket and withdrew a scrap of paper, a photograph. He stretched out his arm. 'Here. Go on, it's yours. It's from the frame that stands on the telly. Take it,' he insisted urgently.

How well did I know this man?

With a shaky hand she slowly reached out, alert for any signs of a trap. Ares had done a great job teaching her how to fight, but she now knew he'd done much more. He'd taught her how to stay calm, think quickly and keep fully alert, as all the time she was reading the man's face and body language. Just a flicker of his eye in the wrong direction would reveal him as a liar and a threat. Ares had told her the Pandora witches were skilled and cunning creatures capable of many dangerous things. If they couldn't get to her themselves, what would stop them getting to her through a friend? Assuming he was her friend. For all she knew he could be one of the Black Queen's minions.

When the photo was within reach and her knife still pointing towards him, she snatched it out of his hand and brought it up to eye level. Flitting her eyes between him, the blade she held in her shaky hand, and the photo, she gasped. The couple were in a bar sitting at a wooden table on which a menu, with *Pub Food* written across the top, sat wedged between a salt and pepper pot. Through the window behind them a row of street lamps shone through the darkness. He wore a silly little hat, she a tiara, and there were bags of shopping spread across the table. A birthday celebration? Both of them posed with their pints of beer held up high towards the camera. Toothy smiles and tipsy eyes. They were snuggled up close, his arm around her shoulder. The couple in the picture looked happy. Although the world in the photograph looked somehow alien to the life she now led, there was no doubt she held a picture of herself and the stranger claiming to be a friend. Yet this memory, the pub, the man were not in her consciousness. Believe the photographic evidence or rely on survival instinct and newly awakened combat skills? Ares would tell her to fight first and question later.

Ronnie half expected her headache to return; a warning that she was getting close to answers she shouldn't know, as that's how it always seemed to go. But it didn't come, and that worried her.

She was about to hand it back and tell him to go and get stuffed, when she saw it; a sign he was telling the truth. Pinned to her white T-shirt, almost covered by her hand, was a tiny splash of red. Her London Bus broach. The same one she saw on the floor of her car when she crashed because someone or something was chasing her. She tilted her head and gave him a long hard look, willing herself to remember him. And when she did she wished she hadn't; for his face was identical to the one she saw in the rear-view mirror. He was the man pursuing her!

Outside a herd of Cahnnox cried a long, drawn out warning of impending danger as they picked up on Ronnie's fear.

Chapter Twenty-Four

'Get away from me!' Ronnie screamed. 'You were the man I was speeding away from when I crashed my car!'

'No I wasn't chasing you, well, not like that! I was trying to stop you doing something you might later regret. You've gotta believe me.'

Her body prickled and still holding her sabre she turned and saw Theo standing there, his massive dark wings unfurled majestically, and then they tucked in. Ronnie blinked, mesmerised.

'He's the one that kidnapped you, Ron, not me!' Tim shouted, snapping her to her senses.

'It's not his fault, he had to do it,' she argued. 'I guess I'm not the person you thought I was. I'm sorry you wasted your time but I'm not coming back. I've got something to do here.'

'Don't give me that, Ronnie Weaver. I know exactly who you are. It's the reason I am here, to put an end to this nonsense and take you back. You don't have to do this,' he insisted.

'You're wrong, it's my bloodline—'

'And what of those pages we found from some old book with your mother's handwriting on? Remember those?'

'Girl, this has gone far enough,' Theo said, calm but firm.

'My mother? Have you got those pages now?'

He shook his head. 'No, but I have them safe. I didn't want to bring them here. Come with me, I'll take you home and show you.'

'I can't, they need me here.'

'What? You'd rather go back to him? The man who took away your life and all your memories? Memories of us!'

'I know all about the memory wipe. It had to be done. I've accepted that.'

'He's cast a spell on you, Ronnie. Don't listen to a word he says, it's all lies. I mean, he's got wings for fucks sake! That ain't normal! I've worried myself sick about you. Doesn't the fact that I'm your boyfriend mean anything?'

She gasped.

'Oh, so he hasn't told you? How convenient.'

Still pointing the sabre at the man Ronnie turned to Theo. 'Please tell me what he says isn't true.'

'I had no choice. I had to think quickly.'

'Why? I thought I was alone and no one was missing me.'

'At the scene of the car crash you were traumatised. I may have been overzealous with the memories I took from you, but I—'

'But you had no right!'

'I did what I thought right, but that doesn't matter now. What's important right now is that you let this go. I know you find this new life hard to believe, but trust me. Put the sabre down, walk away and wait for me in your cell. I will deal with this. We'll discuss it later.'

'It matters to me!' She swung the blade round in Theo's direction, and then changed her mind. Not sure who to point it at, she settled on Tim.

'Yes, Ronnie, put the knife down,' he said.

'Don't listen to him. Come back with me to where you belong—'

'No!' Theo cut in. 'I forbid it! If you go back to the Mortal Realm with him your life will be in grave danger.'

'How do you know?' she asked, desperate and confused.

'Girl, I know more about you than you know yourself. It is why I've been assigned to protect you. It's my job as part of the Destaurian guard. Trust me on this.' He stretched out his wings again, as if beefing himself up for a fight, and for a moment all went quiet as they stood and blinked at the awesome sight before them.

'You're one of them?' Tim laughed. 'How ironic. He's one of the very people we were hunting, and now you're thinking of giving up everything we've worked for to stay with him?'

'What do you mean, hunting—?'

'No! You cannot tell her this right now. She is at a delicate stage in her memory recall. Tread carefully. She's already taken a lot onboard, if you rush too much information to her brain it will be too much to process all at once. System overload. If you care anything for her you'll at least listen to that. Do not harm her, or I will never forgive you.'

'Ronnie, darling, you don't know how happy I am that I've finally found you. It's taken me days to trek here. Don't do this to me. I love you, Ronnie. I always will.'

'Stop it! You'll kill her! You're messing with things you don't understand!'

She looked at Tim and then back to Theo.

'Oh, I understand all right,' Tim said. 'You've wrecked both our lives and now you want to take her away from me and use her for your own sexually deviant purposes.'

'He's the threat here, girl, not me,' Theo insisted.

'Like Hell I am. I know your kind,' sneered Tim. 'And if Ronnie could remember too she wouldn't even be contemplating leaving me for someone as evil as you.'

'Girl, come to me,' Theo ordered.

'I'm the one who loves you, Ronnie. Give me a chance. We can work this out.'

'No! Girl! HPS, now!'

Ronnie hesitated.

'He doesn't care for you like I do,' Tim went on. 'He's using you. Soon he'll have another girl to fuck how and when he wants. That's what he does. That's as deep as it gets with him.'

'No, girl, you're mine now. Stop this nonsense and get over here, or you'll be in big trouble. Enough is enough.'

'I know his type, even if you don't, Ronnie. Come back with me, I'll show you around the institute of—'

'Stop it!' Ronnie screamed. 'Just stop it, both of you!' She raised a hand to her head, a dull ache spreading. Was Theo right? Was this growing headache something to do with the beginning of her demise?

'Girl, I know how bad this looks but you cannot trust him. I am your Learned. Remember your destiny. Get here *now*.'

'Ha! I've heard all about the high and mighty Learned. Well, she doesn't seem to be falling at your feet now, does she?'

But why doesn't Theo do anything to make this nightmare go away?

Trust me, he'd rather die before letting anything happen to you, the voice of Hope said inside her head. *But until you are bonded this important decision has to be yours.*

'Ronnie, for fuck's sake,' Tim urged. 'Your so-called Learned is a *killer*.'

She spun round to look at her Theo, eyes wide and uncertain. Before her was a man who made her go weak at the knees just looking into his eyes. Eyes full of a magical power, shrouded in mystery. And danger. Behind her was a man claiming to be the love of her life on a rescue mission to save her from the clutches of evil, and full of bullshit. But what if he wasn't?

Was she about to get her boyfriend killed?

And what of Theo? How much did she *really* know about him?

All this passed through her mind in a couple of seconds, but it was enough time for Tim to make his move. From behind he grabbed her wrist, forcing her to lose her grip on the knife. It fell to the floor with a startling clatter. Fear coursed through her veins, swiftly followed by a surge of adrenaline. She kicked the blade across the floor, out of reach of both of them, then with her free arm she swung and landed a blow to Tim's throat. He loosened his grip on her wrist and cried out. Shock more than pain, she figured, and with him no longer a threat she turned to walk away. But from behind he grabbed her around the waist and pulled her against him. His clothes felt rough against her bare skin and something sharp dug into her neck.

'Tomorrow, 13 Rivet Avenue, noon,' he whispered quickly. 'Thirteen. Your lucky number,' he laughed. 'Let's talk. Alone. At least give me a chance to explain and show you your mother's notes.'

She pushed against him and he let her go without resisting. She glared back at him with a look of disapproval and then went to where Theo stood.

'Eyes,' Theo commanded, and she stood legs apart, hands behind her back, staring up into his face. No longer did she have to worry what was going on behind her, so she focused her attention on her Learned, feeling safe under his penetrating gaze. Not moving a muscle, frozen like an ice sculpture and with no other thoughts but for her Learned, she waited for further instructions. She'd made her decision, and now she was going to stick by it.

'Go to your room and wait for me there.'

Chapter Twenty-Five

The portcullis rose fast. Startled, Ronnie looked up and stepped into present mode. She hadn't even time to finish getting her sparring uniform off, and still had her knickers on.

Theo strode in with his large wings unfurled angrily, sheer determination written all over his face, not acknowledging her presence. He moved the screen to gain access to his throne, upon which he slumped down, knees apart, hands gripping the carved skull hand-rests. His wings lowered but stayed out. It was the first time Ronnie had seen him seated on his throne, and he looked every bit the king. She searched his face for answers. His eyes fixed on hers with a harsh stare.

'Come,' he commanded in a tone which worried her.

Is he mad at me? she asked herself as she slowly pushed the barred door open, making it squeak. She stepped through.

'Stop dawdling. Get over here now. HPS. Do not make me angrier than I already am, girl.'

So he is angry.

She quickened her pace.

Not once did they remove their eyes from each other, and when she was within his reach he grabbed her round the waist and threw her over his lap. Her heart raced, but knowing he was angry she didn't complain. Nor did she struggle or cry out for him to stop. The book of *Protocol and Etiquette* said punishments were easier to bear if they were not fought against. Time to test out that theory.

Her belly pressed against his leather-clad thighs and her firm breasts hung, pointing to the floor where her fingertips splayed out in an effort to support herself.

Fingers grasped her panties, yanked them down to her knees and left them there. Cool air wafted around her exposed bottom, now thrust high and vulnerable. Her face reddened at the thought of him inspecting her. So closely. With one hand between her shoulder-blades he held her down. A broad palm rested across both cheeks. His touch made her jump.

'Hold still,' he admonished, taking his warm hand away and raising it high above his head. She gritted her teeth and waited for the first spank.

'We have dealt with hundred of girls and we are all aware of the mental strain such a change of life can have upon each and every one of you.' His hand swept down and smacked her bottom much harder than she'd expected. Harder than Artemis had. Not being able to hide her surprise, or the fact that it hurt, she cried out. A stinging sensation spread across her buttocks. That was no playful slap. He meant business. She was sure of it. So squeezing her eyes tight shut she focused on accepting the pain, and what it meant. He'd tell her what she'd done soon enough. If she could only show him this time that she could cope and not make a fuss, he'd have to believe how much she trusted him now.

'You may speak,' he said, bringing the palm of his hand back down on her stinging cheeks. 'And don't try to hold in your pain. I want to hear it. Scream as much as you like. Down in the basement here no one else can hear you.'

A trick? How unfair. If she answered incorrectly he'd slap her harder!

'You deserve a good spanking, whether I like your answers or not. I'm in charge here, not Artemis. Got that?' He spanked her again and a burning pain seared though her bottom, prickling her skin like a thousand tiny needles. So, this was about Artemis? What had the bitch done this time?

He spanked her again, harder. Her eyes shot open with the force of the impact, taking her breath away.

'Yes, my Learned,' she replied, struggling to answer through her heavy breathing.

'Good girl. Now speak freely. What are your concerns about this mission?'

'I'm just a normal girl, my Learned. How on earth can I match up to your expectations?'

He spanked her twice more before he answered.

'You are not as unqualified for this job as you think.' She went to speak but he slapped her again. 'They all have trouble with accepting that.' His hand came sweeping back down. And again. And again. 'But...' she thought she heard him laugh, 'but...' he repeated, 'you seem to have more trouble than most. Do you realise that?'

'No,' she cried out, kicking her legs involuntarily as the next smack took her by surprise. 'No, my Learned,' she added politely. Anything to not rile him on purpose.

'Oh yes, I knew you were trouble. From the day you were born I knew it, which is why you were put under my protection. Procedures were put into place to prepare you. To correct you.'

Spank!

'Just like I am correcting you right now.'

Spank!

'My little PreCent had no idea any of this was going on, did you?'

'No. I didn't. PreCent, my Learned?'

'A human girl chosen for the next Child of Destiny position. I observed you. Followed you. Stalked you.'

Stalked? She wanted to kick and scream for the twisted bastard to get off her – but she didn't. She wanted to find out where this was leading. Did that mean she was twisted, too? Only one way to find out. He smacked her again and she wriggled, as if trying to escape.

'I fed you subliminal messages via various forms of media; books, newspapers, the television, and even while you slept. But do you know what?'

'What, my Learned?'

'I don't even know if any of that worked on you.

But this sure will, girl.' His hand swung down and spanked her in rapid succession, like he was beating out a tune in time to some music in his head.

Smack! Smack! Smack! Smack! She wriggled around on his legs and kicked out, more vigorously this time. Anything to try and avoid his sadistic palm, but through her pain she realised she was rubbing herself against something hard in his trousers.

Smack! Smack! Smack! Smack!

'Who is your learned, girl?'

'You!' she wailed, part excruciating pain, part pure ecstasy. 'You! My Learned! You!' No longer worried how far her screams travelled. Prickly tears welled up in her eyes, blurring her vision.

'Who do you serve?'

'My Learned!' she squealed. Tears dripped onto her arms, her hands, the floor.

He turned up the inner music in his head a notch. The beatings doubled in time to her screams. *Smack-smack! Smack-smack! Smack-Smack! Smack-Smack!*

'Who do you worship, girl?'

'You, my Learned! You!' She gurgled and sniffed, with a vague sense that she must look a right mess. She didn't want him to see her like this, but this was clearly what he wanted. Her fiery pain, her sizzling pleasure, her submitting to his will. Her unadulterated subservience, and by the hardness of his cock beneath her tummy she was finally pleasing him.

'Who do you obey without question?' he asked, on a rhythmic roll. She focused on her own erratic breathing to drive out the throbbing discomfort of his bludgeoning spanks. Blowing in and out she met the tuneful beats of his palm; a screaming, raucous duet of soulful pain and musical pleasure.

'You. My. Learned!' she sobbed in time to his beats. Him the conductor. The driving force. Her the instrument upon which he was beating out a tune.

'Who do you respect?' Layers of pain overlapped, blended, and soon she found the fire which burned within her no longer hurt as much. Well, it did, yet at the same time, it didn't. Impossible. Incomprehensible. All concentration dissipated, melting like ice on a sunny winter's day. Her mind, a white cloud formation, lulled her into its luxurious softness which enveloped and floated away with her into the distance. Her sobs no longer sounded like her own.

Yet still he never let up and played his instrument hard.

'And what of the goddess, Hope?'

'I will…' she moaned, her cloud gathering speed, 'defend her… as if my life… depended on it…' Tears fell from her face like light rain from a cloud.

'What are you?'

'I'm your… Child of Destiny…' Without remorse he spanked her again, several times in quick succession. She wracked her brains to think of more. 'I'll live and die by the SWORD, my Learned.' Her sobs abated. 'It's what I want…' she said, fading fast, her will to stay in control of her answers almost out of reach.

'I need you, my Learned… I want… to be yours… please… I am yours to do with… as you want…' Her voice, like her mind, ebbed away and drifted. Floating higher – further into the skies of pure heavenly paradise, from where only her Learned had the power to return her.

Out of the seraphic white skies in which Ronnie soared, she became vaguely aware that the spanking had come to a halt. His hand rubbed gently against her tenderised skin, soothing and coaxing her back down. Then he placed some fingers inside her, they slipped right in with a wet, squelchy sound. It took a moment for her to realise the slurping noises she could hear was her own pussy as his fingers thrust in and out. Like a ragdoll he moved her off his lap and into a standing position. She watched him fiddle with his trousers and release his restricted cock. It sprang to attention. He smiled. With both hands he reached up to her breasts and pulled her down to him, by her hard, pert nipples. He didn't stop until she straddled his legs, and then sank down onto his sturdy, pulsing shaft.

In an instant her dreamy world made way for a sexual thirst she had to quench. Mindlust.

Theo pinched her nipples spitefully. She arched her back and squirmed on his rigid cock, pushing deeper, wanting as much as she could of him inside. He pulled her by the nipples close to his face, then cupping his hands underneath her breasts he lifted them, roughly squeezing and kneading. A hand reached down to her sore bottom and pinched her. As she yelped her body jerked forward, pushing a nipple against his lips. His wet tongue flickered around her areole, which contracted. He opened his mouth around her hardened bud. He teased it with his tongue, and then clasped it between his teeth. A grown of pleasure escaped her lips as he bit, nibbling, hurting, sucking. He continued for a while and then both hands moved to her trim waist and pulled her backwards and forwards on his cock.

She arched her back, pushing her breasts into his face, urging him to bite her. He did and she groaned, relishing the pain which urged her on, drove her to the edge.

Then Hermes walked into the basement. 'Sorry to interrupt, but we have a situation going on,' she said coldly.

'What is it now?' Theo snapped angrily. 'I'm busy and expecting a Royal visit later.'

'Then I'll cancel that for you. It's Artemis. Apparently she went to the Otherworld, and she hasn't been seen since.'

Chapter Twenty-Six

Samilious grouped the DGU together to brief them on the current hostage situation. They huddled in the living room of a small terraced house which had been evacuated due to the threat of a non-existent gas leak.

'Across the road is a small base of Paraphanites. Our sources have confirmed there's a whole family involved; husband and wife, Adam and Philippa Marshall, and their two children, fourteen year old Callum and Clara, six.'

'Six? But she's practically a baby,' Ronnie said, shocked.

'Don't let their looks deceive you, miss,' Samilious said sternly. 'All have murdered while doing the Pandoras bidding, and despite having been previously arrested they all miraculously escaped custody. Normal civilians do not do that. In addition, we have reason to believe they're holding Art hostage in the upstairs green-black room,' he said. Code for left front room in case anyone was listening that shouldn't be.

Floor plans of the stronghold lay open on a table. 'Okay everyone, places please. The longer we delay this the more time they have to infect her. I want Hestia on communications. Theo's acting as scout, do not lose contact with him and report any new Paraphanite activity.'

'Right, sir.'

'Selene, Eros, Ares and Eos, you'll be in my squad breaching the building. Wear your masks; we'll be using CS gas and possibly flash grenades to render our targets powerless.'

'What about Art, she doesn't have a mask?' Ronnie asked, worried.

'No effect, she's immortal,' he grinned. 'Right, let's move!'

'What about me?' Ronnie asked again. 'I'm new but—'

'Take this,' Samilious instructed, passing her a .338 sniper rifle, one of the many weapons she'd practised with in The Killing House.

'Stay at this observation post with a clear line of fire,' he said, pointing to the window. 'If any of the four come out, shoot to kill.' Then as he and the rest of the team left he shouted back over his shoulder, 'You can do this, Ronnie!'

She looked at Hestia, who stopped to wink and then carried on using a machine on which she was tapping a message to the earpieces of Theo and the others in Morse code.

Ronnie picked up the .338, and through an open window with curtains drawn trained her sights on the top left window, waiting patiently, mentally preparing for her first kill.

A male target, the husband Adam, thought to be the leader, came into view. Calmly she squeezed the trigger, and a second later the bullet struck home. A mist of blood appeared from the right side of his chest. He recoiled, his face twisted in horror, and his eyes flashed with a strange red tinge. *Infected!* Never before had she seen anything like it. He was dead before hitting the floor. Feeling quite at home with her job Ronnie smiled, snapped the bolt, ejecting the spent shell and seating the next cartridge in the chamber, and then scanned the perimeter for her next kill.

'They're moving her,' Hestia said. 'Keep your eyes on the door. The good news is they don't know we're here. Usually moving hostages regularly makes it harder to track them down, but this time we're one step ahead.'

'And the bad news?'

'This is going to make things much harder because they'll all be on the move. Even Art. She's of paramount importance to your future. If she dies, or becomes one of them, it will change your destiny. It may mean we cannot protect you at a later date.'

'But I thought she was immortal. She can't die.'

'We all have our weaknesses. Stay vigilant, and watch for the red of their eyes.'

No sooner than she said it there was a tinkling of glass from across the road and the familiar sounds of flash bang grenades. The door opened again and someone in the smoke moved about. Ronnie aimed her sights on the target, and saw Artemis' face and hands covered in blood. The little girl pulled her about with a strength far beyond her age. Then she saw Theo jump into her line of view, but it was impossible to keep a steady aim on several moving heads blurred by smoke.

They're monsters! she reminded herself. *Don't be fooled, Samilious said.*

'Shoot her!' Hestia urged, also watching the scene playing out before them.

Ronnie aimed her sights on the door again and concentrated on the eyes. In the smoky atmosphere it was her only hope. As expected a pair of eyes flashed red into view of the rifle's telescopic sight and she fired. The target went down. Ronnie panicked. What if Art had already been infected and she'd just killed her?

Ronnie was relieved to hear the whole of the DGU were fine. She had indeed hit the little girl Clara, and after playing the recording for training purposes she was pleased to see the little six year old's face turn totally red-eyed and inhuman. When Ronnie's bullet hit her in the head Clara snarled and spat like an injured wild animal. Something the adult, and even her older brother, had trained to cover up. When Ronnie asked why this was Ares told her it was because the real six year old body of Clara was unable to hold in her true form under stress, something that took practise and tiny children couldn't do. Theo had taken down the teenage boy, who put up a surprisingly fierce fight, and Selene and Eos had the job of taking the only surviving member, the mother, Philippa, to lock her up in an isolated section of Black Ice Prison Tower until further questioning could be completed in relative safety.

Art was taken to The Recovery Tower and kept for observation even though she insisted she was fine.

After the debriefing Ronnie looked at the wall clock and asked if she could go home. She was late meeting Tim, but she had to go. He had her mother's notes and she had to see if they were real, what they said. Plus it felt weird; he was her only connection to the Otherworld, as she had come to call it.

But in doing so she knew full well there would be severe consequences for disobeying her Learned, if caught.

But he won't find out, will he?

Not if you go during your free time, while he's at the High Council meeting, and get back before this eve, a voice in her head urged.

'Are you all right, girl?' Theo asked, looking over people rushing around in front of them.

She nodded. 'Yes, thank you, my Learned. Just a bit shocked by all this, but I'll be fine. Don't worry about me.'

Fuck! I'm lying to him now! Is he reading my thoughts? Does he already know what I'm planning?

No. He's got far too much on his mind, what with the Paraphanites' latest tricks and the Council summoning him to explain why Artemis was nearly killed. Besides, he would have stopped you by now, if he had. You can be sure of that.

Then Ronnie realised she had no idea how to get to Tim.

Silly girl, said the voice in a mocking tone, *you have the means of time travel in that very collar of yours!*

I do? But I don't know how to use it, Ronnie replied, exasperated that another good idea of hers had gone to waste.

No, but I do! the voice of Hope replied eagerly.

Back in her cell she stood still, waiting for instructions from Hope.

Hope told her to stand facing a wall, or any solid surface on which she could draw a door big enough to pass through. *Then with your little finger of your left hand press down on your collar's amethyst until it clicks, while with the forefinger of your right hand you draw an imaginary door where all four sides connect, and recite the magic words – anoichtí pórta – open door. Once the door reveals itself to you and opens, release your collar. Easy when you know how,* the voice of Hope sung, excitedly.

'Anoichtí pórta,' Ronnie said, practising without drawing a door; the last thing she wanted was to suddenly time travel and forget the magic words.

'Anoichtí pórta,' she repeated. 'Anoichtí pórta.'

You must remember once you enter to shut the door behind you, with the command stení pórta to stop anyone following you. Unless you need to, of course, but I highly discourage it. You can always draw a new door anywhere, but you can't always find a door that you may need to shut at a later date.

'Okay,' she said, buzzing with the thought of time travelling.

When you exit make sure it is tightly shut in your

mind and use the same stení pórta command to seal the opening. Chances are the last thing you will want is someone following you home. Oh, and Ronnie...

Yes?

Your plug. Take it out and lose it in the tunnel, otherwise they'll be able to track you down before you're finished.

Ronnie bit her lip. She could get into a lot of trouble for all of this.

The moment you travel that time tunnel you're already in a lot of trouble!

Trying not to think about what would happen she undid her shorts and pulled out the plug with a gasp.

'Stení pórta, stení pórta,' she repeated until she was sure she had it, then she pressed her collar and drew a door saying, 'Anoichtí pórta,' and held her breath.

The outline of the door she drew glowed purple and she felt herself being pulled towards it, although her feet were not moving. Scared she was going to hit the wall and hurt herself she shut her eyes, as gale force winds whipped against her body, her head spun and an incredible overwhelming feeling of lightness seemed to pick her up and whisk her away. She let go of the plug and heard it whoosh away into the abyss.

'Stení pórta!' she shouted, closing the door to her new life behind her. Exhilarated yet scared witless, words flew in her mind in the voice of her Learned, but she struggled to hear them as they were snatched away in the swirling vortex of the time tunnel.

Craven?

What on earth does he mean by that? I'm no coward!

Chapter Twenty-Seven

When Ronnie arrived she found herself standing under a lamppost in a fenced passageway facing a rickety gate, upon which a large white number thirteen had been crudely painted. Thirteen. Her lucky number, so Tim had said. Despite this she felt far from lucky in this neighbourhood.

She looked down both ends of the alley, checking out her escape routes, as Ares had drummed into her. Better to be safe rather than sorry. No one, thank god, blocked either end. No one was standing in any of the windows that overlooked their back gardens. In fact, there was no one anywhere. Not even the sound of passing cars hurtling down the back streets. Yet these terraced houses looked like city dwellings. Was that a good sign for her, like the number thirteen? No one was there waiting to capture her, but neither was anyone waiting to save her.

She tapped her back to check her sword was in place, and without looking reached into the satchel Hestia had given her and pulled out the blade, which called to her as she'd been taught. The Death Blade. How relaxing.

She pushed a gate open and walked through a tiny courtyard of grey slabs and piles of junk. The back door of the house was off its hinge and leaning against the wall, covering a window.

Hardly a secure area, Ronnie thought, stepping

over rubble of broken pots, bricks and smashed wood, and taking one last look around.

On top of a brick wall she spotted a large black bird, not unlike one in Raven's Passage. In its sharp claws it gripped a dead mouse and proceeded to shred and eat it in front of her.

Ronnie turned up her nose and entered the house. All the doors downstairs were barricaded, so she made her way up the stairs clenching tightly her Death Blade for comfort.

Had she made a huge error? She hoped she would live to regret it.

A stair she trod on creaked, and immediately Tim stepped into view at the top of them as if he'd been waiting.

'Alone?'

She looked back quickly, alert for noises behind in case he attacked her. Nothing.

'Please, let's just get this over with,' she urged, looking back up to him.

He nodded.

Ronnie followed him into a dark room, sparsely decorated with only a table, two chairs and a filthy mattress for a bed. She did her best not to sneer with disgust, although she was sure this was not where he lived.

He pulled out a chair for her. She sat down, but he looked agitated and kept pacing the room.

'Sit down, you're making me nervous,' she said.

'You're late. I wanted you here at lunchtime, in daylight. What took you so long?'

'I came as soon as I could. There was a situation I had to deal with. Please, may I see my mother's notes?'

He brushed a hand through his dark hair, ruffling

it up, unable to keep still.

'I'm not well, Ronnie. Something's changed, in me, to me, I don't know, but whatever it is I don't like it. You probably don't care since you no longer know who I am, which you should do by now, but I still care for you. Which is why I wanted to meet. Only now I'm not sure it's a good time for you to stay. I don't want to see you hurt.'

'By you?'

'Truth be told I don't know any more. Strange things have been happening I can't explain. You'd better go.' He walked past her towards the stairs, as if to show her the way out.

'Look, I'm in deep trouble coming here so I'm not leaving until I get answers. You're right, I don't remember you, but when all's said and done you are my only link to this world, my previous life. I don't want to lose that. Or you,' she added. 'My Learned lied to me about you. I'm not sure why so maybe being here now I'll get some answers. Please,' she said, tapping the tabletop, 'sit down and talk to me. You're making me nervous pacing up and down like a caged animal.'

He spun his head round and looked into her eyes. 'That's what they do,' he snarled. 'They have total control over their Child of Destiny. They assume they know what's best for you.'

'And keeping the fact I had a boyfriend in the Otherworld was for the best? What could he possibly gain from doing that to me?'

He walked up to her, put his hand out to touch her and then pulled it back as if he thought better of it.

'In all fairness, Ronnie, your Learned probably needed you to stay strong during your training;

worrying about me would have set you back and got in the way. He really did have your best interests at heart. His type know no other way.'

'But in doing so now I know the truth I'm hurting all over again!'

'And he probably hated doing it to you, but he's a Destaurian Guard, the *mission* must come first.'

'But you said he was a danger, a killer.'

'He is, but not to you. He would never harm you, his protected. I made a mistake. He's not the enemy, it's the Black Witch and her minions, the Paraphanites, you've got to be careful of.'

She nodded, understanding the truth in his words.

'Why are you helping me? I'm your girlfriend, yet I've been living a different life with another man.'

He came back towards her and for the first time stood still.

'In my heart you will always be mine, Ronnie. But we went into this with our eyes open. We didn't know for sure if any of this was true until the car crash. Thank god you came back through time and left me a message,' he said, continuing his pacing.

'I didn't leave you a message. This is the first time I've done this time travelling lark.'

'Well I'm not sure how you managed it, but you did. We always said we'd know for sure you were a Child of Destiny once you came back to me through the passage of time and created a door for me to follow you back through. Time must have distorted. How else do you think I got to Destauria yesterday?'

'You knew all this was going on? *We* did?'

He nodded. 'In our search for answers we

stumbled across a lot more than we bargained for.'

'But I shut the door behind me. How could you have followed me back?'

'I knew you were there, Ronnie. I had a premonition it would happen. The date, the time, everything.' He held up a brick. 'You did try to shut the door behind you, but through your inexperience you forgot to check. I used this as a makeshift doorstop. It's how I kept it open to follow you back.' He grinned, and something in his expression felt so familiar.

'But you turned up before I'd even attempted time travel.' She laughed. 'I can't even believe I'm saying that!'

'Something went wrong with the passage of time. Things got muddled. Whether it was to stop me entering I don't know, but I didn't follow you directly the same way. For anyone without a magic ability it's a maze down there, Ronnie. Somehow I took the wrong turn. I was thrown out into the WildLands and had to make my way to you from there. Thank goodness I was prepared for that. Five nights I spent out there, huddled in a makeshift tent with only a campfire for warmth.'

She gasped. 'That was your fire smoke I saw in the distance when I first got here!'

'Most probably. I never came across anyone else mad enough to camp out there. Anyone human, that is. Believe me, I never want to do it again.' He paused. 'But I would do. Despite all that has happened this was meant to be. I'm losing you, Ronnie, and although this is much bigger than the both of us, I still love you.'

'Oh, how endearing!' a woman's voice sung behind them, and they turned to see the infamous

Pandora herself standing in the doorway.

Theo and Samilious stood in the Surveillance Tower watching the lights on the ART going haywire flicking from green, amber and red in a nonsensical order.

Theo picked it up and shook it. 'Must be broken,' he insisted.

'Impossible,' Samilious said, annoyed. 'It's just a temporary confliction of energies.'

'Like what? If it's magic it must be extremely powerful to prevent its own anomaly readings from being picked up by the tracker.'

Samilious raised an eyebrow. 'Either that or she's time travelling,' he suggested.

'Nonsense. I haven't taught her how to time travel yet, in case she planned on using it to escape.'

'Well, unless her bottom half is able to walk in a different direction to her top half, then I'd say she's either ditched the un-lockable collar, impossible, or the butt plug, disallowed but most probable.'

'But why would she do that?'

'So she can't be found?'

Theo fumed silently as he reflected on the deeper meaning of her blatant disobedience. She was AWOL, time travelling, and had removed the butt plug with the tracking system hidden in it to purposely avoid detection. How could this one girl be so infuriatingly frustrating *and* make his life so difficult in the process? Clearly his usual techniques were not working on her, but once she'd been brought to Black Ice disobedience was supposed to be mentally impossible. On top of that, it was damn near crippling him always keeping her at an emotional distance, and this was how she repaid him.

'What are you saying? You can't track her now?'

'Sorry, Theo, all we can do is sit and wait for whatever's blocking the readings to stop, and then we can continue to follow the progress of the TAG system in her collar.'

'But what if it doesn't stop?' asked Theo, concerned.

'Never happened before, but if it doesn't we'll just have to pray she chooses to come back, otherwise we've got a mighty big search on our hands.'

'But there must be another way!' he demanded, slamming his fist down on the control board. 'You're our attaché and mechanicals expert, are you not?'

'Hey, Theo, she'll be all right. That girl can look after herself. If I didn't know better I'd say she has a mind of her own.'

Which was exactly what bothered Theo.

Chapter Twenty-Eight

Tim looked up over Ronnie's shoulder, his mouth hung open. She followed his gaze. A woman stood before her, short dark hair, black eyes, and an evil smile. No introductions were necessary. Pandora, the Black Witch and High Priestess.

Ronnie stood, amazed at just how beautiful Pandora was, and the witch smirked as if this was the reaction she always received.

Tim pushed away a chair that was between them

and stepped forward.

'Come with me, Ronnie dear,' the witch purred. 'You can have *anything* you want, all the powers in the world with this box.' She held out a hand and Ronnie gasped. In her palm lay a tiny black treasure box, inlaid with ivory and precious gems. It was much smaller than Ronnie had imagined it, and so beautiful.

'Don't trust the bitch!' Tim shouted, not taking his eyes off her. 'Why would that suddenly turn up now?'

'Oh, this is *the* Magic Box of Destiny. I've been saving the opening of it for this very moment.'

'But you can't open it yourself; you're not human,' Tim snarled, stretching out an arm to stop Ronnie getting any closer.

'No, and neither are you, entirely,' Pandora laughed, 'but I know a woman who can!' she said, flashing Ronnie a predatory smile, and with her free hand the witch sent a flash of red light towards Tim. Ronnie screamed and dived across to protect him, and at the same time Tim grabbed Ronnie and pulled her down to the floor. They rolled, sharp daggers of light narrowly missing them both.

'Come, come, my Children. Let's not be hasty about this. Imagine the three of us, our mixed energies combined; there is so much we can do together. My Paraphanites are strong, but with the Spirit of Hope the wonders of the Otherworld would be ours! All you need to do is die for the cause and we can open the box and all live again!'

Don't listen! I've been there! Inside that box. Any wonders that once belonged have long since been suffocated to death by the pure evil which resides within! a voice screamed in Ronnie's head.

Hope?

Yes, I'm with you. I can help hold her back, but I cannot kill her. That's up to you!

Horrified, Ronnie watched as Tim charged for Pandora. In his hand he held a dagger.

The elusive dagger of Andrastus! She'd seen it in the books. How the hell did he get it?

Tim took a dive at Pandora. Her arm thrust forward and the dagger slipped in like a knife through butter. The Black Witch screamed and slapped him across the face with such force he flew across the room. Hitting the wall alone should have killed him, but he jumped up.

Pandora thrust out her hand again, sending another shot of red smoke towards Tim. Angered, he roared, fell to the floor and screamed out in pain. What had Pandora done? Ronnie ran to him but he pushed her away, and as he did his body expanded in size.

Something popped and cracked.

Bones?

He groaned and held his head in agony and the clothes on his body began to rip. First his trousers, then his torso and arms. Muscles grew and kept growing, forcing him onto all fours. His head enlarged, but his glossy brown mane shortened until it became less like hair, more like fur. The facial features darkened, changing from the handsome face she knew to what she could only describe as a monster. His mouth and nose blended together, lengthening, and long uneven fangs sprung out of his slobbering muzzle. It happened so quickly.

The thought of running for the door immediately faltered. If she ran he'd surely catch her with one large stride of those now tree trunk thighs. Her eyes wandered down his legs to his feet; enormous furry feet with claws. She noticed his hands looked similar, clawed and sharpened to kill. What had he become? He towered over her, a giant, half man, half beast. No resemblance of the person she thought he was.

Frightening. Grotesque. Inhuman.

Get out, Ronnie, he's a werewolf! Hope screamed in her head.

For a moment Ronnie forgot the High Priestess Pandora and the immediate danger she was in by letting her guard drop. She didn't know whether to stay and fight, or run. And from which one?

The wolf's glowing eyes rested on her and she fancied she could feel the scorch of fire. She tightened her grip on her trusty Death Blade.

Then his gaze swung to Pandora, and before Ronnie could think what to do a large clawed hand pushed her aside and she rolled under the table as the wolf charged and took a flying leap towards the witch.

Using all her strength Pandora retaliated with a sudden blow of jagged red lightning, which hit the wolf's body and threw it up into the air, slamming him against the ceiling.

His grip on the knife weakened. It fell to the floor. To Ronnie's amazement the wolf stayed where he was, defying gravity, he hovered above encased in a hazy red light. Then he fell to the floor, smashing a chair beneath him.

For a few minutes Ronnie watched in horror as the process reversed and wolf's features crackled and snapped back into shape until all that remained was Tim, sprawled on the floor, still and lifeless.

The light faded from around him, then slithered like a snake, towards Ronnie.

At the same time Pandora's finger shot out in Ronnie's direction and a dazzling strobe of red light flew across the room and punched her in the stomach. With the force of the impact she fell to the floor, dazed and winded. The blades in her satchel clattered together. Her eyes streamed and she tried to breathe. Fear of dying clung to her throat and choked her. Then she glanced at Tim, limp and lifeless, and anger pumped through her veins.

She looked up. A wild fire burned in Pandora's eyes and she let out an inhuman laugh. Another blow hit Ronnie's right shoulder, knocking her sideways towards the table. Fighting against her pain Ronnie continued moving and rolled under to safety. A quick glance at her stomach and she realised she was all right.

A heavy bolt of power hit the tabletop. She smelt wood burning and felt the heat from above. She looked up. Through her tears she noticed something taped to the underside of the table. She wiped her eyes and took a better look. Next to a large black singe mark Ronnie spotted an empty dagger holster!

The dagger! It's the only way you can kill her. The wolf man hurt her, she's weaker, but you have to kill before she changes and gets her strength back.

Ronnie's gaze desperately searched for the dagger, remembering Tim had dropped it while hovering near the ceiling. Then she saw it. Not far from where Tim lay, glinting in the corner of the room was the Andrastus Dagger. She had to get it.

It was her only chance.

She darted out from underneath the table and reached for it. Another bolt of red lightening hurtled towards her and she jumped aside. It narrowly missed her and cracked the floor where it hit.

She rushed to the dagger and grabbed for it while glancing at Tim. A wisp of smoke resembling the form of man weaved its way towards him, changing form as it glided past her eyes, even as her fingers closed around the dagger.

The smoke drifted across his chest and disappeared into his open mouth, just as another sharp bolt caught her shoulder and she cried out in pain.

With all her might Ronnie fell forward, the dagger held tightly in one hand and rolled, narrowly missing yet another bolt. Not thinking she threw the Andrastus Dagger towards the Black Witch, and spinning, yet on a straight and deadly course, the weapon embedded itself in its target's chest.

Pandora screamed, her body flickered as though she tried to disappear but could not do so. She fell to the floor, her beautiful black robe settling softly around her still form.

Get out now! Hope screamed. *Draw a door! Get out!*

But Ronnie scrambled over to Tim and searched for a sign of life. He was still breathing!

Leave him! You must get out now before she regenerates and her power increases.

No! Ronnie shouted at her in her mind. 'I'm not leaving him!' she said aloud. *Besides, he's the only connection to my old life. I need him.*

Quickly she drew a door, saying the magic words, and it opened easily. She crawled through, dragging Tim's heavy body with her. A another flash of lightening charged towards her as she pulled Tim right in and frantically climbed over his body, desperate to retrieve the box and the dagger.

Pandora lay almost transparent. The knife fell to the floor as if there was nothing left of her to hold it any more. In her hand, still gripped tightly, Pandora held the Box of Destiny. Clearly the last lightening bolt was Pandora's last attempt to kill her, Ronnie thought as she grabbed the dagger and thrust it back into the witch's body.

The knife went right through Pandora and the action caused her long fingers to uncurl. Ronnie grabbed the box, put the dagger in her belt and scampered back through the doorway where Tim lay unconscious.

She imagined the door she'd just come through slamming tightly shut and no bricks wedging it open this time. With the closing magic words she locked the door and thought of Black Ice, and within seconds the light around the closed portal faded.

Desperate not to leave him behind she clung to Tim. Suddenly she felt lighter, Tim's body seemingly weightless in her arms, and Ronnie knew they had begun their trip back through time. Away from the witch, away from danger. A moment later they arrived in the Black Ice assembly hall with a bump.

Tim's eyes flickered open, then closed. He groaned.

'Stay with me, Tim! Stay with me!' Tears clouded Ronnie's vision.

Tim groaned again, his eyes flickered. He was rapidly losing consciousness.

'Eros will know what to do.' Quickly she tilted his head and checked his airways. All clear. She then began to put him into the recovery position, when a voice broke her concentration.

'Take him away!' Theo boomed angrily across the hall.

By the tone of his voice something was wrong. Puzzled, Ronnie looked up and saw Ares and Samilious advancing towards them. 'Take him where?' she asked Theo, clinging even tighter to Tim. 'He needs a hospital. He might have broken something. At least get Eros!' She looked up at Theo with pleading eyes. 'Please, my Learned, *help* him!'

'Let him go, Ronnie,' he said, ignoring her pleas.

Ares bent down and grabbed Tim's shoulders, avoiding her eyes, while Samilious walked around to pick up his feet.

'Don't move him! Didn't you hear what I said? He might have broken something. He needs medical attention. Please help him.' She fixed her eyes on Theo's stern face and he gave her that tight-lipped, uncompromising stare she knew all too well.

'Girl, get yourself over here, now.'

She hesitated and stood up. Ares dragged Tim to his feet and Samilious lifted his legs.

'But where are you taking him? What's going on?'

'What you did going to meet him was irresponsible. Not to mention downright disobedient. Knaala!'

Ronnie walked over to Theo, with her eyes to the floor, and knelt at his feet.

'Eyes!'

Instantly she looked up.

'He's dangerous, Ronnie. To you. To our mission. To all of us.'

'But he's my friend, my Learned. He's no danger.' She frowned.

'We can't take that risk. Do you know how much danger he put you in? He needs to be dealt with, and fast.'

Ronnie's eyes widened. 'Dealt with?'

'He'll have to be destroyed.'

'Please, no!' she implored, searching his face for a speck of compassion. 'Please!'

'We have reason to believe he's now one of the infected.'

'Infected? With what?' *Did he see him change? Did he read my mind?* 'He looks fine to me,' she added cautiously.

'He's a Paraphanite. You know they don't look any different on the outside, but inside he's an evil deviant; a bomb ready to explode.'

For a second she almost blew out a sigh of relief. Desperate to spare him she blanked her mind from all further thoughts of the creature she saw, in case Theo used his Destaurian Eyes on her. That he changed into some sort of wolf before her very eyes would not bode well. Not now. Perhaps not ever.

Theo nodded to his guards and they took Tim out of the room.

'Or is this not about Tim, but about us?'

'What do you mean, girl?'

'Do I mean so little to you that you cannot spare

this man's life just because he's my friend?'

'That's nonsense and I will not have you speaking to me like that.'

'If I may be so bold, my Learned, you wrote the ruling that no single Destaurian Guard should allow love to come into their lives. I think it's an excuse not to get hurt.'

'I still stand by what I said. He's dangerous.'

'With all due respect, my Learned, many a wonderful thing has happened on account of love. Menelaus battled for ten years to get Helen back during the Trojan War. Can you not spare one man's life for me?'

'He cannot be allowed to live.'

'He saved my life. Would it not be right for you to thank him by sparing his?'

'He did?'

'Yes, Pandora turned up. I fought her but she was strong. If it hadn't been for Tim she would have overpowered me and I wouldn't be standing here telling you all this now.'

'Impossible. He's human.'

'Wait, please,' she said, remembering the dagger and the elusive Magic Box of Destiny. She rummaged around on her person, but to her horror could not find the box. She checked her belt and hunted through her satchel, even though she knew she put it in her belt, it wasn't anywhere to be found.

Shit! Must have lost it in the time tunnel! Oh, my goddess! If he finds out I had it only to lose it five minutes later I'll be in big trouble!

She pulled out the blade. 'He used this on her.'

Theo gasped.

'This is the Andrastus dagger, is it not?' She held

it up and he took it from her, totally awed. 'Where on Tartarus did he find this?'

'I don't know, my Learned, but if you spare his life maybe he'll tell you what he knows. Please?'

'That dagger changes everything, girl.'

'It does?' She smiled and relief rushed through her body in waves carrying her fears away in an instant. 'May I ask how?'

'In Destauria we have a rule. If any creature saves the life of one of our hosts they are immediately bestowed with an immunity from harm and treated as one of us; a friend.'

'Oh, thank the gods above!' she exclaimed, tears of relief trickling down her face.

'Although that makes you happy, of which I'm glad,' he said, wiping her tears away with a thumb, 'it does cause us more problems.'

She looked quizzically into his dark eyes. 'But everything will be all right now, surely, my Learned.'

'No. For with this ruling we are also forbidden to kill him even if he does turn out to be one of the infected.'

'So what can you do? You'll be able to save him then, my Learned? Find a cure?'

'One step at a time, girl. One step at a time. First I will send Hermes to tell my guards to transfer him from the Prison Tower and take him to the Recovery Tower for tests.'

The Prison?

'If we are keeping him alive we'll need to do some rigorous checks on him, and from thereon we can decide what to do. But I can assure you he will be treated with the care and respect he deserves.'

'Thank you, my Learned. Thank you so much.'

'Don't thank me, thank the gods, they created the life for a life rule, not me.'

Then without warning he wrapped his arms around her in a fierce embrace. 'And if you *ever* disobey me like that again I will not be held responsible for my actions. I thought I'd lost you. Understood, girl?'

Ronnie nodded, tears streaming down her face, wetting his bare chest. So many mixed emotions filled her.

After a long while he let go and instructed her to resume her 'present' position. His eyes studied her face intensely. 'Time for your punishment, girl.'

Besides all that had been said and done it was what she wanted; a chance of redemption and to show the man she loved how sorry she was. To make things right.

'Oh, I nearly forgot,' he added. 'After your punishment you will go to your cage and read book three of *A Child of Destiny's Guide to Serving her Guardian; Protocol and Etiquette of the Bonding Ceremony.*'

Ronnie gasped, and her face lit up with joy. 'Are we to be Bonded soon, my Learned?'

This was big news. Their Bonding would finally cement their relationship. Was this his way of showing he really did care, or was it because Tim was on the scene and could now be seen as a threat to him that he wanted to secure her as his?

'Yes, girl, in the morrow our Bonding Ceremony will begin. Now, go immediately to the Punishment Tower and select the whip with which you will be beaten. Assume the position in the centre of the room and wait. You've been naughty and need to be punished with some serious Whip and Cock training.'

'Yes of course, my Learned,' she obeyed, unable to hold back a smile.

Ronnie waited for what seemed like ages, forehead pressed to the floor, bum raised high in the air. Resting on her elbows with the crop she had chosen laying in her open palms, her nipples hardening as her pussy became wet. To wait for her punishment in such a position in a room which resembled a dungeon was a punishment in itself, but also excited her beyond belief. And knowing the walls were covered with whips, chains, manacles and other scary instruments of torture which Theo could use on her if he wished only intensified her horniness. But more than anything she needed it, to repent. To prove to him she was sorry for her disobedience. She wanted to feel Theo's control over her through pain, to have him tighten those invisible chains around her body, rendering her powerless to do anything but beg his forgiveness.

Although she didn't hear him enter the chamber the hairs on the back of her neck prickled as they always did when he was near. With a limited view her eyes flickered around the black polished floor, trying to catch his reflection so she wasn't taken unaware. No such luck!

He was watching; she could sense it.

She shut her eyes and listened for any movement in the shadows. Soon he would come close enough to pick up the crop and she'd hear him then.

But without warning the palm of his hand came swatting down on her bottom and she shrieked with shock and pain.

The crop disappeared from her upturned palms

and Ronnie tensed, waiting for the beating to begin. The moment he placed it firmly on her back she jumped. He then proceeded to tease her by running it all over her body, never letting it stray from her flesh.

He turned the crop sideways and slowly ran the leather slapper down her bottom crease, against her rear entrance and down to her labia, parting her swollen lips. Then the crop lifted and she knew he was inspecting it for her juices.

'Tsk, tsk! What a slut you are, getting wet in anticipation of your punishment. What say you?'

'Yes, my Learned, I'm Sorry I'm such a slut but I couldn't help myself,' she whimpered, as she waited for the first strike on her bottom. But to her surprise he slapped her pussy instead. She yelped as the pain between her legs burned like molten lava and tears instantly formed in her eyes.

'That's to remind you this is a punishment not a reward, and you are not to enjoy but learn a lesson on proper behaviour.' His voice was gruff. Uncompromising.

'Yes, my Learned,' she replied with a nod, and a hollow feeling in the pit of her stomach.

He smacked her pussy again. Despite the pain she tried to keep still, for if she moved just an inch more trouble would ensue.

'Communication is an exchange,' he stressed, cracking the crop through the air and swiping it down on her bottom. 'The key to unlocking any problems you may have. From now on whether I ask or not you will tell me exactly how you feel. Whether something is troubling you or you are extremely happy, I want to know. If you want to meet anyone outside Black Ice you must ask my express permission, and not until it is granted may you leave these grounds. I am your guide, your voice, and I will even think for you if that is what it takes to get the message across. Do you understand, slut?'

'Yes, my Learned!' she cried as he cracked the crop down again and again, stinging her backside as tears of remorse streamed down her face. Then he roughly pulled her up by the hair and stuffed her mouth with his growing penis. While she sucked and snivelled he brutally thrashed her arse, sending electric shocks straight to her enlarged clit. Pleasure and pain became one.

'I will not tolerate disobedience in any form,' he insisted, striking home the enormity of what he was doing.

Quickly he released her hair, pushed her facedown to the floor with a hand on her neck and struck with an even greater force, etching crisscrossed welts on her pale, heart-shaped bottom.

Theo then grabbed her hair and pulled her mouth up to his cock so she could suck it again. The more excited he became the quicker he swapped over. One minute he'd pin her down and thrash her, the next she'd be pulled back up by her hair onto his cock, almost suffocating her, its length and girth stuffed to the back of her throat.

He came in her mouth, and then gruffly pulled out without warning to splash more spunk over her face. After he made her lick him clean he pulled the sobbing slut up and held her tight. Tears of arousal, shame, resentment and gratitude meandered down her cheeks, wetting his bare chest.

He slipped his fingers into her wet slit, just long

enough to make her groan longingly, and then pulled them out.

'I don't want to have to do this again, Ronnie, but if forced to I will, only worse. Go to your cage and think about what you've done. There'll be no release for you today.'

Chapter Twenty-Nine

In the Royal Bonding Hall of the Floating Kingdom of Nuvola, Tim sat facing the large black altar waiting for Ronnie to appear. Out of the corner of his eye he saw Theo looking his way.

No doubt he's waiting to see me squirm with embarrassment as my girlfriend masturbates for him in front of me and this huge audience.

Theo leaned closer to Tim, and because of the growing rowdiness of the audience shouted in his direction.

'Tonight I shall, er, how do you Earthlings say it? Fuck both my Goddess of Hope and Ronnie in front of you all, so we can bond as one true being.'

Tim gritted his teeth and managed a feeble smile, which he desperately hoped looked convincing.

This man, Theo, her Learned, her soon-to-be-bonded-life-partner annoyed him to hell. He hated the fact Theo had his girlfriend under his control in such a Destaurian way she was powerless to resist, just as he had been powerless to stop Ronnie becoming one of them.

Had Theo asked Tim, the only human in the room, for the 'pleasure' of his company at his Bonding Ceremony on the pretence of thanking him for saving Ronnie's life, when in fact he wanted to make him suffer and rub his nose in it? After all, Theo now owned Ronnie, but technically she was still his girlfriend, since they hadn't officially broken up with each other.

Tim wasn't sure. But not wanting to go into Destauria without all the facts he'd thoroughly researched the Bonding Ceremony Day. It was a part of a whole series of sexual events lined up and celebrated by all Destaurians. The festivities began early in the morning in Nuvola, and ended with a grand finale in the Bonding Hall. To his amazement he discovered Destaurians were into the humanisation of statues for entertainment. How that worked with human girls like Ronnie he couldn't find out as many parts of the ritual were sacred, but that made him curious.

What he did know was a lot of preparation had gone into getting Ronnie this far into her training, and by the way the spectators' staged seating was majestically decorated in Royal Blue tones etched with gold, they'd pulled out all the stops for what they deemed a very important occasion.

Thankfully the Andrastus Dagger had helped keep both of them alive, and there was nothing Theo could do to physically hurt him because of the immunity granted to him by the gods for saving her life, but that didn't stop Theo having the one thing he didn't. Ronnie.

Luckily Ronnie had not told Theo about his change, otherwise he wouldn't be sitting in the middle of them right now, having since discovered that werewolves were in the Destaurians' top ten list of enemies. How the shape-shifting change happened he did not know, but when this was all over he vowed to get to the bottom of it and find out.

But first he needed to get through today in one piece, and be there for Ronnie. He owed that much to her for saving his life, not that he didn't want to be with her anyway, but he had to be careful at night, when his darkness grew.

A frenzied chorus of cheers and clapping burst from the crowd, interrupting Tim's thoughts. He leaned forward in his seat and blinked as what looked like a block of ice was lowered into the centre of the stage in front of the altar. Inside stood a beautiful perfectly carved ice sculpture of a woman. Some supporters were eager to see more and stood up, forcing those behind them to do the same. So Tim stood up to get a better look himself.

In the centre of the display case stood Ronnie, as though frozen in time. Immortalised like one of them. There was something strangely beautiful about the way she'd been transformed into an artificial-seeming being dressed to titillate. No one could take their eyes off her.

Tim's cock tingled, hardening in his trousers. Betraying him every way he thought impossible. She was once his girl... he wanted to feel angry, at everyone in the room, at her. He wanted to wallow in his shame of not being able to stand up for her and end this fiasco. To stop them staring! But as much as he tried to deny his feelings she looked so damn fucking hot!

Then Theo stood up, distracting Tim from the scene before him. His stiffening cock ached in his pants. In a vague attempt to cover up any signs of his growing lust he sat again and crossed one leg over the other and leaned forward, covering the bulge. It didn't work. Theo glanced down as if he knew the truth before even looking, and grinned. He then looked away, turned to face the audience and addressed them all with the words, 'I've changed my mind!'

Tim baulked. Theo was going to put a stop to all this after all? Perhaps he'd misread him.

'Tonight I propose to do things differently.'

The crowd gasped and murmured amongst themselves.

Tim glanced at Ronnie as she stood there strapped up and unable to move.

'Before I let her out of her display case, allow me to explain. I will skip the threesome fuck-fest and go straight to the meat of the matter, of which I know you've all been waiting.'

The Destaurians cheered and whistled agreeably.

'Now as you all know reproduction is a physical impossibility until Ronnie is not only Bonded, but collared by me, therefore, men, this is your last chance for some time to ravish a Child of Destiny without fear of impregnation. So those of you desiring to avail themselves of my girl in the closing ritual please come to the stage and wait until I present her.'

Time almost stood still as Tim looked back, shocked and amazed at the number of men in the room rising, keen to use her body indiscriminately.

A finger tapped Tim on the shoulder. He turned. It was Theo.

'Please,' he said, taking hold of his arm and firmly lifting him out of his seat, 'won't you join us?'

Tim thought for all of two seconds. If Ronnie was going to do this and enjoy it he'd rather be involved than just watch. So he nodded, stood up, and made his way to the front of the stage where he took his place in the queue with the rest of the sex-craved animals eagerly waiting for the go-ahead to join the two pieces of meat on stage.

With a growing sense of agitation Tim looked at his watch. Dusk falling, he could feel his hunger rising. He hoped he could get his turn in before he turned.

Encased in a glass container unable to move except for her eyes, Ronnie was lowered through the roof of a huge auditorium and placed on a podium in the centre of a stage. Thousands of staring faces filled the football stadium-sized Bonding Hall, restlessly waiting to get a better look at her naked, motionless form.

Theo came to the display case and opened the door. Wherever she looked a wave of expectant faces turned her way, accompanied by tumultuous applause and a stomping of restless feet from an unruly crowd.

With her limbs and head immobilised she could only watch as Theo lifted her, attached to a stand, out of the case. He carried her to an altar carved from Black Ice and set her down carefully, as though she might crack and crumble if dropped. Every inch of her body had been cleverly painted to resemble translucent white ice, and she couldn't remember it ever being done. Mindlust?

Remember, slut, you are a living breathing ice sculpture unable to move without help, Theo said.

Strangely his harsh name-calling turned her on even more, as if she needed any help.

While Theo unhooked her from the stand she

spotted Tim and thought how far apart his and Theo's worlds were, yet she belonged in both their lives and wouldn't have it any other way. Tim was a reminder of her roots and there was so much she could learn about herself from him, once they'd had time to catch up. He held the key to her forgotten life, if only her Learned would allow him to unlock it. Given time, maybe he would.

Although free from all her restraints she was far from free. Other than Theo putting her into a desired pose, she kept perfectly still. Her job now was to act like a mindless statue incapable of movement or freewill, so she emptied her mind and tried not to think about what was going to happen.

To her horror Theo cruelly pushed a vibrating dildo into her pussy, and then switched it on.

'Do not move and do not come, slut!' he ordered, his voice booming around the Bonding Hall. Amplified, his voice broadcast across the auditorium. Every grunt and groan was going to be heard. She then saw a screen on the wall enlarging her immobilised image that looked more like an effigy of Aphrodite than her. If she orgasmed at the wrong time everyone would see!

Oh, my Goddess, my Goddess, my Goddess! Please, if you never do anything for me again, please just help me!

Ronnie waited for an answer.

Nothing.

Her mouth felt dry. She wanted to lick her parched lips, swallow and take a deep breath, but it was not allowed; a replica of Theo's cock was stuffed into her mouth and invisibly tied to prevent it.

Ice sculptures do not move.

Hope? asked Ronnie.

Tis I, the beautiful Goddess of Hope smiled back.

The woman Ronnie had felt such a strong connection with, her inner goddess, stood at the bottom of the altar looking every bit as beautiful as she did in her dreams. Only during the Bonding Ceremony was the goddess able to come back and be with her true love, Prometheus, and for only a very short while could she stay in human form. A warm and intense feeling of love spread through her body.

That's the combination of our minds and energies converging with one common goal, Hope whispered in Ronnie's mind, as her naked body climbed up the steps to the altar, hips swaying, and kissed Ronnie's gagged lips, exciting the spectators further.

It is simplicity itself, yet simple things can produce complicated results, the Goddess of Hope said, cupping Ronnie's vibrating pussy. Ronnie did her best not to shudder under her sensitive touch. She must keep still!

Oh, goddess, how long am I going to be left with this thing inside me, trying not to come? Ronnie pleaded. Right now, one touch of her sensitive sex and she wouldn't be able to hold back.

I will remove it before you come, slut, Theo said, pulling Hope's face closer to his while he groped Ronnie's breasts.

With a mixture of jealously and Mindlust Ronnie watched her Learned and Hope hungrily kiss each other. Two souls reunited for this one short ceremony. Her own body faintly trembled with the pleasure of a fast approaching orgasm that only her Learned had the power to allow or stop.

From now on I will remain in both your hearts and minds as though we are one single intelligent powerful life force, Hope said. *But remember, both Prometheus and I need you as a host to help guarantee my continuous safety, and you need us to teach you how to survive in our world and save that of your own. In short, we all need each other to survive.*

All Ronnie could do was blink in response.

Everything is linked, even though you may not see it straight away. Things come into being from the bottom up, Theo said, now concentrating on Hope's breasts, squeezing them with his possessive hands, his teeth tugging at her nipples making her groan with pleasure.

Gods I'm close! Ronnie said, watching them together, feeling the vibrating cock suddenly bringing her orgasm to the edge.

I must go, Hope said, as Theo pulled out the dildo, which did little to ease Ronnie's agony of needing release, although it subsided a little.

Remember, gradual degrees produce a large sequence of relatively simple steps, resulting in something much bigger than us all. A power mightier than one person alone can handle, Hope said in Ronnie and Theo's head, as her physical body flickered and vanished.

Theo then picked up Ronnie and lay her supine on the altar.

Do exactly what I say and you'll get through this just fine, he said.

He sat her up so her feet hung over the edge of the altar, and spread her legs wide apart. He picked up her left hand and put it behind her back, and fed Ronnie's forefinger up her own anus. He then opened her mouth and told her to keep her eyes on his, as he used her right hand to masturbate herself, sadistically keeping her on the edge at all times.

When satisfied she was close to coming he stopped, pressed her back down on the altar and entered her wet pussy, smoothly and slowly, savouring every inch that slipped into her velvety channel.

Happy not to think for herself Ronnie gladly obliged. And then she saw several men of all ages, shapes and sizes walk up onto the stage and gather around the altar. Some were undoing belts and unbuttoning trousers. Others were already naked and playing with their erect cocks; all of them pointing in her direction.

No, please! she cried, suddenly realising they were all there for her.

Your body is mine to do with what I wish. Lie still, slut, Theo ordered.

The men crowded closer.

No escape!

Relax, girl, he said, removing the gag from her mouth. *Remember we three are one, you are not alone. You can do this.*

But there are too many of them. It's so degrading.

Underneath Theo's pumping cock, Ronnie's body was nudged to the end of the altar with each wet, squelching thrust, until her head was hanging back over the edge. An old grey-haired man shuffled forward with his trousers bunched around his knees and fed his soft, age-spotted cock into her gaping mouth. At first she wanted to spit out the limp organ, but suddenly in the dark recesses of her mind a perverse flame ignited and a sexual jolt of both revulsion and excitement rushed through her body.

Good girl. Remember you're doing this to please me, Theo said sternly, *as your lineage dictates you vacate all limits. Let them use you. Don't think. Become a statue.*

That Theo was capable of exerting complete control over mind and body to such an extent she couldn't think for herself was a powerful aphrodisiac.

The geriatric gripped the altar's lip with one hand and worked his cock into her mouth with the other, steadily wanking himself until the stem of flesh took on a life of its own. Soon the surprisingly large swelling in her mouth was that of a young stud, not an aged plough horse, and it threatened to asphyxiate her if he didn't slow down. His sagging belly ground back and forth, pressing around her face, increasing her difficulty in breathing. Who was the man, she briefly wondered, with the cock of a stallion and the body of an old pig. Suddenly an engorged cock was thrust into her hand and Theo's voice told her to *make me come, slut,* so she tugged as best she could until she got a rhythm flowing when another cock, slick and hard, slipped into her other hand and she was ordered to play with that too.

Wait a minute. If you have your cock in my hand, who is inside me?

Not being allowed to move, and with her head hanging back over the edge of the altar, her mouth filled with the elderly man's cock and both hands busy, she couldn't sit up to look. She groaned as someone moved her knees higher into the air and she blocked all thoughts out of her mind and became their living, breathing, plaything.

The elderly man weaved his fingers through her short hair and hung on while he pumped spunk into her mouth with intermittent grunts. Then immediately the geriatric removed his cock from her mouth warm, wet seed spurted across her belly from both sides, and that familiar salty, pungent smell drifted to her nose.

Someone flipped her over and aggressively thrust his cock into her from behind. Nails like claws roughly scratched and squeezed her breasts, while more fingers rubbed and slapped her wet slit. From every direction slippery cocks prodded and poked her body, inside and out. Cold spunk from several men coated her ice-painted belly and dripped onto the black altar.

She heard Theo's voice order his slut to stretch her body out to take more cock. She did, and found herself lying on the slab of Black Ice, pulsating against her cheek pressed uncomfortably against the hard surface, while her hands milked two new erections.

The man fucking her from behind gripped her hair harder and pulled her head back so that her mouth opened, and another rigid cock filled it instantly.

'You look so fucking hot with another man's dick in your mouth,' Tim's voice growled in her ear as he belligerently fucked her so vigorously she thought she might split in two.

Tim!

His fingers worked roughly at her wet vulva. Ronnie felt so horny, so helpless, with no choice but to experience the arousal they forced upon her. The coherent thoughts of her mind quietly faded into the distance, leaving her as a frozen, living, breathing orgasmic sculpture of Black Ice for everyone to use. Mindlessly obedient.

Tim rode her fiercely like a wild animal spurred only by instinct and a need to release his pent up dark energies, until his throbbing cock ejaculated inside her and his thrusts abated. And that she'd just been fucked by a wolf-man excited her intensely.

No sooner than he had withdrawn his cock from her sore pussy another's engorged tip rubbed against her slick hole, using her juices to make himself wet, but he didn't enter her. Instead his cock nudged up to her bottom hole, and without any regard for her pain he forced it into the tight, puckered orifice.

Tears stung her eyes while she desperately tried not to make a noise as his thick cock pushed its way deep, not stopping until it was fully embedded. The friction burned yet excited her, and the pure bliss of her helplessness emptied her mind and froze it into one incoherent, unfocussed sensual haze.

At one point Theo's slut had a cock up her arse, her pussy, in her mouth and one in each hand, but as time went on more and more men were crowding the altar, preparing themselves to use her body to dispense themselves upon or inside her, in the most depraved way possible. But by this time she didn't care. She was an empty vessel to be filled.

She had no idea how long it lasted, only that sometimes her body was posed into awkward positions and she fought a desperate need to come. Sometimes Theo placed her on her knees to suck an engorged penis. Sometimes he put her on all fours to be fucked, and once she was held upside down while someone licked her dripping cunt while another pumped her mouth with his cock. But always with an unknown cock stuffed into every orifice or against her, and always being explored like some attractive object able to satisfy their curiosity and Mindlust. Having lost the ability to obey orders of what to do and whose cock to suck, they just moved her into the required positions like she was their dirty little fuck-doll without a mind or a will of her own.

Ronnie hardly noticed when it came to an end, and everyone except Theo had returned to their seats. Used, sore and dripping with sperm, he helped her up and placed her into the knaala position, giving her a few moments to recover before they moved onto the final part of the Bonding Ceremony, which would tie them together forever.

Chapter Thirty

'Knaala at my feet, Child.'

Ronnie knelt, spread her thighs apart, and placed the palms of her hands on her thighs. Her pussy lips felt gloriously sensitised and sore. Theo nodded for her to start reciting the sacred Bonding words.

'With a free mind and open heart I, Ronnie Weaver, request that you, my Learned and Destaurian Guard, rightfully and judicially accept the submission of my will unto yours and take me into your care and guidance however you see fit.'

He nodded, and looked down with pride written over his face as she knelt before him, tears of happiness in her eyes.

'What do you offer me in exchange, girl?'

'I promise to satisfy your wants, desires and whims, which are consistent with my desire as your Child of Destiny to be found pleasing to you,' she said, with a slight shakiness to her voice. She hoped her nerves were not showing because she might forget her lines, the last thing she wanted to do during the locking of the Collar of Commitment around her neck. It meant too much to both of them for her to mess it up.

'How do you propose to do that?' Theo asked sternly.

'To give you the use of my time, talents and abilities as one of the owned, devoted and fully committed to only you, my Learned.'

'Girl, as a Child of Destiny, a host for Hope, do you accept the power vested in my role, and the keeping of your body for the fulfilment and enhancement of my sexual, spiritual, emotional and intellectual needs?'

'I do, my Learned,' she nodded. 'I request that you guide me in any sexual behaviour, both together with, and separate from you, in such a way as to further my growth as your subservient property; your Child of Destiny.' Ronnie paused to wipe a stray tear from her eye, took a deep breath and carried on. 'My Learned, I beg of you to make use of me. Mould me, shape me, assist me to grow in strength, character, confidence and being.'

He smiled, and looked deep into her grey eyes. 'Do you accept your irrevocable surrender as my property, with sincere humility and understanding, that you will always belong to me, unless I choose otherwise?'

'This, I Ronnie Weaver, do entreat with lucidity, and the realisation of what this means, both stated and implied, in the conviction that my offer will be understood in the spirit of Hope and Devotion in which it is given.' She swallowed and blinked back another tear, trying hard not to burst into tears in front of all the witnesses.

'No other man shall own or touch me, unless your permission is granted or you give me away, my Learned.'

If he ever washed his hands of her and gave her away to someone else to keep, she swore she would never survive.

'Very well. I accept your offer of complete surrender, which under Destaurian law shall serve as your contract of consent and bind us together.' He looked over to Artemis. 'The collar.'

In her hands Artemis held a plush, red velvet pillow, on which sat a steel band set with an amethyst gemstone in the centre. He picked it up, opened the ring at the hinge, and walked round behind Ronnie.

'In recognition of our bond, my ownership, and the attachment between us, I lock this Collar of Commitment around your neck to signify your permanent place in my life as your Guardian, and owner. May it serve as a powerful reminder of the control you have surrendered to me as my Child of Destiny – my property.' Cold metal touched her skin, and snapped shut with a satisfying click.

She shut her eyes for a couple of seconds and smiled, wanting to remember this part, lock it away into her memory for the rest of her life.

'Locked in place the Collar of Commitment will keep you within your bond and exclude all others' powers over you. If anyone tries to come between us I will destroy them. I hereby declare in front all every witness in this room, and in accordance to Destaurian Law, you are now *mine*.' He leaned closer and whispered in her ear. '*Mine*,' he repeated with a breathless voice, which made her pussy quiver.

'A toast to my Bonded, my Child of Destiny!' Theo said, taking a glass of Ambrosia from Artemis. He raised his drink to the audience; first those seated around the stage and then up to those in the galleries. Then he turned to his newly bonded, held up his glass and said, 'To Ronnie! May you Live and Die by the SWORD's Code of Honour!'

To which every Destaurian in the room chanted in unison, 'Serve! Worship! Obey! Respect! Defend!' And the Bonding Hall, to Ronnie's amazement, erupted with cheers and whistles drowning out anything they tried to say to each other from thereon. The noise was deafening but Ronnie didn't care, for amidst all the commotion she just looked up at her Guardian and smiled, happy in the knowledge that whatever had gone on in her past would be revealed as and when, and if her Bonded should allow her to delve into it. Until then none of that mattered any more for locked tight, and resting gently around her throat, was the cold steel Collar of Commitment. Finally the honour of being truly his, by law, was hers.

Epilogue

'When we return from our Bonding Holiday I am taking you to your place of work. It's time you started living your life as normal. Well, as normal as can be for a Child of Destiny.'

'My place of work?' she said excitedly.

'Yes, your office, your desk, your stacks of paper.'

Suddenly her face fell. He noticed.

'What's wrong? Don't you want to get back to normal?'

'Does this mean you don't need me around any more?'

'Of course not. Girl, you are my Child of Destiny. I own you. You are mine. Nothing can, or ever will, change that. It's in your bloodline. I *love* you.'

She breathed a sigh of relief. 'Oh, thank goodness. For a moment—'

'Don't you want to know where you work?' he asked excitedly.

'Do I like it?'

'Time will tell. You worked for a University library, Ronnie. But as of next week I've a new line of work planned for you. One I guarantee you will like much more.'

'Me? I was a librarian?'

'A total bookworm. Don't worry, in your new job there'll be plenty more books, but I'm afraid it won't be quite as dull as your previous job.'

'How do you know, my Learned?'

'Because while you worked in the library you had a hobby, and soon that hobby will be your job.

It's complicated, but you'll find out after our holiday.'

Ronnie grinned. 'And now that you've teased and intrigued me you are refusing to tell me anything else until then, my Learned?'

He smiled. 'You know me too well.'

'What about who I work with? Can you at least tell me that, my Learned?'

'Next week you'll have all the answers.'

'What about Tim? Will he be expected to leave Black Ice now?'

'He will always have a home here, Ronnie. You'll just have to wait and see, but I assure you he'll be looked after as promised.'

Ronnie grinned animatedly again. 'Thank you my Learned, you are so good to me. Right now I am so happy!'

Just then Artemis walked in. 'Sorry to interrupt, dudes, but this is important. I've got something for you.'

Theo held out his hand.

'No not for you, silly, this is for Ronnie.'

'For me?'

She passed her a small package, wrapped in gold paper and tied with red ribbon. 'Yes, for you. It's a bonding present. It's traditional. Go on, open it.'

Ronnie took the package, and with shaking hands undid it. Inside was a jewellery box. She looked up and stared at first Theo and then Artemis.

'Don't worry, it won't bite,' Artemis encouraged.

Ronnie looked back at Theo, who held up his hands. 'Don't ask me, I have no idea what this is. It's all Art's doing.'

She opened the box. Inside was a glittering ring. Artemis helped her get it out.

'Read inside. There's an engraving.'

'To my beloved wife, Hazel, always and forever yours, Henry.' Her mouth fell open. 'My goodness, that's my mother's wedding ring!

Artemis nodded proudly.

'But where did you get it?'

Artemis bit her lip. 'You know the day I got kidnapped, blah, blah, blah? That's what I went back for.'

'Oh, gosh! You shouldn't have.' But as soon as the words were out she realised what she'd said. She couldn't have hoped for a better bonding present.

She squeezed it on her little finger and held it up to the light. The band of white gold looked so small and dainty.

'It's beautiful. Thank you. You risked your life to get me this. That means a lot. Thank you doesn't seem enough. How will I ever be able to repay your kindness?'

'Oh shush! No need to thank me. You deserve it. It belongs to you.'

Tears of happiness meandered down Ronnie's face, and if she didn't know better, Art looked pretty misty-eyed too.

Artemis flung her arms around Ronnie, squeezing her tight. Then she let go and stepped back. 'Now get back to the party. They're all waiting for you. I'll see you later.' She winked and marched out of the room leaving Ronnie with Theo. He reached into his pocket and pulled out a hanky.

'Wipe your eyes, and when you're ready we'll go back in. Art's right, this party is for you. They're all waiting to see my Child of Destiny. My bonded.' He paused. 'Oh, nearly forgot. When we return you'll also meet your sisters.'

'My sisters?'

'Yes. Why, did you think you were the only one?'

After the shock settled in Ronnie pushed all questions from her mind, wiped her eyes, took a deep breath to compose herself and smiled. Nothing was going to spoil her day. Whatever her Learned wanted she would happily oblige, because all that mattered was pleasing him. He knew what was best for her and although she still had a long way to go and her training would never end, what mattered most was that she trusted his decision implicitly, finding a sense of security and happiness in servitude that she never dreamt possible. Ronnie's heart swelled with pride.

Through his guidance and protection he'd moulded her into someone new, fixed the broken person she was and repackaged her. Without her realising he'd made her look into herself, at her fears, doubts and uncertainties. Now these had drifted away into the abyss where her past lay locked away like the dark secrets of the elusive Magic Box.

And best of all, she'd come into his life with nothing, and even though she still did not possess anything material except her collar and now her mother's ring, she'd gained so much more; a real purpose to her life.

'Ready?'

'Yes, thank you, my Learned.'

Proudly he clipped a chain to her collar and led her out of the door back into the Royal Nuvola Bonding Hall, for the final reception before they were sent off on their Bonding Holiday.

She thought of Artemis, her kindness, and how she had misjudged her. She wondered about her sisters, and found herself looking forward to meeting them. So much had happened and so much more was going to happen.

Witches, angels, demons and shape-shifters, indeed! Whatever next? she mused. If she could get through that with her Learned by her side, she could get through anything. But most of all, what really resonated with her was what her Learned had said earlier.

I *love* you. I *own* you. You are *mine!*

Whatever happened, wherever she went, those words would always keep her going. They stepped into the hall and everyone cheered.

'Go on,' Theo said, unclipping her lead, 'take this opportunity to mingle. For this nigh we leave for our holiday.' With a tender kiss on Ronnie's forehead, which reminded her of the day they first met, each went their separate ways into the crowd.

Ronnie hoped the pretty dark-haired girl she spotted earlier was still in the Bonding Hall, as she really wanted to ask her where she obtained that beautiful necklace, and perhaps show hers off too. What was her name again? Such a mysterious one, Ronnie thought as she scanned the crowd trying hard to remember.

Oh, yes, Darkita, and there she is!

The End... or is it?